Escape from the Belfry

Second Edition

Escape

from the Belfry

Second Edition

Doris Gaines Rapp

Daniel's House Publishing

Daniel's House Publishing
P.O. Box 623
Huntington, Indiana 46750

Library of Congress Control Number: 2017905141
ISBN: 978-0-9988590-0-2   (second edition paperback)
ISBN: 978-1-4808-0056-4   (first edition paperback)
ISBN: 978-1-4808-0054-0   (hardcover)
ISBN: 978-1-4808-0055-7   (eBook)

Contact Daniel's House Publishing at:
www.danielshousepublishing@gmail.com

Table of Contents

Dedication

Escape from the Belfry is dedicated to all the children in my life. We must all learn to handle life in honest and noble ways. We all have someone beside us, giving us counsel. Adam Shoemaker called him Shaddy, the Spirit of the Belfry.
Doris Gaines Rapp

Acknowledgements

Thank you my sweet husband, Bill, for patiently waiting for me to look up from my laptop. You are the joy of my life.

Thanks to Vicki Borgman for reading the book and giving wonderful suggestions. Your careful attention to time sequencing was vital to the flow of the story.

Also, I give a special "thank you" to Mrs. Borgman's sixth grade class at Central Christian School in Fort Wayne. You were the first to hear *Escape from the Belfry*. You are a great bunch.

Bobbi R. Madry, your friendship and encouragement are personal blessings. Your years of experience as a gifted book editor have been a professional gift to me as well.

Thanks to Debi Lindhorst of The Type Galley in Warren, Indiana for the wonderful new cover. You always see what I'm thinking.

Thank you to Bonnie Tobey Manning who took the great photo on the back cover. You are gifted. www.printroom.com/pro/btmanning.

To all the women in the writers group I attend, I say, "Thanks for your suggestions, support, and patients." You are all indeed a rare find. I am blessed to know you all.

Prologue

Fifteen-year-old Adam Shoemaker lives alone in the dark belfry of the Church on Cranberry Street. He is cold and confused. It's December 1945. Why hasn't Pops come home from World War II? The war in Europe is over and most of the troops have come home already, but not his dad. "Could Pops be a deserter?" That would be a humiliation he could not face.

Adolf Hitler, the butcher-tyrant of Germany, brought ruin and death all across the European continent during the war. In a desperate effort to save his family's reputation, Adam changes his German name from Schumacher to the English name— Shoemaker. Will everyone in town forget that he was a Schumacher not long ago?

Moms is in a sanitarium, recovering from tuberculosis. There is no one on the family farm now. His secret hiding place in the belfry is the only spot he can think of in which to hide, to make sure no one sends him to an orphanage.

Late at night, Adam hears someone in the church. Again he is conflicted. If he checks to see who is there, he could be discovered. If he reports it after they leave, how will he explain why he was also in the church at night?

Adam's existence in the belfry is desperate at times. He must handle all the twists in his life. A stranger stalks him, bullies try to intimidate him, and he struggles to choose the right way to handle it all.

Chapter 1

A Hot, Icy Day

Wednesday, December 19, 1945

Adam slithered into the Cranberry Street Church through the furnace room window he had left unlocked earlier. *If I had some place else to go, I wouldn't be here,* he thought as he listened at the basement door. He was trapped. Someone was coming down the stairs.

He watched from the safety of the darkness just inside the furnace room, as the janitor, Alfred Gunderman, walked in.

Mustn't be found, Adam worried. *I can't rebuild the family's reputation from inside an orphanage. What would Fritzy think of me then? There aren't any foundling home kids in Frederica Breman's family. Fritzy's home is near perfect. There will be none in mine either.*

Oh, Spirit, make Mr. Gunderman go away! Adam pleaded. The furnace room was hot and he still had his cap and coat on! If he tried to wiggle out of his heavy jacket, he might make enough noise to be discovered. *Spirit, help me stay still and silent.*

Was the spirit a fantasy? Maybe. But, the world of reality was too lonely for Adam to care. So, he listened.

13

"In time," the spirit promised. "Everything in time." And—that's what Adam needed to hear, even though he was the only one who heard it.

Farther down the back hall, Adam saw dark shadows begin to move toward the old man who didn't seem to notice them. But, Adam could see their black eyes. They were as hollow as the hole in his heart.

"Let us deal with the old one," Adam heard a shadow hiss. "We'll trip him on the stairs. He'll never come back. Hiss."

Adam heard a loud, groaning noise above the building. It rattled through his backbone as the shadows passed. The branches of the oak tree near the back door of the church, scraped on the slate roof. It reminded him of the rattling of ghostly chains he had heard in a dime movie.

Make him go away, Adam pleaded again. He didn't think the spirit heard him. He couldn't feel the warmth inside or sense the heavy presence that had come upon him before, when he was sure he heard the spirit speak to him.

Adam's heart pounded as beads of perspiration dripped in his eyes. *If I stand here any longer, my skin will singe.* It felt like he was roasting.

"Too cold to hurry outside," the old man muttered to himself. "Thankfully, it's still early enough for the coal to be hot in the furnace. It's warm in here."

You'll be fine, Mister, Adam mocked silently. *You have a home to go to. Fritzy has a home and a family. I have nothing.*

Adam's only companion in the cold, musty belfry was the spirit he had called on. If he didn't have the spirit, he would have no one. Real or imaginary, Adam wanted the spirit to stay. Some day he would ask the spirit to help him escape from the belfry, and help him avoid contact with the shadows he had seen in the church.

Maybe none of it was real, including the spirit. But, Adam chose to believe in fantasy rather than face the real world.

14

Through the far window in the basement, he could see sleet assault the pane and almost force its way through the tiny space between the glass and the frame. That image didn't cool him, however. He was still nearly scorched. Suddenly—he saw Mr. Gunderman pause and turn.

"What was that?" The old one stopped and listened.

Adam watched from the darkness. *He hears me. He knows I'm here.* Adam winced. *I must not be found.*

The heat from the furnace steamed around the door casing. *I can't stand this anymore. I am hot! I have to move!* Adam eyed the exit sign on the other side of the building.

"Spirit of the Belfry, please make me invisible so I can get out of here," he whispered into the darkness around him. Then Adam felt a warmth again, not furnace room warmth, but as if someone were standing so near he could feel their closeness. A presence of power filled Adam, all the way from his heart to his shoelaces.

I am invisible! I must be, he almost cried out.

Adam took a deep breath, then slipped from his hiding place and made a silent dash toward the outside door. He cringed, thinking his steel-plated clodhoppers might tap on the concrete floor. As he ran toward the exit door, he heard nothing. The spirit had created the silence he had needed.

"Who's there?" the janitor shouted into the darkness.

As Adam darted across the room, a pale light beaming through the closed window revealed his slim, lanky figure.

Adam burst across the room with more speed than he knew he could muster. *I can't get caught. If they catch me, it's all over.* He could see the outline of the outside door ahead and gave one last burst of speed.

"That looked like a young kid. Where did he go?" Alfred Gunderman mumbled.

Adam sailed out the outside door into the frosty air. He could hear the old man huffing and puffing behind him, trying to reach the door before it slammed closed.

15

By the time Adam heard the outside door close then fly open again, he had managed to clear from view all but his left clodhopper as he slipped in the snow and sludge then rounded the corner of the church. Adam stopped in the darkness under a tree, looked around the trunk and back at the church. The old man stood in the doorway and shook his head.

"I bet those steel-plated shoes are soaked now," Adam heard the old man shout after him.

As Adam crouched behind the tree, the wind was so still he could hear the man say, "Sorry. Bless him, God. Keep him safe and warm in this awful storm. I don't wish ill will on any of your children. That kid looked terrible thin."

Chapter 2

Frederica Breman Just Slid In

After his dash from the Cranberry Street Church to make sure he wasn't discovered by the janitor, Adam was out on the street again. From the hot furnace room to the icy white street, he struggled to adjust to the bitter cold even with his jacket on.

As Adam walked along the sidewalk so he could re-enter the church through a different window, the battering wind beat against his face. His thoughts went back to the warmth of the farm house in the winter and the closeness he shared there with his parents. Folks here on the home front received notice if a loved one had died in a battle, but Moms had heard nothing. There had been whispers that Pops might be a deserter, which made Adam's life even worse.

He wanted to be at home and smell the sweet hay of the barn and the aroma of Moms' apple pie baking in the oven. But, he knew he couldn't stay on the farm without his family. Just as his thoughts wandered up the lane to home, he heard a friend from school call his name.

"Adam Shoemaker!" Frederica Breman shouted. "Wait up!" Her fur lined mukluks thumped like small kayaks through the deep snow.

"Sure, Fritzy." He pulled his stocking cap farther down over his cold, red ears and waited for her to catch up. What else could he do? He had no reason for being on the cold sidewalk outside the church. He hadn't been able to find his gloves so he jammed his hands back into his jacket pockets that had retained a little furnace heat.

"Where ya goin'?" she asked. "I thought you live the other way."

"I was just out for a walk," he lied as he started to walk in the direction of Fritzy's house.

"Out for a walk on a dark evening like this?" she gasped. "It's been snowing all day. I nearly landed on my backside a minute ago." Fritzy added.

"You'd better go in. It doesn't look like the snow's gonna let up. Your cheeks are getting really red." Adam turned and started to punch fresh holes in the crust-covered snow with each step. "Why are you still out?"

"I walked over to my grandparents' house after school. Grandma and I made a fruitcake. She'll take it out of the oven in an hour. I can almost smell the spices all the way over here. We weren't paying any attention to the weather. Wow, it has gotten bad."

"Fruitcake? I thought nobody liked fruitcake." Adam smiled a little. His mother's fruitcake was wonderful, but, at school, it wasn't popular to say that you like the Christmas cake.

"Well, I like it," she snapped back. She skipped a little to stay up with Adam's long stride. Then, with a slip and a slide, like a duck on an icy pond, she up-dumped and landed on the padded side of her snow pants.

"Fritzy! Are you okay?" Adam scooped her off the frozen sidewalk.

"Yes!" she sputtered angrily as she brushed herself off. "I am fine, but my pride is broken! Why don't these people have their sidewalks cleaned off?"

18

"Are you all right?" A voice called from the house.

"No!" Fritzy shouted back. Then she squeezed her eyes closed and held her breath when she saw the man in the doorway. "Thanks, Mayor. I'm great—just cold. I fell on this nasty sidewalk."

"If there's anything broken, you let me know," the mayor waved and closed the door.

"You amaze me, Fritzy. Even after that fall on the sidewalk, you had enough spit-fire left in you to tangle with the mayor," Adam teased.

"All right, Adam Shoemaker." She jerked off one of her knit gloves and gave Adam a playful smack on the cheek.

"I accept the challenge, Mademoiselle. I have demeaned your abilities. Shall we say dueling pistols at thirty paces." Adam removed his cap, swung it across his body, and bowed.

"Good," she lifted her chin. "I'll name the place and you make sure you're there on time." Fritzy took a few steps and grabbed her hip. "Oh!"

"Are you hurt anywhere, except where you cracked the ice back there?" Adam grinned.

A loud screech interrupted their playful exchange. Down the block, car breaks ground to the metal, followed by the loud crash of assorted auto parts as they slammed together.

"See. Did you hear that? I told you it is slick out here," Fritzy added as if she needed an excuse for her fall.

Adam watched the snow blow sideways in the glow of the street lamp. He could feel the cold on his teeth every time he opened his mouth to the icy air. He began to worry. "I'd better get you home. Then I can get in out of this blizzard too." Adam didn't add that he would have to turn around and walk all the way back to the church.

19

"You don't have to take me home. I'm a girl, not an infant." Fritzy lowered her head and brushed ice clusters from the blond curls that stuck out from her parka hood.

"Fritzy, I first met you in elementary school. You've always been able to take care of yourself. I remembered when we were in the sixth grade and you walked in front of Mr. Grouch's school bus. He waved his fist at you like always. He would always get real mad when people didn't obey traffic laws."

"You don't remember that, Adam Shoemaker," she teased.

"Oh Yes, I do. You yelled back, 'I have to get to the other side of the street, don't I?' Then you raised your hand and waved politely like you were so innocent."

Adam smiled. He thought she had been spunky then and she was even spunkier now.

"We're here, Adam." Fritzy nodded at the white frame house. "I'm home."

"Oh, right. Let me help you up those icy steps," Adam offered.

"You mean my dad didn't shovel ours either?" she grumbled.

"It looks like they were cleared and a new layer of snow and sleet have piled up again."

"Well, okay. Thanks for the offer of a big strong hand, but I'm perfectly able to walk by myself."

"Yeah, you've already demonstrated that," he teased.

Fritzy grabbed the step railing and slowly eased herself up the slick steps. Her boots skated all five treads to the porch. Mr. Breman stepped out of the house and reached for his daughter.

The aroma of sizzling hamburgers drifted through the open door. Adam breathed in all the deliciousness he could mentally create. He was hungry.

"Thanks, Adam," Fritzy called back as she hurried into the warmth of her brightly lit home.

"Thank you," Mr. Breman added as he closed the door.

Adam turned around in front of Fritzy's house and started to trudge back to the church. As he walked in the winter evening, he thought of warm summer picnics and juicy hamburgers piled high with onions and catsup. But, it wasn't summer and there was nothing on a grill. The snow, which had now changed to sleet, continued to pepper his face.

He would be inside soon, but not through the front door of the church on Cranberry Street. He wasn't a member. He was an intruder, a common squatter. He was a homeless fifteen-year-old who sought refuge at night in the drafty, unheated belfry of the church. That bell tower was also inhabited by the sinister shadows that filled each dark corner and hung like bats from the rafters. He believed they were kept in check by the ever present spirit of the belfry. Alone in the cold with his imaginary companions, Adam would wait out another night.

Adam had no key, so rather than entering through the window of the hottest room in the church basement, he ran around to the back of the building and re-entered through the kitchen window over the sink. He scooted silently down onto the large drain board. Thankfully, it was completely dry, which spared him of an embarrassing wet spot on the back of his pants. After swinging his feet around, he slithered down carefully from the counter until his feet were planted firmly on the concrete floor. He opened the kitchen door a crack and took a peek to see if all was clear.

From the tiny opening in the door, Adam could see that Mr. Gunderman was just coming into the adjoining, multipurpose fellowship hall as Pastor Silverman's tabby cat, Gertrude, came out of nowhere and skittered between the old man's legs. She nearly knocked him down before she darted across the room.

"Gertrude, you huntin' church mice?"

Adam watched as the man followed the cat across the floor and into the corner near the main entrance. The janitor looked around the whole area that led to the wide stairway beyond the double doors. "How many mice we got in here?"

"The blustering wind is rattling the stained glass windows. I hope that old lead channeling holds those glass pieces in place," Pastor Silverman said as he came down the steps and into the Fellowship area. "It's really bad out there, Alfred. You'd better go home. This will go down in history as the blizzard of the century."

Gertrude tiptoed over to Pastor Silverman and draped herself through the pastor's legs. "Gertrude, what are you doing in here?"

"She thinks she smells a mouse," the janitor said.

Pastor Silverman picked up the cat and cradled her in his arms. "Alfred, I was thinking about another blizzard, one just like this, when I was a kid. Dad sent me over here to check on you. That night you helped God save my soul. You made me see that the promise of Christmas peace is for me too."

Helped God save his soul? Adam wondered how that was possible. *God is probably dead anyway. He might have gone down in one of those fighter planes, like in the news reels at the movies. Or, an ace pilot pierced the sky and God fell out. At least, any god I believe in would have slipped through a crack in Heaven.*

Adam's muscles tightened and clinched. *If there was a god, I wouldn't even be here. He'd give me somewhere else to go. A kid with no place to live gets placed in a children's home. Then, what would Moms do? I wouldn't be able to visit her in the hospital.*

He heard the lights snap off as the two men left the room. Adam stepped out of the kitchen and watched through the basement window on the other side of the fellowship hall as the snow continued to come down like giant clumps of white, frozen feathers. He could see the icy glitter on the sidewalk. It sent a shiver up Adam's back. He hurried up the steps and slipped across the floor. He paused at the bottom of the belfry ladder and wondered if the spirit had really made him invisible.

As he hurried up the ladder, rung by rung, an old doubt took over. *Maybe the spirit isn't real after all. Maybe I imagined the shadows, too.*

Chapter 3

The Lonely Belfry

Adam still had doubts as he eased off the ladder and slipped into the bell tower room. Was the spirit real or just an imaginary friend to make up for his loneliness?

The small enclosed hideaway, just below the open-air space where the church bells hung, had a small window where ice crystals had formed on the pane. All around him was silence, the achy kind that sets in when emptiness is everywhere. There, in the cold, dark, rough room is where he slept each night.

Adam knew the rooms in the church below the belfry were warm, but people came and went at all hours. Like a honeybee hive, there were always activities in the church besides the Sunday morning worship. He would lie on the floor and listen to the happy voices of people as they bustled in and out just below him. Not tonight. After the janitor and Pastor Silverman left, no one else was around. The weather was awful.

Normally, he had to stay out of sight, invisible. If he were eighteen, it wouldn't matter. He could live wherever he wanted. But, that was three years away. People would never let a fifteen-year-old live alone, regardless of how well he could take care of himself. Adam could plow a straight line, plant a field, and do any kind of farm work, but he wasn't old enough to choose where he would live.

"I don't need to be taken care of. That's gray-haired thinking," he complained to himself. "That's why I have to hide from those meddling, old fuddy-duddies who won't mind their own business."

Alone in the belfry, Adam had curled up on the cold wood-plank floor the first few months he had slept there but found no comfort. The bell tower's bare floor in December was like an icy barn stall on the farm, but with no hay to cushion his head or animals' breath for warmth. There in the belfry, his jacket was all he had to cover him from the cold.

Earlier that day, when there was no movement downstairs, and before time for Mr. Gunderman to come in, Adam had selected three blankets and a pillow from things the church members had donated to the Christmas rummage sale. World War II was over and goods of all kinds were in short supply, so the church members cleaned out their dresser drawers and closets to help returning vets and families in need. That holiday season, Adam would have felt blessed, if he believed in a god who blesses.

To meet his own need to have some things of his own, he found a new basketball and a small, forty-eight starred American flag attached to a stick on the donation pile. Up in the belfry, he made a pallet on the floor with a pillow and some blankets he had rescued from the pile. He put the ball near his bed so he could see it was always there, and wedged the little flag in a chink in a rafter beam. He reviewed the nation's colors, and a sober smile escaped his tight lips as he wondered about his soldier dad.

The day had been long and tiring and Adam had to get some sleep. He had school the next day. His room was as ready as he could make the dark, cold space in the church belfry.

My own room, Adam mocked himself.

26

The snow outside had stopped momentarily. The clouds parted and let a small beam of light stream through the tiny window and illuminate his space. Large, rough, hand-hewn, hand-scraped beams provided the rafters of the old church, and long wooden pegs held all the old timbers together.

"The rustic space is kinda pretty," he admitted, "if you don't mind the dark, the cold, and the awful dampness."

He looked around the dim space that shimmered with air-dust the moonbeams revealed as they streamed in the window. Huge cobwebs sparkled like the webs of giant, furry-legged spiders that clung to the corners of the barn. They added a mystery that felt both intriguing and eerie.

"The heavy cross-beams in the ceiling remind me of our old barn," he mumbled to himself. "But, it smells more like pigeon hooey than sweet straw or new mown hay."

Suddenly, Adam heard a rattle in the darkest corner of the rafter room and shuddered. He knew that the shadows were in the church. Earlier, they had even been downstairs and now he thought they were back in the belfry. His Grannie O'Hara had said the spirits that smell bad can be ordered to leave if you show them you are not afraid.

"I command you to get out of here," he demanded, but he could smell no odor and saw no movement.

Not the shadows? Then, a thought came to his mind that disturbed him more than having to deal with the shadow entities.

"Rats!" He shrieked with disgust. He hoped he was wrong. He hated rodents of any kind.

"Spirit?" he called to the darkness. "Please make me or the rat invisible. I don't want to see the ugly thing." But, the spirit didn't answer.

Adam heard the flapping noise again and sniffed the air. It was too cold to smell anything including the shadows, and that was good. So, the noise couldn't be those demonic shadows.

27

I can't go to sleep until I know what is trespassing in my tower. This is my space! I am king here!

"Take courage my son." Adam heard what sounded like the wind whispering through the thin, single-pane window.

Adam calmed. "Yes, Spirit."

Creak! The old boards announced Adam's movement as he searched for the source of the sound.

What if someone comes back into the church downstairs? He screwed up his face with each step, as if a frown would silence the wood as he stepped. It felt he had anvils laced to his feet, not clodhoppers. *Wish I had taken these boots off.*

But, his steps were not silenced. Had he really run silently across the basement floor to avoid Mr. Gunderman or had he imagine it? As he neared the corner of the belfry, he stopped. He knew there was something in the darkness. *Nasty old things, rats.*

"Where's Grandpa's shotgun when I need it?" he wondered. Then, he laughed at himself. "The blast would reverberate across the ice and snow like a civil war canon. Right! Sneak around in the dark, then blast away at a mouse with a machine gun. Good thinking, Shoemaker."

Suddenly, something darted at him from the peak of the roof like a dive bomber from a corner of the black sky. "Bats!" he shrieked without a thought or care to who might hear him. He swung his arms wildly in the air around his head and shoulders. "Get off me!" he ordered as he smacked at the space within his reach. "Spirit, help me!" he bellowed again.

"Courage, Son," he heard the spirit whisper. "Courage does not need a gun," the spirit encouraged him.

Thud! Just as quickly as the winged menace lunged at him, the thing dropped to the hard floor.

Adam squinted in the beams from the moonlight to see if the creature was a bat or a Cooper's hawk that had attacked him. It had to be huge. But, there on the wood-plank floor was a little ruby-throated hummingbird. The tiny bird did not move but lay there at the tip of his shoes.

"A hummingbird? You're supposed to be gone by now, Little One," Adam whispered as he scooped up the small green feathered creature. "With all those bright feathers, you must be male."

He stroked the little bird's ruby fluff and blew short puffs of breath over its green head. It felt downy soft beneath the first layer of feathers that waved like grain in the field as he blew.

"You should have left in September along with the rest of them," Adam whispered. "Grandpa planted sweet honeysuckle along the orchard fence just for you hummers. I can smell the nectar even now. Grandpa and Grandma, Moms and Pops are all gone from the place now. Guess the flowers are gone too."

Despair crept into Adam's voice as he thought of all he had lost. Adam smiled faintly as he remembered a time when he had a family. Both Gramps and Grandma Shoemaker had died in an automobile accident. Then Pops had to serve his country in the war and Moms had become ill shortly after. Even the neighbor who had farmed for Moms said he was unable to continue. He gave no reason. Now the farm lay empty. Moms had to sell their horses and cows too. Adam had no one, no income, nothing. He hung his head and remembered why he had come to live in this church belfry. He felt defeated again.

Adam knew he could have stayed in the Shoemaker farmhouse. His family had lived there for generations, but he would be too far from town to get to school. Besides, he couldn't stand to be isolated on the farm. Not because of fear—just the unbearable loneliness of it. Now that winter was here, the house would be cold. The empty coal bin and lack of electricity made the farm house uninhabitable.

He knew he wouldn't be able to get the two miles from the farm into town every day or the extra five miles to the hospital where his mother received treatment if he had tried to stay on the farm. The key to the old truck was in Pops' cuff link box but it would do Adam no good until he got his driver's license in another four months. Also, people living on nearby farms would notice him and perhaps call the Child Welfare League that cared for war orphans and other abandoned kids.

"Adam," the spirit called on a drafty waft of air, interrupting his thoughts, "cover the little bird with your hand."

The spirit was so close, the breath of his words filled Adam with hope.

Adam placed his hand over the little bird just as the spirit instructed. The belfry hovered around Adam like a warm presence while the frigid air whistled outside the window. The small amount of light that shimmered through the window was focused on the bird he held in his hands. The glow was a golden color of hope. Adam stared at the tiny hummer in his hand with trance-like vision. The little bird appeared to be dead. Then, like a second life, the tiny hummingbird began to move.

Adam didn't know if the miracle he was seeing came from the spirit's wise words, the warmth of his own hands, or, if he had inherited his grandfather's knack of healing animals, but the hummingbird's wings moved slightly.

Another amazing thing—the little bird didn't try to fly away. He lay there in Adam's palm nearly motionless. Then Adam had an idea. He had watched from a distance one day when Mrs. Bee Bee Brumble donated a funny little woven wicker basket she carried as her purse, to the charity drive.

Adam had overheard Bee Bee's husband say. "Beatrice Bianca, the time has come to put that purse to rest. I am tired of the guys asking me if we've trapped anything yet." That morning, they plopped the purse in the donation box.

The boy felt he could not lay the bird down for fear the little fellow might try to fly before it had healed. The hummer had to be protected. Adam decided to get that basket from the mission pile. He wanted to keep the little bird around for a while and the protective basket-purse would make a safe nest for him.

He slipped back down the ladder with the bird in his partially open hand. Silently, he crept on down below to the fellowship hall. A delicate bird in his hand and steel-plated shoes on his feet did not make his silent shuffle easy. Adam also had that toed-in athletic stride that was as agile as a thoroughbred on the basketball court and as clumsy as a new born colt everywhere else.

"Guess you've been scrounging for food, the same as me. But, I don't eat a steady diet of flower nectar," Adam said to the little bird as they came to the tables of sale and free items. "All the flowers have been gone for weeks."

Adam reached the rummage table that boasted items which included Mrs. Brumble's basket-purse. He found a small washcloth for the bottom of the basket and carefully placed the bird on it inside the cage and closed the lid. "Gramps taught me all about you little hummers and by this time you should be down Mexico way."

He searched in the church kitchen for something the little bird could eat. From the cupboard, he took a small cup and stirred in a little sugar he found in one of the many sugar bowls in a kitchen drawer. On the shelf next to the cups and saucers, he spotted a little jar of honey and added a small amount to the sugar before stirring in a tiny amount of water. "Homemade nectar," he spoke to himself under his breath.

Adam was careful not to swing the basket too much as he carried the make-shift birdcage back up the ladder to the belfry. Once he got to the top, he paused next to the trap door and listened for any sound in the rooms below.

31

"Just for tonight," he whispered to the bird, "considering your injury, I'm going to leave the trap door open so we can get a little heat up here." He placed the basket on the floor beside the bed he had made. "Don't get used to a warm bed though, Little Hummer. It won't be safe to leave the trap door open all of the time. If folks saw the opening, we would soon be found. You wouldn't have a comfortable basket to sleep in then, and I wouldn't have this glorious mansion to call home."

Adam rolled over onto his back and stared into the blackness above and around him. The darkness made him feel even more alone. The empty nights would soon roll into Christmas, with all the memories of a time when his family was real. Adam knew he would not be celebrating the holidays this year. There would be no iced cookies or brightly lit tree and no presents under the branches in his life. He thought of how the bird had remained motionless in his hand and the new breaths the hummer finally took. *Will the spirit breathe new breath into me too?*

As thoughts danced in his head, Adam pictured Fritzy Breman again. He imagined that Coach Breman, Fritzy's dad, and all their family would have a wonderful celebration, complete with juicy roast turkey and warm, pecan pie.

He smiled to himself as he thought about Fritzy. She had talked to him more than usual recently. There was something different about her words and the crinkles around her eyes.

"God," Adam prayed as he had each night for four months, "I've prayed a lot lately, but the truth is I don't really think you're there. But, Moms says you are and something happened with that bird that I don't understand. Maybe you are. If you haven't died in the war, please help Moms. She needs your healing. She's at the West Slope Hospital, where they treat tuberculosis. I know you can find the large white building. There's a Christmas star on top for the holidays. You know all about Christmas stars. Her name is Bridget Schumacher, but she might be going by Bertha Shoemaker now. I know I've changed my last name. With the war and all, there are too many bad feelings about names like ours. And God, I know you don't have pockets full of money up there, but I've got to get some cash real soon. If I can pay the deposit on a load of coal, I can get heat back in the farm house and Moms can come home. But, the hard part is, we'll still need an indoor bathroom. That is a must, her doctor told me, before they can release her. Well, if you're there God, help Moms. Thank you for the blankets and pillow. And—let the little hummer live. Another living thing would be nice to have around here when I get home from school every day."

Adam closed his eyes and hoped that God was still there. But, he didn't see how that could be possible. He had absolutely nothing left of his life. Would God allow that to happen? But, he had to admit, his life had just gotten a little better. He had a few things: some blankets, a pillow, and a little bird that flew in from the cold. Would they be able to stay warm together?

"Sleep well, young one," the now familiar voice of the spirit whispered into the cold night as Adam's breath formed an icy wreath around his head. "And remember—take courage."

Adam looked around for the source of the voice, but in the moon light, only a comic book with a muscle man in blue and a red cape gazed at him from the cover.

"Are you tired my son?" the voice whispered.

"I don't know. But, I wish—"

"One day, you'll know who you are and you won't have to wish," the spirit whispered softly.

"Spirit, what is your name?" Adam had wanted to know but had been afraid to ask.

"My name? Some have called me, Father."

"My father has not come home from the war. Some have said he may be a deserter. Will you leave me too?"

"I will never leave you, Son," the spirit assured him.

"Then, I'll call you Shaddy. Pops said Shaddy means *all powerful*."

"That is close, young one. That is close," the spirit with the new name answered calmly. Adam squinted in the dark hoping to get a glimpse of the spirit. "Shaddy, maybe I don't know who I am yet, but I wish I had the power of Superman. Shaddy, I'm not wishing, I'm asking."

"You will have all you need, when you need it," Shaddy answered as the voice seemed to drift away on the rhythm of the blowing wind.

All I need when I need it? Adam wondered if that would be true. For now, he would trust the wise spirit of the belfry who whispered in his ear. If Shaddy were really a powerful spirit, like his name, then somehow, Adam believed he would have Superman powers when he needed them.

Chapter 4

We Need You Shoemaker

Thursday, December 20, 1945

Aoogha! The next morning, a car horn in the street blared out reveille. The snowstorm had stopped for a while during the night and sound carried for blocks on the thin crystal clear air.

"Hey, Barbara, get a wiggle on!" Adam heard Charlie Baker shout from the street.

Aoogha! There was urgency in the insistent, tinny car horn.

"Okay, okay," Adam also answered reveille's call. "Great, another day already," he moaned as he resisted opening his eyes to his dank existence. Often, he was afraid ice might form across his eye balls if they were exposed to the bitter cold of the belfry. That morning, the small amount of heat that drifted up during the night through the open trap door was welcome. It raised the temperature a few degrees. His mouth tasted stale. He'd have to find water that wasn't frozen.

Aoogha! Another blast of his make-shift wake-up alarm horn.

The day broke like most other days in the recent months of Adam's world, fragile and jagged. For Adam, his mornings startled rather than started. At any time, he could be moved away from all he knew, away from Moms, away from his school. His life would change forever if he were found.

He heard the chimes of Agnes Coffee's fancy grandfather clock in the Agnes Coffee Lounge downstairs. He wondered why the clock couldn't be loud enough to awaken him in the morning. Its tone was much friendlier than the aoogha of Charley's A Model Ford.

Why did everything have to be so hard? Then he listened again. From high up in the belfry the tones of the old clock sounded more like a funeral dirge than a cheery wake-up call. Adam decided to stick with his original plan—the A model's *Aoogha*. "Hoping for change for change's sake never works out," Gramps had said.

In spite of his Spartan living, Adam had worked out a weekday plan. Each school day, Charlie Baker picked up Barbara James out in front of her house, across from the Cranberry Street Church, long before school started. Charlie and Barb liked to spend time over fizzy, chocolate sodas at the fountain in Lally's Drug Store before school. The lunch counter had opened early during the war to provide breakfast for workers in town.

Charlie's rooster crow was predictable enough to give Adam time to wash up in the men's room of the church. It was a small area with only a toilet and a sink that mounted on the wall. But the water was hot, which made it a tropical paradise to Adam's thinking. Then he would hurry out the back entrance before Alfred came in the front door.

That morning, Adam slid down the ladder like a fireman on a firehouse pole with a foot on each side of the rails. Back in the church kitchen, he ran a little water in the small dish he had taken up to the belfry the previous evening and sprinkled a bit of sugar over the surface then stirred in the sweetness. A tiny bit of honey was added as before.

"I think I saw—," he thought out loud as he opened a small cabinet that smelled like vanilla, cinnamon and other rich spices. "There it is." He fished around behind the salt box and brought out a small bottle. He removed the lid, tipped it up and added a few drops of red food coloring to the homemade nectar. "Flowers are colorful," he reasoned, "so the bird might be more attracted to the sugar water if the liquid is bright."

He hurried back up to his space and opened the basket. "Oh please Shaddy," he whispered as he held his breathe. "The hummer has to be okay." Adam wouldn't be able to handle the loss of something else.

The little bird lay motionless in the basket. Adam's chest gripped with fear so tightly it felt like he had just been stepped on by a mule. He said nothing but starred at the hummer. Then, the tiny bird fluffed his feathers and stood up. To the boy's surprise, the hummingbird didn't try to fly away. Adam held out his hand and the little hummer hopped up and perched on his finger, midway between his first and second knuckles. The bird's trust was amazing. How could the little thing warm up to him so quickly?

After seeing the bright, flashing eyes and colorful feathers, Adam didn't want to leave the little fellow to go off to school. If he had a choice, he would have chosen differently, but he had learned to take care of responsibilities first and play second, if there was any time lift.

Adam placed the bird and the synthetic nectar in the basket, closed the lid, wrapped his blanket around the basket leaving a crack for fresh air and looked around the belfry. The space looked different in the daytime. Every corner was lit in light.   All of the shadows were gone. It was still cold and colorless, but the light added life and brightness against the dull walls. He had to leave. He slid down the ladder again and darted out the back door just as a key turned in the front lock.

Adam loped through the alley, past the back of Donley's Furniture Store. It was harder to walk back there, but he thought the short cut was worth it. Suddenly, a souped-up pale blue jalopy skidded up behind him and sent cold, heavy snow flying around Adam's head and shoulders. Some of it slid down his collar.

"Sorry, Schumacher," Ernie Clifford mocked out the jalopy window. "Hey, has your Daddy come home from Germany yet? Or, did he decide to stay in the Mother Land?"

"What did you say to me?" Adam bellowed. As he clenched his fist in the air, his rage foamed within him.

"You heard me, Kraut!" Ernie shouted back as he sped off.

Shadows, the color of Adam's anger, darted out of the shack behind Donley's store. They were as black as bitter-weed, puffed up and mean. Their odor was foul, and Adam wanted to gag from the stench of them.

"We will lock his brakes and make him crash," the shadows seethed.

Adam refused to look at them and jerked his eyes to the ground. Suddenly, the sun slipped out and shone through the clouds in his heart. The bright rays drove the demons back into the gloom of the shed.

Adam shook his shoulders and arms to release the anger that had strangled his body. *Shaddy, get the rage away from me.*

He kept his focus on the icy rocks and gravel in the alley and kept moving until he came out on Norman Avenue. His head down to brace himself against the cold and the dark influences around him, he chose to think about the hummingbird and smiled.

A lone cardinal twittered from the top branch of a leafless maple tree, the only spot of color in the all-white world around him. He thought of the hummingbird and wondered if

Ruby would be a good name for him. *No, he's a boy. I'll call him Rudy.*

"Shaddy, take care of the little hummer," Adam whispered. "You're always in the belfry when I need you. Be there for the little guy too. Right now, Shaddy, the little hummer is all I have."

Out on Norman Avenue, the whole town looked like a cover from *The Saturday Evening Post*. The curbs were buried in deep white drifts so Adam couldn't tell the sidewalk from the street. Normally, school would have been cancelled due to a snow storm like the one the previous night. It was close to Christmas, so Adam figured the school superintendent wanted to press on. He often started a speech, "In my day, we weren't afraid of a little snow."

"Good morning, Adam Shoemaker," Fritzy called as she hurried out her door to the clatter of a large jingle bell that hung on the knob. "Who were you talking to?"

"Just the bats in my belfry I guess," he smoothed over the slip. *Right big-mouth, walk around talking to yourself. That's impressive.*

They hit a patch of ice and teetered in their balance. "Careful there. The sidewalk has gotten very icy and the curbs have disappeared altogether," Adam warned.

"You would pick me up if I fell, wouldn't you?"

"Your pa wouldn't like that very much."

"Well, he wouldn't want me to lie in the snow on the cold, hard ice, would he?" she giggled as she took wider strides to keep up with the tall, long-legged boy.

He said nothing as he trudged through the deep snow that crunched as he broke through the icy top layer. His smile was evidence enough of his feelings for the girl. More words could have produced silly giggles to accompany the grin—and a truly awkward moment.

"How's your mother, Adam?" Fritzy asked.

"Doctor says Moms has to stay in the hospital another couple of months, 'til the weather warms up a bit." That was true, but the real problem was, the house had no heat. And, Adam had no money for a deposit on the coal that would get the old farmhouse warm again. He was very aware of that fact with his cold hands in empty pockets. There would be no need for furnace heat in the warmer weather of spring. And, there was the problem with the bathroom. There was none. Adam didn't know what he was going to do about that.

Fritzy tried to match his steps, stride for stride, crunchy boot beat by boot beat. "A long stay in the hospital must get awfully expensive. My grandma was in the hospital for a whole week and that cost hundreds of dollars."

"I don't know what her stay will cost when she is finally done with treatment. The bill will be a lot. I know that."

"How—?" Frederica stopped. "Oh crumb. I'm sorry. I shouldn't ask. Your family's accounts are none of my business."

"That's okay." He thought about the stack of bills that already stuck out of every cubby of the roll-top desk in the farm parlor. "I don't have any idea about the cost of things or when she can come home." He really wanted to say, "And, I don't know where the money will come from either." But, he was from a family of private people, and Adam had learned to be silent. The sound of the empty wind was all he heard. *Maybe that's all Shaddy is, the winter wind.*

"Sorry to get nosy." She hurried, slipped and slid as she pressed deep footprints in the fresh snow of the sidewalk and seemed to try to catch Adam's eye whenever she could.

He slowed and touched her sleeve. "Wait, Fritz." Maybe he could trust her. He had to talk to somebody. He and Fritzy had been friends since early grade school. Lately, he had begun to feel silly around her, awkward.

He let go of her coat as quickly as he had made contact. What if she didn't want him to touch her?

40

"The problem is just that, my dad—well, I never told you—but—" he caught himself before he continued. "Never mind." How could he tell her that his dad had been missing in action for more months than he could remember?

His grandfather had always said, "Your name is your ticket to the good life."
A kid with no dad and a sick mom was not part of the pedigreed families. Adam believed that.

If Pops is dead, that's one thing, he thought again and again. *Death is okay. It has respectability with it. People sympathize with the family when a loved one dies. But, if Pops is a deserter, that's a whole other thing.* If Pops is a deserter, the Shoemaker name would be shattered like broken glass and there would be no hope of their reputation ever being mended.

Adam knew that Fritzy would wonder why his dad hadn't come home in the several months since the war had been over. He wanted to tell her.

"Pops—" he started again. "Forget it, Fritzy. I'm talking way too much."

"You! Talking too much? You put fewer words together than anyone I know," she laughed. "Besides, I can't say I know how you feel 'cause I don't. Daddy's eyesight is what kept him out of the Army."

Adam had to change the subject. *Shaddy, help me,* he pleaded silently. Immediately, a distraction on the street presented itself, like the spirit had waved a sparkling wand.

"Hey, Shoemaker," a high school boy leaned out of his car window at the four-way stop, "you goin' out for basketball or not? We've already played some games, but Coach said he could still use you."

A delivery man in a milk truck honked his horn, so the boy in the jalopy drove on. As he moved on down the street, the boy shouted back, "We need you, Shoemaker!"

"We need you, Shoemaker," Carl Benton mocked from the open door of his milk truck.

"We need you, Shoemaker," an eight-year-old boy teased as he darted across the street to make his getaway.

"Watch out!" Fritzy shouted as the second-grader stepped into the deep snow of the cross-street and into the path of a large truck.

The truck driver slammed on his breaks and geared down, but his swift reaction was too slow for the treacherous road. The sound of metal on metal cut the air. The truck was a torpedo aimed at the second-grader.

Shaddy, speed! Let me fly. Adam flung himself into the busy street, both arms extended toward the boy. The velocity felt like flying as his body shot through the air, but it happened too fast for him to grasp the wonder of the miracle.

"Adam! No!" Fritzy screamed.

His body flew horizontally across the road, with enough speed to propel him directly at the boy. He grabbed the child and tucked him under his arms like a large, leggy football. Instantly, Adam aimed for a high snow drift beyond the street and hit the ground in a roll. Adam laughed as he let loose of the boy.

"Wow!" The kid jumped to his feet and shook his head. "I thought I was a goner!" he squealed. "Thanks Adam, thanks. We must have been flying." Just as quickly as he had slid into the street, the boy slipped and slopped off in the direction of Pasadena Grade School.

"Adam," Fritzy gasped as she grabbed his arm, "you just saved that boy's life. It all happened so fast. How did you do that?"

"I don't know. We do what we have to do, when we have to do it," Adam said.

Then he remembered. *You will have all you need, when you need it.*

Chapter 5

Hummingbirds, Basketball, and Party Time

"Here, Basketball Star," Carl Benton, the milkman, laughed as he tossed a glass pint bottle of fresh milk to Adam. "Ya gotta keep up that Superman strength, Boy. Looks like you have a lot to offer football or basketball, either one. I saw you shoot baskets when I picked up my son from school. You're good at that too."

"Thanks," Adam shouted back, more thankful for the milk than the compliment.

"Adam that would be great! If you can fly, you can certainly jump. Join the team! I would come to every game," Fritzy giggled a little more. "I happen to know the coach personally, and I'm going to tell him what you just did for that boy."

Adam wanted to change the subject. He didn't know what had happened. Had he actually flown across the street like a super hero? He could still feel the air beneath his body, holding him in flight.

"Oh, you know the coach do you?" he teased.

"We get along alright, as long as I take out the trash, help Mother, and keep my grades up. Dads are dads. You know how that goes," she laughed.

"Sure," Adam agreed. But, he thought, *No, I don't know how that goes. I haven't seen Pops in almost three years.*

"Come on Adam, join the team. What's stopping you?"

"No, I—I can't." Adam never planned to say anything out loud about his family's problems, not until he heard himself say, "I don't have any basketball shoes."

He wished he hadn't said it. The words stuck in his throat like he had swallowed Rudy, all feathers and prickly orange bird feet.

"What about your uncle? Can't he get them for you?"

"My uncle?" He stumbled over his words. He was beginning to forget all the lies he had told.

"You told me you're living with your uncle. Uncle—Harold I think?"

"Yeah Fritzy, Uncle Harold." Adam knew he was lying, and he didn't lie well.

Fritzy went on talking and didn't seem to notice. "Couldn't he give you the money for the shoes and help with your mother's medical bills?" She asked then stuck her tongue out to capture a few fresh snowflakes.

"He's gone a lot." He smiled a knowing smile. "Fritzy, you don't know where that snowflake has been."

"Yes I do. It has been in the pure air of a snow cloud."

"You hope it's clean," he joked.

"It is," she insisted.

"Uncle Harold works hard, but he doesn't make much money." He stopped when he realized what he was saying. That turn of the conversation could be a problem. He couldn't cause people to think that no one else was at home. "Of course, he's home every night. He's just late."

"What does he do?"

"He's a traveling salesman. With the roads so bad this winter, travel is slow. He's home mostly to sleep. I get my homework done then—now Fritzy, that's another thing. I have so much to do. I clean the house—"

"Apartment."

"What?" Adam was confused. He put his hand to his face and tried to think it through.   "You said house, Adam. You meant apartment. You live in an apartment, right?"

"Right—an apartment." He had to talk about something else before he slipped and fell over his own fabrications. In spite of the cold, embarrassment was beginning to make him hot.

"Maybe if my dad," she started, "no—I have a better idea. My brother, Jimmy is away at college. His basketball shoes are on the floor of his closet. I'll bet you could have them."

"That's nice, but I have so much on my mind right now, so much to do, I wouldn't be able to focus on the game."

"But, it's—"

"Are you and your family going to Florida right after Christmas this year?" Adam quickly changed the subject. He would have to redirect her before he got his stories all tangled up and choked on them.

"Florida? I'd love to go south again before school starts, but Grandma wants to stay up here until after the first of the year. She wants to enjoy the snow for a week or two. Besides, vacation break is so late this year."

"So you're stuck here?"

"Not stuck. I haven't had a white Christmas for a long time. I'm looking forward to sparkling snow on holly wreaths and fluffy white trees."

Crack! Whump!

"Yikes," Fritzy yelled as a large icy branch snapped off from high up in the tree just ahead of her.

"You okay?"

"Yes, just mad," She stopped and stared at the fallen branch.

"Mad? At a tree limb?" Adam laughed and grabbed the biggest end of the frozen wood.

45

"Well," she fumbled, "I didn't expect it."

"You wouldn't have expected it to land on your head either. Thank goodness it didn't."

She picked up the other end and together they hoisted and drug the limb to the side of the walkway. "What are you and your uncle going to do?"

"Do?"

"For Christmas, Silly," Fritzy kept the questions coming.

"You don't stop talking even in the middle of an emergency, do you?" he laughed.

"Emergency?"

"It would have been if that limb had parted your hair for you."

"But it didn't, so there's no emergency. You just want to change the subject. What are you going to do on Christmas Day, Adam Shoemaker?"

"Not much. I plan to spend most of the time at the hospital with Moms."

"At the hospital? Won't you get tuberculosis?"

"No. Moms has passed the contagious stage. She's just weak."

"Will your uncle take you out there?"

"Sure," Adam lied again. The only way he was going to get out to the sanitarium would be to walk the five miles, since he had no Uncle Harold to drive him anywhere. He knew he could hike that far. He had trudged out there often. Maybe this time, with all the snow and cold wind, he would be able to hitch a ride. But, he wouldn't tell Fritzy anything about that. No one knew he lived in the church bell tower, and no one would, not even his mother. He shook his head and tried to get his mind off the impossible.

"Guess what I found—a hummingbird."

"You did not, Adam Shoemaker. They left months ago."

"Yes, I did. He flew right at me."

"Where? Where were you? Where did you find him?" Her excitement began to bubble out again in double time.

Adam stopped. How could he explain that the bird had been high up in the beams of a church belfry? He had to think up a different location. "The garage," he offered. "He was up in the rafters of my uncle's garage. He dove at me, then, hit the ground."

"The apartment has a garage? That's great, especially with this kind of winter."

"The apartment is in the upstairs of a home, and we have one of the spaces in a three car garage." Lies, lies and more lies. "With the boys home from Europe and Japan, housing is scarce."

"Is he okay? The hummingbird, is he alright?"

"He snapped out of it. I gave him some sugar water with food coloring mixed in to attract his attention." How could he tell her that Shaddy had helped him heal the little bird?

"Maybe he was in torpor," she chattered on, caught up in the excitement of the find. "They do that you know, when they don't have enough to eat."

"They do not." He stopped. "What is torpor anyway?"

"My dad's a science teacher, remember."

"Oh—that's right. Okay, so what's torpor?"

"Hummers eat one and a half to three times their body weight in food every day. When they don't have enough to eat, they go into a sleep-like state called torpor. Their body temperature drops by 50 degrees and their heart rate can slow from 500 beats per minute to less than 50. They may even stop breathing for a while."

"He was sure wide awake when he flew at me."

"Then, that rules out torpor. Hummingbirds don't respond to an emergency when they're in torpor. When you came upon him, that was an emergency for the hummer."

"Sure is a pretty little thing."

"They are fascinating. Daddy keeps a hummingbird feeder outside our breakfast room window. I could watch them all morning."

"Maybe the bird is one of yours." Adam didn't like the sound of that. He wanted the bird for himself. He might have to give the little fellow back if he could find its owner.

"Couldn't be. They flew south in September."

"Yeah, to Mexico." Then Adam thought a moment. "Ask your dad how those little things fly all the way to Mexico."

"Everyone believed that hummers fly south on the backs of northern geese. Some stories even say that they piggyback under the geese's wings. But Daddy says—"

"Don't tell me the story isn't true." He blew on his hands to get a little warmth back into them. "I like the way you told it first. For a little bird to find shelter under a large, safe wing sounds jake. I like that better." Adam always preferred the fantasy to reality. He had enough reality all around him in the bell tower.

She slipped her hand through the crook of Adam's arm and tromped through the deep snow a little harder until she matched his stride—almost. "So, the little hummer found another bird who can fly on miraculous missions, Adam—you."

"Well, I don't know about that, but I like the story of the hummingbirds."

"I like that story too. Aren't little fables wonderful? They take your mind off harder things."

"Harder things like basketball games and Algebra tests," he added. He liked walking with Fritzy. Maybe that's why he wanted to keep the conversation going. "I got a basketball last night."

"Have you been practicing?"

"Not yet."

She seemed to gulp in air as she shot back a plea. "Let Daddy give you Jimmy's shoes, Adam, please, for me."

"For you? You wouldn't fit in those shoes, Fritzy."

"You know what I mean. Stop being abstruse."

"So now I'm a fancy word for confused?"

When Adam and Fritzy got to the school door, they stomped off as much of the snow that clung to their boots as they could. Through the school doors, they entered a world of polished hardwood floors, smooth tile walls, and brick arches that defined the staircases. It smelled clean, not sterile, but clean. School was the home Adam did not have, and housed the only healthy adults in his life. School felt safe.

"Adam, look!" Fritzy squealed.

"What?" He looked around to see what she was so excited about.

"The New Year's Eve Party—I nearly forgot!" She pointed to the poster prominently displayed on the wall.

"I thought they cancelled that, since this is the first Christmas so many of the dads will be home," Adam said as he thought of full dinner tables and the smell of Moms toasty homemade, yeast rolls. He thought of families gathered by the fireplace after dinner, where they rested off their meal.

"Look at the date," she giggled some more. "The party is on December 31, the same day as my sister's wedding shower. This will be the first party since the War."

Fritzy nearly jumped up and down with party possibilities for the first time in years. Her verbal speed increased by twice its rate. "It's not a Christmas Party, like before the war. It's on New Year's Eve. With the party that evening, the chaperones will have Tuesday, New Year's Day, to relax and recover from the holidays. Sarah Jane's wedding shower is on New Year's Eve too, so everyone will be celebrating," she looked so excited, she seemed to bubble over as she babbled.

"Can we go?" she begged. "A party would be so much fun, with games, food and music! Everyone will be there. Will you take me?"

Adam's head swam and it felt like he could be taken under. He would have to tread water fast. He wouldn't have the money for a corsage for Fritzy or the tickets. He wouldn't have proper clothes, and he couldn't drive. He had no one to pick them up and drop them off.

"I'll bet we could double date with Charlie and Barbara," she prattled on. "They'll have games and—Adam, if you can fly like you did when you saved that boy, we would win all of the games and win some prizes."

"How much are the tickets?" He knew the price wouldn't matter, even if it cost nothing. He still wouldn't have money for flowers.

"The tickets were two dollars apiece, but the parents committee has decided to make it free. And—I don't need flowers."

"Fritzy—" Adam whispered as other students breezed past them.

"I have an idea, if you won't be insulted,' she lowered her voice. "My church needs someone to help the janitor for a few weeks during the holidays. There are so many programs; he can hardly keep up with everything. You would set up and take down tables and chairs, haul out the trash, sweep the floors—you know." She chattered on and on.

He saw no magic or dark shadows. Shaddy had not whispered in his ear, but, Adam's luck had changed. Maybe he had a job!

For the first time in months, he felt a sliver of hope stir within him. Had Shaddy, the spirit, put thoughts in Fritzy's head? How else was she able to have an answer to all of his problems? Was Shaddy providing what he needed, when he needed it, like he said?

"Where, Fritzy? What church do you attend?"

She beamed, "The Church on Cranberry Street."

Chapter 6

Going Home to Emptiness

"Don't push, Bobby," Kathleen Snyder ordered as she elbowed the eighth-grader who always pushed and shoved his way out to the school bus stop at the end of every school day.

"Yeah, yeah, yeah," the red-headed kid with the orange stocking cap fired back.

Adam saw shadows pass, glare at Bobby and seethe, but move on. He shuddered at the sight of them as he stood just inside the west door and waited for everyone to leave.

The snow beyond the school's windows still drifted halfway up the mailbox posts. He didn't even know if the road to the farm would be clear?

After everyone had cleared out of the building, except the floor sweeping crew, Adam started to walk toward the farm. He was almost sure no one had seen him slip out of town. He had hurried down back streets, away from the traffic. He didn't want anyone to know his business. He definitely did not want anyone to know that the farm was empty. The neighboring farm families might notice, since they look out for one another, but, they also respect the need for privacy.

The day was Thursday the twentieth, but the date wasn't important to Adam. What mattered was the mission he was on. He hadn't been out to the farm in months. If his mother was going to be released from the hospital soon, he would have to make sure everything was ready.

The country road out to the farm was a roller coaster ride on summer days. Gramps would drive back from town at just the right speed to leave Adam's stomach suspended in mid-air about every tenth fence post. The blizzard might make walking impossible. The blowing snow rolled into five foot drifts in the open fields where they waited for excited kids to get home from school and dig tunnels beneath the peaks. The weather couldn't stop Adam today.

The farm was a couple of miles out of town. Farm trucks had flattened deep ruts in the snow that made walking easier if he stayed in the furrows. But, even the warm sun hadn't melted much of the snow, just enough to leave some sloppy ice that caused him to slip occasionally.

"Shaddy, walk with me please and protect me from the bitter wind." Adam felt the same warmth come over him as before. It started in his heart and spread throughout his body, both inside and out, from his hair to the soles of his clodhoppers.

"I will remember your gloves for you," Shaddy promised.

Carl Benton slowed his milk truck as he pulled up beside Adam and opened the door. "This is no afternoon for walking. Want a ride?"

"That would be jake." Adam put one foot on the step of the delivery truck.

"Adam?" A familiar voice called after him on the cold air.

"Fritzy, what are you doing here?"

"I'm sorry. I truly am." She swished in her black snow pants and stomped through the snow inside her fur-lined winter boots as she caught up to the truck. "I had to come and find you. I walked all the way out here because I'm suspicious.

There's something going on with you, and I'm your friend." She stopped and stomped her foot. "Talk to me, Adam Shoemaker! Right now!"

"I don't know what to say," he blurted out.

"Begin by telling me why you were hiding from everyone when you left town." She jammed her gloved hands as far into her pockets as she could.

"I wasn't hiding," he began another lie.

"You were too, Adam, so knock it off." Fritzy pulled her hands out and placed them on her hips like a schoolmarm in an old movie.

"Okay, okay," Adam's shoulders fell as he opened up a little. He trusted Fritzy more and more. She was real. "I'm going out to the farm to check on everything. I didn't want anyone to see me. Maybe people won't notice there's nobody around the place," he confessed.

"Adam, I already know your mom is sick, your dad is gone, and you live in town with your uncle. Who else would be living at the farm anyway—spooks—little men in black?"

Adam shuddered as he thought about the shadows. "I guess you're right. But, I don't want anyone else to know."

"Why?" she demanded. "Who cares?"

"I care. I don't want people to know my business. You'll just have to accept that," he whispered insistently.

He gave Fritz a hand and helped her into the truck. "Thanks Carl." He rode in silence with Fritzy's background patter chattering beside him.

Finally Adam said, "We'll have to hurry. Your dad is going to kill me if I don't get you home before dark."

"No he won't. I told mom I would be late because I was going for a walk."

"A walk! All the way out here?" He chuckled a little.

"When I get back, I'm going to help Mother with Christmas cookies."

"Christmas cookies? That sounds good." What he really meant was food of any kind would taste like a feast that afternoon.

"She picked up some multi-colored sprinkles and green food coloring for the icing this afternoon," and on she chattered.

Carl had remained silent but, when cookies were mentioned, he spoke up. "Now you're making me hungry."

They arrived at the farmstead and hopped out of the truck. "Thanks again Carl," Adam said. The short lane that led to the barnyard had been plowed. By the looks of the tracks the tractor tires left, the good neighbor was either Nate Parker, down the road, or Sidney Crammer from the next farm over. Adam recognized the tread tracks and both farmers had the same kind of tractor.

The wind whipped through the willows and dripped their icy jewels all around the yard, from the road to the barn. The house looked cold and abandoned.

"It gives me the shivers," Adam admitted as he pulled his jacket around him.

"I think it's kinda pretty. A beautiful winter scene. All it needs is a light in the window and a little smoke from the chimney." Fritzy stopped and smiled. "Doesn't it remind you of a Grandma Moses painting?"

"Beautiful?" he gasped. "It doesn't look like a painting to me. It just looks empty, abandoned."

Adam pulled the house key from his pocket. He had carried it all the months the family had been off the place. The key represented access to a life that used to be—a life that was no more—a life of warm pancakes, with hot butter and syrup dripping down the side once the morning chores were done. He looked toward the house, but it looked dark and cold.

"Let's start in the barn and check on the cats." His choose the barn first because it was too hard to go into the house. He grabbed Fritzy's hand. Together they slipped and slid up the earthen hill of the bank barn.

"I should have brought my ice skates," Fritzy laughed. "I'll bet I could have been Sonja Henie—if I didn't fall down all the time," she giggled some more.

"Don't try out for the Olympics until you get a little more practice," he joked.

"Maybe if I practice off the ice," she suggested with a grin.

"Right, an ice skater who practices away from everything frozen," he shook his head in disbelief. As they reached their goal, Adam pushed the double, cross beamed barn doors open. The perfume of the old barn still clung to the walls and hung in the air—sweet bailed hay, clean metal milk cans that still boasted the aroma of fresh raw milk, and leather harnesses that hung from wooden pegs driven into the huge barn beams.

The tractor was still in the barn with a partial tank of gas. The oat bin was half full of grain, but the cows had been sold. Off to the side, on the barn floor, the coveted 1937 Diamond T truck waited for Adam to come of driving age.

"Looks like the cats still play in the hay mow. They must have found food by hunting mice." A few of them, including Adam's favorite calico, bounded over to them and nuzzled his leg. "They look okay."

"It all looks the same, yet everything is different," Adam whispered as he fingered the house key in his pocket. The key to the house was something he could hold on to. It would never have been left behind.

"Come on. We can't waste too much time. The dark will be comin' on soon, and I came to clean."

"Well, me too. I'm no weakling." She looked toward the house. "Looks like the porch steps are going to be another assault on frozen peaks."

He found a flat-nosed grain shovel in the corner of the barn and carried it to the house. "This should do it."

"I can help. I shovel the walk at home sometimes."

"I can get it done faster." Adam insisted. He shoveled the snow until his fingers nearly froze to the handle. He stopped and blew warm breaths into them as he cleared a path up the steps. They stepped up on the wide porch that wrapped around two sides of the house like a man wrestling a bear with biceps of icy steel. Adam nearly slipped onto his backside while Fritzy still clung to the frozen porch railing. Her feet slid in every direction, like a slapstick comic in the movies.

"Careful," she laughed. "I don't think I can pick you up off the ground or this porch."

"Me? You look like the one who is walking on ball bearings."

"At least if I fall, I'll do it gracefully."

Shadows came, waited for an accident to happen and watched with their blank, black eyes. The porch smelled foul, like a dead possum was under the boards.

"Get away from me," Adam commanded the darkness.

"Done well, my son," Shaddy encouraged.

Fritzy didn't hear the spirit. "Sorry!" She threw up her hands in resignation, then grabbed the railing again.

"Not you," he stammered.

"Who then, Adam—the ghosts?" She looked around the barnyard.

"Something like that," he whispered, embarrassed.

With the coal shovel, he pushed the snow from a large section of the porch but not to the front door. The parlor door was only for company and few people were considered company to Moms. He cleared the path to the second door. Adam turned the key in the lock at the side entrance that led into the sitting room and let them both in.

The house didn't feel like home. There was no warmth and the rich aroma of homemade noodles and chicken wasn't coming from the kitchen. Moms's African violets had withered and dropped their dry blossoms. A layer of dust blanketed everything.

"This is lovely," Fritzy admired.

"This is all dirty is what you mean."

"Dust isn't dirt, Adam. Dust is more like heavy air that has settles in the house."

"Heavy air?" He looked at her with amazement. Then he turned to the details of the room itself.

"Let's get you guys out of here," Adam talked to the plants as he hustled them to the back porch. Fritzy followed close behind.

The enclosed porch always smelled of tart pie apples, no matter the time of year. "It smells wonderful in here," she smiled as she inhaled the fruity aroma.

A bucket of black walnuts still sat in the corner. The green hulls had been removed but they had waited there, uncracked, for over a year. Moms had gotten too weak to think about walnut meat that still clung to the shells.

"Maybe we can crack these nuts for your mom sometime."

"Sure," he responded automatically as he sat the skeletal remains of the violets on the tin counter-top of the old wooden cabinet. He grabbed up some cleaning supplies and looked around.

"The electricity may not be on now, but I can chase some of the dirt around with these rags and out of the carpet with the broom."

"I'll take the dust rags," Fritzy offered.

"One of them—I can dust too," he grinned

"Wow, what a man," she teased.

In the parlor, he focused special attention on the bookshelves. "Moms always said, 'Adam, don't just push the dust around in front of the books. Take each book down and dust the shelf underneath it.' Moms was always particular about a clean house." He removed each book then stopped.

"Huckleberry Finn" he read from the book's spine. "Moms you—" his voice cracked, and he wiped his nose on his sleeve. "Good ol' Huck," he smiled and shoved the book back into its assigned slot.

"Anne of Green Gables—Adam, did you read the Anne stories?" Fritzy asked surprised.

"No," he laughed. "They were Moms' favorites."

"The fireplaces will be a big problem," Adam admitted. "I left the house in early spring when the dampers were still open. I was in and out through the summer because we had a problem with the farmer who was to do the planting. I got so overwhelmed with all of that, I never closed the dampers. It looks like snow and leaves have fallen through the chimney and picked up a lot of soot as they fell." He stared at the hearth, took a deep breath and began. With one of the dust rags, he polished the brass fireplace tools until they shone.

"That looks great, Adam. I'll use the broom on the carpet. That way, we won't chase dirt from the carpet back to the fireplace." She grabbed up the broom and didn't wait for Adam's approval.

"The little shovel, and the rest of these andirons, will get rid of these leftover ashes," Adam's voice was soft. "Moms asked me to clean the fireplaces after the last cold spell in the spring, but, as usual, I didn't refuse, I just didn't do it." He leaned his hand on the mantel and stared at the hearth. "I would do anything that you asked me to do now Moms, if you could just come home."

"I am so sorry, Adam."

"Pops—why, why did you leave us?" Adam spoke so soft, it had to come from a hidden corner of his memory.

Fritzy tried to encourage him and picked up a framed family portrait from the thick beamed mantle. She saw smiling parents and a happy son with stubborn brown hair. "Look at

58

the cute kid with all the hair. Your family looks really happy," she offered.

"Were happy," Adam corrected. The picture brought back memories and unanswered questions Adam thought he had forgotten. Pops was several heads taller than Adam when the picture was taken.

"I wonder who the tallest is now." Adam whispered as he took the picture and carefully dusted the surface. A faint smile crossed his face. How could he hate someone he loved so much?

Suddenly, there was a strange presence around the house, a foreboding. He had seen the shadows in the barn and on the porch, but not in the house. What was it? He didn't see anything, but he could feel it. He suddenly felt trapped, like the house was closing in on him. The foreboding made his skin rise with chill bumps.

"You okay?" Fritzy asked.

"Sure," Adam shrugged it off. "I'm just jumpy today I guess." Then he hurried to finish cleaning the house as it grew even colder.

Adam was soon lost in his thoughts. He had fears he didn't share with anyone. *What is it? Who is here?*

He shook off the uneasy feeling and tried to concentrate on the work at hand. There were two dual fireplaces in the house. The first one was there in the sitting room that shared a chimney with the fireplace in the parlor. The same was true upstairs. A fireplace in Adam's room was back-to-back with the one in his parent's room.

"Let's get busy," Adam said. That afternoon, the two friends shoveled and whisked all four fireplaces, vigorously pulled and raked the carpets with the broom and carefully ran a dust cloth over all surfaces. Then he checked his watch. "The time is flying. It could be dark by the time we get home."

"Adam Schumacher, you here?" A voice called from downstairs.

He sounds familiar, not sinister. "I'm here," Adam admitted, then wondered if he should have kept Fritzy and himself hidden. Their presence was out now. "I'll come down."

"Gloves," Shaddy whispered as he had promised.

Adam grabbed his gloves from his top bureau drawer in his room and started down the stairs with Fritzy close behind him. When they got to the foot of the steps, he was surprised to see Sidney Crammer. The man stood just inside the sitting room door where he dropped snow from his hat onto Moms' good sofa.

"I let myself in. Your dad had given me a key when he asked me to farm for him. I thought I saw you walking up the lane earlier."

"We were just leaving Mr. Crammer. We have to get back to town."

Fritzy came quietly down the stairs and stood at a distance.

"Haven't seen you or your ma around the place in months. There a problem?"

"No Sir. We—well; we don't tell everyone our family's business, Mr. Crammer. I hope you understand." Adam started toward the door which caused Crammer to retreat. Adam reached for Fritzy's hand, opened the door and headed out.

"Sure, Adam." Crammer paused and followed the two as they walked out onto the porch. Adam locked up. "I talked to your pa a couple years ago about buying some of the farm. He wanted to put in running water and a bathroom with the money."

Adam stopped and studied the man. He certainly knew there was no indoor toilet. It was a major condition in Moms' ability to come home, and he had walked the slippery path to the outhouse on many cold nights. But, he never heard anything about selling part of the farm.

"We put in electricity back in 1939," Adam said, "when the rural service came down our road. Guess Pops was thinking about a bathroom too."

"Yeah, he was," Crammer agreed.

"He didn't tell me anything about it. Moms neither."

"Well, he told me, Son. I'm sure he didn't want to bother you." Mr. Crammer squared his shoulders and looked out over the barnyard. "You sure have a pretty place here."

"Yes, Sir." Adam searched his memory for any hint that Pops was thinking about bringing the privy into the house. "Pops told me about everything, Mr. Crammer. We didn't talk about the bathroom. He never kept secrets from Moms and me." *Crammer must be the source of my crowded feeling, I feel pushed.*

"Won't argue with that, Adam. Since your dad—well, is still gone, don't know how you're going to pay to have a bathroom put in your house."

"Adam has a job now," Fritzy interrupted. "He's not a child. He is employed."

"That's my point, Adam. If part of the farm is going to be sold, you and your mom are the two I should deal with. As a matter of fact, your dad had talked about selling off the creek and the bottom land adjacent to the water's edge."

Adam felt a knot in his stomach. "The creek?" He looked at Fritzy and motioned for them to move on down the porch steps. Sidney Crammer scampered close behind like a yapping dog unrelentingly nipping at their heels.

"Yes, of course, the creek," Crammer cracked.

"We've got to get back to town, Mr. Crammer." Adam had to nearly push the man aside so they could be on their way. They were running late.

Sidney Crammer stood in the lane as the young landowner and his friend headed back to town. The wind had come up again while they were inside. "Think about selling,

Adam," Cramer shouted after them. "Letting go of some of the land was what your father wanted," the man hollered again.

They had walked half way down the dirt lane when Adam turned and put on his gloves. "I'll talk to Moms. I can't promise you anything. I'll tell you this, I'm against it." He turned and didn't look back.

"Everybody knows that land with water is the most valuable," Fritzy chimed in again.

"That's right," Adam agreed. He knew Crammer's offer didn't sound right. His grandfather's voice echoed in his ears, and the message was the same as the one from his own father. His father and grandfather had been through the Great Depression. Each knew the fear and desperation of poverty, but they always had one thing of value.

"Maybe one of your neighbors could farm the land for you and your mother," she suggested. "I know many farmers work other people's fields. They make money for both of them."

"That's it, Fritzy. Crammer had farmed the land for us after Pops was drafted. Then suddenly he said he couldn't do it anymore."

"Well, that was convenient. Now you and your mother are in a place where you might be forced to sell some land." Fritzy's voice was hoarse as they hurried along the lane.

"Well, it won't work," he stated flatly. "Gramps said, 'Adam, it's the farm.' Pops and Grandpa taught me clearly. They both said, 'The land is all you have between hunger and prosperity. Hang on to every acre. The ground is a living solution.' Crammer is not going to trick us into selling one foot of this farm."

Chapter 7

Blue Car Man

They would have to hustle if they were going to get back to town before darkness fell. Adam had Fritzy with him and, to his way of thinking, he was responsible for her, at least that evening he was.

A clear mind and clear vision are different things. When the sun sets in the country, it is dark, seriously dark. They had to reach town before the sun touched the horizon. They stepped up their pace as the temperature began to drop. When they had passed Raymond Bryson's farm, six lanes down the road, a blue car slowed down beside them.

"The weather's starting to get bad. You two want a ride back to town?" the driver asked.

"That's okay," Adam refused and didn't look up. The timbre of man's voice had an eerie echo that was unnerving as the sound bounced along on the clear icy air. The goose bumps on Adam's arms stood at attention again. *First, Crammer pushed me, now this guy. I can't get Fritzy involved in this.*

"Look behind you, Son," the driver suggested.

Early evening moonlight allowed Adam to see that a squall had gathered in the west. "Even in the dark, that doesn't look good."

"It looks bad." Fritzy huddled up close to Adam and buried her head in his back to protect her face from the wind.

"There's another blizzard pushing in. You two had better hop in and let me take you back to town." The man was pleasant enough.

Adam would have acted without paying attention to his gut in the past, but it was different this time. He had never seen the man around before and Fritzy was with him.

"I'm so cold. You get in the front and I'll climb in the back. I can still get back in time to help Mom finish the cookies," Fritzy said as she reached for the door handle and got in.

Adam had little choice. He got into the car with a sickening feeling in the pit of his stomach. Country people hitch rides into town all the time. In a small community, everyone knows everybody else. This time the situation was different. He was sure he did not know Mr. Blue Car.

"The name is Smith," the man offered.

"Adam Shoemaker. Thanks Mister."

"Fritzy—"

"She's just Fritzy," Adam stated bluntly.

"I have a last name, Adam Shoemaker," Fritzy snapped as she pushed her hood from her head.

"Strangers don't need to know everything," Adam said softly.

"But it's okay if he knows your last name?" she snapped then yawned.

"Yes, it is," Adam smiled.

"That sound like very old thinking to me," she shot back.

"Shoemaker?" Smith looked at the boy a moment then turned his attention back to the road. "It's a little slicker out here since the sun has gone down."

Smith? Adam puzzled. *There aren't any Smiths in Middletown.* "You from around here, Mr. Smith?"

"No, Son, I'm not. You live out this way—you and the Little Miss?"

Adam felt uneasy. Why was the stranger asking him where they lived? Who was he? Adam didn't like the whole situation, but he really didn't know why, except he had Fritzy to think about. If he had to jump out of the car quickly, he couldn't leave Fritzy behind.

He answered in a monotone droll, "No, I live in town. We were visiting the Crammers." More lies but they seemed to be the safest response.

Shaddy, who is this guy? Why does he give me the creeps?

Nothing more was said for a little while. In the reflection on the side window, it looked like Fritzy had fallen asleep.

"This is the first Christmas without war since 1938," Smith broke the silence.

"That's right I guess. I hadn't thought about the holidays like that."

"Did you folks get along okay back here?"

Back here? Adam wondered what the stranger meant. He decided facts would be safe.

"Most of the men and boys were gone. My dad shipped out almost three years ago. First, we thought he wouldn't have to go. He was a farmer and food was necessary. I guess they ran out of available men."

In the dim light, Adam could see the snow-covered jagged fence posts in the side window as they got closer to town. They flew by like skeletons standing guard. Adam focused on the falling snow that bombarded the front windshield with kamikaze impact.

"I'll bet you're glad your dad's back home."

Adam was not interested in talking about his father's absence with a stranger. He didn't know why his father hadn't come home. He definitely was not going to say that Pops might be a deserter. It was easier to think that he was dead and the war department hadn't sent his body home. Not even his dog tags.

"Is there anything I can do to help out?" Smith sounded caring, helpful even. But, who was he?

"No, we're getting along okay." Adam gripped the passenger side door handle and nearly jumped out of the car when they slowed at the first stop street inside the city limits. Then he thought of the sleeper in the back seat. "You can let me off at Fritzy's house."

"This is Cranberry Street?" Smith looked up at the street sign. "Tell me where to go."

"Three streets up. Norman Avenue." They road on in silence.

"I'll take you home then," the man offered.

"No, that's okay. I live down the street." Adam insisted.

When the car stopped, Adam hopped out and opened the back door. "Fritzy," he nudged her shoulder. "Wake up."

"Oh," Fritzy slowly opened her eyes and looked around. "We're home? Thank you. I'm going to the church for a while later this evening, but I'm starved."

Mr. Breman opened the front door. "Glad you two are back," he called out as he hurried down the steps to help his daughter inside. "Your mom said you had gone for a walk and I said, 'Impossible. Not on an afternoon like this.' Did you have a good time?" He reached out his hand to Adam. "Good to see you. I knew she was in safe hands."

"Yes Sir."

Coach Breman looked into the car and gave a friendly wave.

"Coach, this is Mr. Smith. He gave us a ride when the weather turned bad."

"Thank you," Coach waved again.

"You are most welcome." Smith said. "Say, you don't know a Schumacher family around here do ya?"

Coach looked at Adam and back at the blue-car-man. "No, I'm sorry. I don't." Then, to Fritzy he said, "Come on, Honey. Let's get in where it's warm."

"Thanks, Adam. I had a good time," she smiled then thought again. "I am really hungry, Daddy. Did you save my supper?"

"We were just ready to eat. Do you want to stay for supper, Adam?" Coach Breman asked.

"Yes. Come in for supper," Fritzy begged. "You must be as hungry as I am, and I could eat anything that doesn't take a bite out of me first."

"No thanks. Gotta get back." He backed away, putting distance between himself and Mr. Blue-car. "Bye, Fritzy."

Adam motioned to Smith to drive on. "I can walk from here. Thanks." Adam had to get away. He was tired of the questions, and sick of the cold. He was relieved he had told Smith to let him off at Fritzy's home. It was just a few blocks down and over from the church, and he could walk the rest of the way. There was something about the man that made him feel uncomfortable, but he didn't know what.

Smith coasted his car along the curb behind Adam as he walked on the sidewalk. Adam feared the man would follow him all the way to the belfry. He walked up to the first house that had no lights on and pretended to try the front door.

"Back door," he shouted over to Smith and waved him off. Adam walked around to the back of the house then, he ran up the alley and over the fence into the neighbor's yard. He was glad Morningstar's dog wasn't out. That big black mutt chased anyone and anything off the place. Adam could hear the dog bark even though the animal was inside the house.

In Morningstar's back yard, Adam could see that moonlight had begun to burn through the heavy snow clouds. In the dim light, he saw a path stretched out before him, defined by tiny bits of sparkling green dust. He followed the crystal path, darted across several back yards and came out on the next street, more than a half block from where he had entered. When he circled around and got back to the church, he finally breathed a sigh of relief. His satisfaction at arriving back on Cranberry Street was quickly squashed. Every light in the church was on. He dare not go in.

"You are home, My Son," Shaddy whispered in his ear.

"Home," Adam mumbled to himself. "Only a god who would speak to me would call a cold, lonely belfry a home, a home I dare not enter because good people are here."

Chapter 8

Christmas Cookies and Precious Art

Adam walked to the back of the church building. He couldn't enter through the kitchen window. A group of women worked rapidly and buzzed between the oven and the counters. There was nothing Adam could do. He considered the coal room window but thought it would be too risky. The church women liked to have all the lights on so the hall would be brightly lit. Adam leaned into the doorway of the back entrance and crouched down to make a smaller target for the wind and flying snow. He lost track of how long he hid in the dark outside the church. He dozed off in bits and snatches.

Wait a minute, there is no reason why I can't go in where it's warm. I refuse to be found frozen stiff in the morning.

Adam went to the front door and stepped inside the church. He had figured it right. Every light in the church was on.

Even though the street lights had come on, the usual time for folks to be home for the evening, the church on Cranberry Street was alive with activity. Adam followed the sweet aroma all the way to the kitchen door. He quietly stepped into the warmth.

Women of the church hustled to place hundreds of freshly baked and iced cookies into large tin cans decorated with festive Christmas scenes. The cookies were then covered with wax paper before the tin lid was secured on the top.

There were three fragrances that made Adam's knees buckle: burning leaves near a fall woods, sawdust ribbons freshly shaved, and Christmas cookies just out of the oven. Festive shapes of sugar cookies were all over the kitchen waiting to be iced.

"Adam, I'm so glad you're here." Fritzy wiped her flour dusted hands on her apron as she looked up. "How did you happen to drop in? Daddy had my grilled cheese sandwich ready and I wolfed it down in the car while he drove me over here," she paused just a second. "Would you like a cookie?" Without waiting for an answer, she popped an extra Christmas stocking into Adam's mouth. "I'm sure this one won't fit in the tin," she smiled. "We're finishing up with the cookies while some of the men set up the Nativity Scene."

"I know, I know," Adam said with little enthusiasm, "a doll in a manger."

"Adam, our baby Jesus is a work of art, a masterpiece, carved from a Lebanon Cedar, brought back from the Mediterranean. The artist, Samuel Morris, was one of the greatest wood artists ever. The carving is worth a lot of money, but more important, the Baby Jesus was given to us by Mr. Morris himself. He used to live here in Middletown. That carving represents our very own Christ Child."

"I'm sorry, Fritzy. I didn't understand how much it means to all of you. It is the Christmas Christ Child, but it is a piece of priceless art as well, given by the artist."

"That's okay. You didn't know," her eyes twinkled, "and now you do." She untied her apron strings, folded it carefully and laid the bright cotton cover-up on the kitchen counter top. "Have you ever tried to carve anything?"

"Me? No, never."

"Mother let me carve a few big bars of Ivory soap," Fritzy smiled. "Mrs. Becker, the art teacher, told us to draw a picture on paper the size of the bar of soap. We put that image on the soap and traced the edges with a tooth pick that left an indented outline on the bar. Then, we used a paring knife to shave away everything that wasn't our drawing. Carving soap is fun. I can't imagine how hard it would be to carve something as beautiful as the Christ Child out of hard wood? That carving of the babe represents all of our Christmases past."

Adam said no more about the carving. Fritzy's description of her own artful whittling and explanation about how much the figure meant to her, only made Adam feel worse. A baby doll in a wooden food trough hadn't seemed very precious to him in the past. He didn't expect this Christmas to be any different, but he couldn't tell Fritzy how he felt.

There was silence. Then she added, "It's getting late. If more snow comes in like they say it's supposed to, the walks will get even more slippery. Daddy is going to meet Mom and me out front. I had better be going."

"I wish I could drive you," Adam offered.

"Then none of us would be safe," she laughed.

"I will have you know, I have been driving the tractor on the farm for five years, since I was ten. You would be very safe with me."

Fritzy smiled. "A real race car driver!"

"I might not be ready for the Indi-Five-Hundred." Then he thought about all of the people who were still milling through the church as they began to finish up and clear out. He couldn't very well be the last one in the building. After all, how would he explain that?

"I'll walk you to the door so you can wait for your dad," he offered.

They slipped their coats off the hangers near the front door and put them on. Together he and Fritzy stood for a

71

moment by the leaded glass window in the door where they could see out to the street. They didn't say much. They shared small talk about school, the day, and the holidays. They spoke a lot of words but the conversation would not have sounded special to anyone who happened by. To Adam, their being together was great. It wasn't just because he was talking with Fritzy, but because he had absolutely no one else to share a thought with except the hummingbird. The hummer was not no-one, he was a no-thing, and that was vastly different.

"More snow?" Mrs. Breman shook her head and scolded the darkness outside. When Coach Breman pulled up to the curb, she grabbed her coat from the coat rack and joined the two. Adam walked to the curb with Fritzy and helped her and her mother into the car. What should he do? There were still others in the church.

When the Bremans' car neared the corner and turned, Adam slipped back into the church and into the sanctuary where he slouched down on a pew. Like a common street bum, he stayed in the darkness of the sanctuary and waited for the sound of happy friends to fade. He was not one of them. He was an interloper, a fraud, a liar. He feared he would be caught in his charade.

"Why do I even care?" he whispered into the vacant places all around him. He should not have cared about Fritzy or about the Christ Child carving. Caring about someone else felt like he was standing on an ice-covered pond as the hardness snapped and the crack chased him across the surface. He could barely stay ahead of the split that would take him under and steal away his new sense of security.

"What next?" he whispered into the night. "Shaddy, will I ever stop running from breaking ice?"

Chapter 9

The Basketball Shoes

Friday, December 21, 1945

"Shoemaker," Coach Breman came up behind Adam in the school hallway the next day and put his hand on the boy's shoulder. "My daughter tells me I might be able to snare you for the basketball team."

"I don't know, Coach. I don't—"

"She also said you could use Jim's basketball shoes."

"Coach, I can't pay—"

"Who said anything about payment? Besides, Jim has grown two inches taller since he has been in college. He now wears a shoe two sizes bigger than the ones sitting in his closet at home. You would be doing his mother a favor by helping her clean out some of the things Jim doesn't need any more. Today is Friday. He will be home tonight for Christmas break. Maybe you could stop by the house on your way home and pick them up? Sure would help Mrs. Breman."

What could the boy say? He had no more sharp excuses left in his quiver.

"Then there is still the team. Adam, George Barnard already left town with his parents for the holidays. Eric Fox is

73

sick at home with mumps, and Gary Jefferson is down with a head cold so bad he can't breathe through his nose. We have one game left tonight before Christmas break. I want you to play, or we may have to forfeit the game."

"Coach, no. I haven't even practiced with the team."

"Yes you have, Adam. You play with the guys every day after school for a half hour or so before the team practices. I have seen your free throws and lay-up shots. You're a natural."

"I shot baskets every day all summer out at the farm. Pops had put up a hoop for me before—I'll think about it, Coach." The bell rang to announce the start of class. The halls began to empty.

"I'll talk to you more at the house. Now you stop by for those shoes, Adam." Coach Breman hurried into the Biology Lab and starting lecturing before he pulled the door closed.

After school, Adam darted out the north door and started down the freshly shoveled sidewalk when Fritzy caught up to him. She had to move fast. The legs that went with her five-foot four-inch body could not cover nearly as much ground as those that matched his six-foot two frame.

"Adam, why are you running?"

"I'm not running. Just out stretching you." He laughed and waited for her to catch up.

"Daddy said you were going to stop by the house and get those shoes. Right?"

"Right," he added with apprehension. His father had taught him to work hard and not accept charity. He had wrestled in his mind all day about whether to accept the shoes, about the team, about being beholding to people. Now, he was on his way to the Breman home and the decision seemed settled. Was he helping Mrs. Breman, or was Fritzy's family helping the needy, abandoned kid? He couldn't tolerate the thought that the Bremans might think of him as poor. He was temporarily out of money, that was true, but he was not poor.

Pops always said that poorness is a state of mind, not a state of the wallet.

When they arrived at the Breman home, Fritzy's mother met them at the door. "Would you like some milk and cookies, Adam?"

He laughed to himself. Milk and cookies sounded like a kid's snack but a hungry man couldn't be choosey.

Without waiting for an answer, Fritzy led him into the kitchen and pointed to the table and chairs. "You sit here," she commanded in her fun-loving way as she sat down.

He slowly studied the room. There was a four-burner electric stove against the east wall, a sink built right into the kitchen cabinets beneath the window that looked out over the back yard, and an electric refrigerator in the corner, not an ice box like his family had on the farm.

No ice man stops here, he thought.

"Here we go," Mrs. Breman offered as she brought over a small plate of cookies and glasses of cold milk.

"Tell me, Adam, what's your mother's name? I think I may know her," she began. "I believe we belonged to the Child Welfare Club together when she first came to town. She was a good friend. We served as room-mothers together when you two were in first grade. I heard she is sick."

A good friend? I didn't know Moms had friends. All she does is work all day long, every day. He snapped his mind back to Fritzy's kitchen. "Yes, Ma'am. She has tuberculosis."

"Where do you—?"

"I'd better hurry along. My uncle will be wondering where I am."

"Oh, I don't remember that your mother talked about a brother."

"No, Ma'am. He's not my mother's brother. He's my father's brother. Moms is from the East" He looked up at the clock above the sink.

"Sit down, Adam," Mrs. Breman said as she patted his shoulder. "You have plenty of time."

Adam sat down at the table as directed, drank the full glass of milk and took a few bites from one of the cookies. "Wow, these cookies are good, but I really have to go."

"Please, let's look at those shoes first," Mrs. Breman protested and led the way to her son's room and his overstuffed closet.

"I just know they'll fit you," Fritzy babbled as she wrapped some cookies in wax paper. "You can take some with you." She looked up and then added three more to the package.

The bedrooms were on the second floor of the colonial style house. Jim's room was on the north-west corner and was decorated in coordinated shades of blue and brown with matching bedspread and curtains. Trophies were displayed everywhere, across the top of the dresser and on special shelves designed just for them. Adam could tell the cabinets were strong and designed to hold many statues that testified to Jim's ability. There were basketball, baseball and track trophies of various heights and designs. He didn't want to stare, so he only glanced quickly about the room.

"Well, these are the shoes." Mrs. Breman stretched and pulled the pair from the back of Jim's closet. "Oh," her face distorted as if in pain.

"You okay, Mrs. Breman?" Adam saw her wince. He was always aware when Moms had done too much. There was a time, when the world was sane, that he thought he might like to become a doctor. He liked to draw pictures of all the muscle groups of the body. In the last few months, he just hoped to survive another day.

"I was cleaning the closet this afternoon, and I pulled a muscle in my back crawling around. I was trying to drag the stuff out of the back."

"Here, let me help you." Adam squatted down like a weight lifter before the big pull. With his long arms, he scrambled everything out from the floor of the closet with one scoop.

"Oh, thank you," she chuckled as she started to bend over.

"No, Ma'am. You sit there on the bed, and I'll lift all this stuff up to you." He gathered up the now infamous basketball shoes, a tennis racket, a pair of black dress shoes, two baseball caps—one white, one dark blue—both with appropriate team logos prominently attached on the front, all mixed in with half-used notebooks, an older pair of sneakers and single socks with an occasional pair, mostly in plain colors and one argyle.

Mrs. Breman quickly sorted all the items into categories, with subdivisions of clean and soiled. "There, the task took us a matter of minutes when we did the job together." She reached over to pick up the shoes that were on the floor and then smiled and stopped. "You had better get them, Adam. They're yours now anyway." Then she put her hand to her mouth. "Oh, they are size 11. I hope they fit."

"Yes, Ma'am," and his eyes twinkled. "I'm sure they will." He turned his back as if he were going to sit on the edge of Jim's desk chair. "Shaddy," he whispered low, "increase their size by a half."

"Blow in them, My Son," Adam heard Shaddy whisper in his head.

Adam tipped up the shoes and pretended to look inside for stray laces.

"There may be dust inside them. I am so sorry," Mrs. Breman apologized.

Perfect. He turned his back to the two, "Don't want to get any dust on you two. He took a deep breath and blew into the shoes and felt the leather give and expand between his fingers. He pulled the laces on his clodhoppers, kicked them off and slid his feet into the basketball shoes. They fit perfectly.

Thank you, Shaddy. Neither Fritzy nor her mother seemed to notice the power of Adam's breath. The size 11s had become 11½ with a puff from Shaddy the spirit.

"They seem to fit you," Mrs. Breman smiled. "And, for helping me, a bonus," she added as she carefully rose, straightened her back, and went to the dresser. "Jim has grown so much his shoes are two sizes too small, so his socks would be short too." She reached in the drawer and pulled out half-a-dozen pair, most of them athletic white. "Here you are." Quickly she added, "Thank you so much for helping me get rid of this stuff. That will leave room for Jimmy's stuff—things that fit him."

"Ma'am—"

"Adam, you don't know how much you have helped me. This is at least something I can do in return. I—don't have extra money. It helps me a lot to be able to give you something of value in return, even if the shoes and socks are used—junk."

"Oh no, Ma'am. They're not junk. I appreciate your generosity." Adam picked up each item as if it were a precious gift. He remembered what his grandfather had said, "When people are generous, the recipient is generous in return by valuing their gift, no matter how small."

"Are you ready?" Fritzy beamed as she came into the room.

"Ready?" Her mother asked.

"I'm going to take Adam over to the church. Mr. Gunderman needs some help with his work, and I thought Adam would be a good job candidate." She latched onto Adam's coat sleeve and tried to ease him out of the room.

"I thought you were kidding about a job." He had no idea there were any jobs available around town. Since so many returning veterans found no work when they got home, Adam did not even apply anywhere. The message was always the same. "No openings."

Adam suddenly became excited. He had a strong sense of responsibility, and he might now actually be able to put it to use with a real job.

"Maybe you shouldn't leave. Your mom seems to need more help," Adam protested gently. He used to be a helpful, thoughtful person, before the entire world learned what hate was.

"I'll help you when I get back, Mom. Adam is going to talk with Mr. Gunderman about helping out at the church over the holidays."

"That's very nice, Adam. I'll get a sack to put those things in, and a few other items I see here on the floor. You get your package of cookie and then you two can run along."

"Thanks," Fritzy sang as she pulled Adam out of the room.

Adam turned back and looked one last time at Jim's warm room with walls and a ceiling. His own bare attic room in the bell tower flooded his mind by comparison. The only warm spot in the belfry was inside Mrs. Brumble's purse, that small hummingbird that slept in the basket. And the only one to talk to was Shaddy. He was always there.

Chapter 10

A Real Job in a Secret Place

The front door of the Cranberry Street Church! Wow! Not the back entrance. I can enter through the door that respectable people go through.

Adam's experience with the church was vastly different on most other days. He didn't usually go through the front door. He wondered if the kings of old ever went through the back door of the cathedral or crawled in through the coal room window. Today, as he entered with Fritzy, he felt like one of those kings as he walked through the double doors. He wondered when he had stopped feeling noble, respectable.

Again he thought of his grandfather's admonition. "Always keep your name clean. Nothing is more precious than your reputation." Adam felt stronger than he had in months, stronger and cleaner.

"Mr. Gunderman," Fritzy called out from the narthex without proceeding into the church. "You here?"

"Fredericka Breman?" a voice called out from the room below.

"Yes, Sir," she echoed back.

They waited. When the old man came up from the Fellowship Hall below, Adam realized that Mr. Gunderman was breathing hard as he climbed the stairs. Each step on the treads seemed to be in time with the music from the sanctuary. The church was awake this time. The boy took it all in. Off in the sanctuary, the organist was practicing for Sunday services. Adam was mesmerized by the melodies he had forgotten. She usually practiced during mid-day and he wouldn't hear her since he was in school at that time.

Alfred Gunderman huffed and puffed to the top of the stairs. "It's you, Child," he chuckled like the Squire of Christmas Eve, right down to his rosy cheeks.

"This is Adam Shoemaker, Mr. Gunderman, and he would like to apply for that assistant janitor's job. I came along to tell you that my parents and I recommend him very highly for the position."

"Oh you do, do you?" Alfred smiled mischievously. He looked down at Adam's black leather, high-top clodhoppers, then met him eye to eye. "You an honest boy?" he quizzed.

"Yes, Sir, I am." Adam straightened his back and tried his best to meet the old man's gaze, blink for blink.

"You been arrested for anything?" Gunderman continued. "Vandalism—trespassing—pilfering?"

Adam felt a discomfort in his skin, like he had seen a spider and couldn't stop brushing an imaginary one off his clothing. He had already said he was honest, but he definitely had been trespassing in the church. The question included the word *arrested,* however. "No, Sir. I have never been arrested for anything."

He felt his eyes lose contact with the man's, and he snapped them back again. He knew he was playing with words.

A man's word is the most important thing he has, he remembered his father saying in a distant time. Gunderman probably knew his father and grandfather. Their good word would have gotten him the job easily. However, Adam didn't want to bring up the family name. He had buried that in the past.

"Never been arrested, never stole anything." Alfred repeated. "Now that is a blessing! And, accepting a gift of charity is not stealing."

Adam thought of his new basketball and the basket-purse. He could feel a bead of sweat on his forehead. *How could Alfred Gunderman possibly know about the ball or the purse?* His mind raced as he tried to stay ahead of his story.

Shaddy, he begged silently. *Help me get through these questions. Soon I won't remember which story I told. Keep my face honest, even if my words aren't.*

"Quit teasing, Mr. Gunderman," Fritzy coaxed, completely unaware of the agreement that had just been etched between the old man and the boy. "I know he's a fast worker Mr. G. He can almost fly," she laughed.

"Well, we can always use a good pilot, Son. The one additional thing I require is about those clodhopper shoes." Mr. G. said.

Adam held his breath. They were the only shoes he had.

"I know every one of you boys wear them. You had too. The metal heal and toe plates kept them from wearing out. You only got two pair of shoes a year during the war, they had to last. But, they scratch up the hardwood floors somethin' awful. When you're here in the church, you'll have to wear something else."

Adam felt his heart drop to the floor. "I don't have any other shoes, Sir."

"Of course you do. The good basketball shoes are for the gym floor, but Mom through in an older pair that would be perfect to work in," Fritzy reminded him. "Here, Adam, I'll take the sack while you tend to business."

Alfred Gunderman stuck out his hand, and Adam responded meekly in kind. "We have an understanding then, Adam," the man said as he continued to pump the boy's hand with a viselike grip.

Rather than feeling pain in his hand and discomfort in his conscience, a new feeling of manly pride welled up in the boy. This was Adam's first contractual agreement. No lawyer was required to draw up the details. Adam knew what was expected of him. His hand shake was his bond.

Shaddy, give me a grip of steel. As Adam felt his handshake firm to a confident clasp, Alfred smiled.

"You savin' up for a nice Christmas present?" Gunderman winked and nodded in Fritzy's direction.

"We're going to the New Year's Party," she bubbled. "Right, Adam?"

"Right," Adam agreed but his mind bounced around like the ball he had gotten the evening before. *Money for party clothes—coal for the farm.*

Winston's Coal Company had said they would accept a deposit on a load of coal. Adam had a real reason for getting the job. He wasn't a kid anymore. He felt responsible for his mother with Pops gone. "All in all, I guess I need about twenty dollars."

Alfred eyed the boy with a squint and a sparkle in his eye. "I tell you what, if you can work during the holidays, help set up, clean up, and tear down, maybe you'd like to keep the job. I could use you several hours after school even after the Holidays. Naturally, you would have to keep your grades up. What kinda grades do you get, Son?"

"Mostly A's and a few B's." He hadn't thought to lie about grades. He was a good student. It came naturally to him, especially science, math and the creative arts.

"Adam, that's wonderful!" Fritzy said. "Are you going to college after high school?"

"Don't think so. A high school degree, especially from Middletown High School, is a great education. I can get a job anywhere I want to when I graduate."

"No hopes of becoming a teacher or doctor or anything like that?" Alfred pushed.

"Medicine—I had thought about becoming a physician—but—"

"You can do anything you put your mind to, My Boy." Mr. Gunderman spoke with determination and authority.

"If my brother can get passing grades in college, I know you can," Fritzy said as she patted him on the arm. "Besides, you're good in science and, well, everything. You can do whatever you put your mind to just like Mr. G. said."

"That's what my Grandpa Shoemaker used to say." Adam could hear Gramp's words of wisdom in his head. Recently, however, he thought only about school work and how to stay alive. He didn't believe in the future any more. He only felt empty inside.

"I'm not getting any younger, ya know,' Alfred admitted. "The ol' ticker flutters, my back and knees hurt. Well, never mind about that. I leave the complaining' to the young folks."

"What?" Adam's attention focused back on the immediate. "Yeah, right. Leave the complaining to the young folks."

"Are you all right?" Fritzy pulled on his sleeve.

"Yes, sure," Adam smiled sheepishly.

"Mr. G., Adam can help you run up and down the stairs, lift the heavy tables and put them away. He can help you do everything," Fritzy prattled on.

"Now see here young lady, I am not ready to retire," Alfred made clear.

"No, Sir," Adam jumped in.

"Oh, Mr. Gunderman, we're never going to let you retire. Just keep Adam around to do all the things you don't want to do," she giggled.

"Fritzy—" Adam stopped before he said something that would jeopardize his new job.

"Well, now Young Man, you pay no never mind to Fritzy. Are you interested in the job or not?" Alfred was a practical man. "Job or no job?"

Adam could not believe what he was hearing. He could have a job for now and maybe for the next few months. "Yes, Sir," he smiled, "that would be great, now and later."

"You know they'll find out about the lies," the shadows tormented as they rose up from the stair well and glared at Adam. Thankfully, no one else heard them.

"Don't ya want to know how much you'll be makin'?" Gunderman teased.

"They will just cheat you," again the shadows hurled dark emotional bombs meant only for the boy.

Shaddy, I don't want to hear them. Immediately, he experienced a selective deafness. He saw the shadows' mouths move but heard no sound, except Alfred's words.

"Of course you do, Adam. Everybody wants to know what they'll make," Fritzy forced herself into the discussion.

"Yes, Sir, I do," Adam smiled sheepishly. It was hard, but he tried to keep Mr. G's words separate from the faces the shadows made as they passed by. "I didn't think it was polite to ask."

"I like that Adam," Alfred smiled. "You're more interested in the work than the pay. But, in business, you have to know if you're getting a good deal or not."

"Yes, Sir," the boy stuck out his chest and stood as tall as he could, which was several inches taller than the stooped little man who held his future in his hands. *I wouldn't know if I'm getting a good deal or not.* But, he asked, "Tell, me, Mr. Gunderman, how much will I make?"

Fritzy giggled and grabbed Adam's arm. "That was very manly. Good for you."

Adam blushed and stared at his shoes again.

"Well, the minimum wage for most folks is forty cents an hour. That seems fair. You should earn a man's wage. I'll expect a man's effort in all your work, so forty cents an hour it is."

"That should be enough." Adam spoke out loud but his head was full of marching numbers.

"Enough for the party?" Fritzy grinned with the innocence of one who had no worries or cares.

"Yes," Adam agreed, "at least part of it, and, I need some for stuff at the house." To himself he mumbled, "Twenty dollars," but in his mind he was thinking, *Twenty dollars might be enough for Moms to be able to come home soon. It will take a long time to save up that much.*

"Twenty dollars, huh?" Gunderman smiled.

Adam was startled. He hadn't realized he had been heard. He wanted to keep his family life private. "Yes, Sir."

"Well, with all that has to be done, you can get in about twenty-five hours by the time of party. You wouldn't be working on Christmas Day of course. You'd have about ten dollars. You'll not have the full twenty before Christmas, that's in four days. But, remember, this job will carry on after school starts again."

To Adam, Christmas was just another holiday without Pops, but Moms had always been there. Pops had inherited the Schumacher farm, and the family lived a comfortable life before the world went crazy. Adam wished his mother could be home by Christmas Day, but he would have to be patient. This year, he would visit her at the Sanitarium on Christmas Day and that would have to be enough. "That will be fine, Sir."

"Okay then. We have a deal, but Son, I expect you to do a man's job. Don't wait to be told. If you see something that needs to be done, do it. If I have to tell you everything, I might as well do the work myself."

"I understand but how will I know—"

"I'll give you a list of chores for each day of the week plus an anytime list. Picking up paper off the floor and keeping snow away from the entry are anytime tasks, not something you wait 'til Thursday to do. You do a good job here and you will have learned how to work for a lifetime." He slowed then asked, "Your folks know you're gettin' a job? Is it okay with them?"

"He just found out today, Mr. Gunderman," Fritzy protested.

"Okay, but—"

"Moms has been sick so she'll have to write a note." Adam had to control the contact his boss would have with his family. He would work out the details somehow. For months, he had been making do. If he had to, he would write the letter himself and have Moms sign it. He would do a good job for Mr. Gunderman and prove himself to be the best worker in town. Goodness knows he lived close enough to the job to never be late.

"I'm very pleased to have such a conscientious young man work for me, well—for the church. If you are helping to take care of your mother, you have my vote."

What an unexpected turn! Adam hadn't even applied for the job, but the job had found him.

"Here ya go," Alfred smiled, handed him the broom handle and walked away. "Work in your sock feet or change your shoes first," Mr. G. shouted back.

"You are a working man, Adam. The older shoes are in the sack with the other stuff. Change into them and start your new job. I'd better let you get your work done," Fritzy smiled. "Later, you'll have just enough time to get ready. Daddy said you might play in the game this evening. I hope so. I'll be there." She started to leave than added, "Say you'll come."

"I'll see." Adam waved, and then pushed the broom around the entry. "Is this just some kind of joke, Shaddy? If it is, it is definitely not funny," he whispered.

What you need, when you need it, is not a child's game. Trust, My Son, trust," Shaddy breathed on the *swish, swish* of the broom.

Chapter 11

Hometown Hero

"Charlie, Charlie!" The fans shouted from the gymnasium stands that evening.

Charlie Baker shot from inside the keyhole. Everyone held their breath, then—the crowd roared as the ball swished through the basket. It was the fourth quarter. The score was close. Oakridge High School was up by three points. The Middletown team was getting tired.

Coach Breman watched each play as he thumped a rolled up program in his hand. Perspiration rolled off the players exhausted bodies, but they still tried hard. There were just too many absent high scorers.

"Shoemaker," Coach called to the bench, "you're in."

"Me, Coach?" Adam swallowed hard. He had already been in during the first quarter. *Made a fool of myself already. What more do you want?*

From the corner of his eye, he saw one of the shadows ooze onto the glistening floor. "You can't do it Boy," it jeered.

He tried to shake the doubts from his mind. *Shaddy, close my ears to the clanging ones and to the crowd too. They scare me as much as the shadows.*

"You're our man," Coach smiled and pointed him onto the hardwood with a wave of his hand. "You're the man of the hour."

"You didn't have to say that, Coach," Adam smiled nervously.

"Mr. Foul-out?" One of the members of the Oakridge team poked fun at Adam but knew enough to keep his distance.

"That's me!" Adam pretended to boast. "I'm the foul-out champion!"

"If someone makes fun of you," Pops would say, "join in the fun, and the other person will lose their ammunition. They won't be able to embarrass you. You can't humiliate someone who won't be humiliated."

Johnson snapped the ball to Adam who dribbled the ball down the court and executed a lay-up shot that was absolute beauty in motion. Slam—dunk! The crowd jumped to their feet and the din was intoxicating.

From just behind the home bench, a piercing whistle split the air and Adam knew. Only Fritzy could whistle with that earsplitting pitch. He could recognize her blast anywhere.

A call for a time-out brought the team over to the sidelines, into the coach's circle. The huddle smelled like sweaty gym socks and teenage adrenalin.

Adam was within a few feet of the noisy fans. He tried hard to stay focused but he had never had all eyes turned on him before. In fact, he felt invisible most ordinary days.

The timekeeper's buzzer brought all the players back into center court. Middletown was down by one point. The ball was snapped back onto the floor and the players started down the court when an opposing team member fell into Adam. That meant one thing. Adam would have to stand alone inside the key.

Adam stood at the free throw line, frozen in anticipation, positioned to take his shot. The free throw was a one and one. If he made both, Middletown High would be one point ahead. He bounced the ball a few times and eyed the basket. A dark shadow hung from the rim. At first, Adam broke eye contact with the target. He bounced the ball again and tried to regain focus. The gymnasium was silent. Adam aimed, let the ball go and watched it arch in the air. Thump. The ball hit the rim. A gasp from the crowd held their collective breath in mid-air.

Adam's heart hit the floor faster than the basketball. From the hero of the school to their greatest disappointment, his rise and fall were dramatic. He was embarrassed beyond anything he had ever experienced. He preferred being out of the limelight. In the dark, a hidden figure has no form for others to admire or ridicule. A star can lose some shimmer and shine very quickly. But, he knew he did not belong in the shadows. He was not one of them.

Adam tried to regain self-control as he took his place on the floor and guarded the man assigned to him. He raced up and down the floor for the next few minutes. In his mind, he felt like a character in slow motion on the neighborhood movie screen. His energy was gone. His heart for the game had been pierced. The crowd sounded like the wind whipping through the bell tower, magnified times half a life time.

No matter what the players did, neither side could add one more point to the scoreboard as time ticked past. Charlie fouled out and had to take the bench. Adam looked around the floor for an opening. There were only twenty-five seconds left on the clock.

Adam dribbled slowly down the floor as he looked for someone, anyone he could pass the ball off to. He popped the ball to Bill Collins who dribbled a few bounces then snapped it back to Adam again as he neared the keyhole. There was no one around, at least not in Adam's world of panic and doubt.

"Fly, Adam, fly!" Fritzy yelled from the bleachers.

"Fly, Adam, fly!" The crowd joined in. "Fly Adam, fly!"

Shaddy, he whispered, *levitate me. Let it be so. Let me fly like everyone is yelling.* He felt a weight lift from his body and a new energy rushed in. Step, step, leap, shoot, and—swish!

The crowd jumped to their feet as the time-clock blared. A flood of cheering fans leaped down to the basketball court and lifted Adam onto their shoulders. He scanned the crowd around him for the one face he wanted to see. Then, there she was.

Fritzy grabbed his hand as the crowd bounced him in the air. The shouts continued while Fritzy ran along beside him, as they made a victory lap around the gym floor.

What did he hear? What was the crowd saying? Could their words possibly be true? Was his name the one they shouted? Was he actually visible?

Chapter 12

Work and Lies

Saturday, December 22, 1949

"Adam! Adam! Adam!" The rhythmic canter of the crowd echoed in Adam's ears throughout that night. No matter when he awakened in the dark cold belfry, the thoughts that flooded his sleeping mind were of smiling faces as the crowd sang his praises. How long would the good feelings last? Adam believed he had been invisible for months hidden away in the church belfry. Being noticed was a new experience for him and he didn't know what to think of it. He knew he liked the warm feeling he had inside.

Adam stayed on his pallet and listened for the sound of the wind beyond the cold stone walls. He smiled. The snow had stopped falling by the time he awakened to victory.

Saturday was here already, December 22. Adam opened his eyes a few minutes later than he would have on a school day. He had to be up early enough that Mr. Gunderman didn't see him come down the ladder from the belfry. A few extra minutes of staying in bed and thinking wouldn't hurt. Still, he could not get caught in the church at an inappropriate time. Things were balanced wobbly in his life, and he had to keep all the dominos lined up until the final one was in place. Each story had to be carefully positioned. Each black tile represented a different lie he had told. If he weren't careful, the whole thing could collapse.

Adam's mind had a way of flipping like spit on a hot, greased griddle. He quickly forgot the thrill of victory from the previous night and began to wonder if the only thing in his life that was real, was the little hummingbird there in the belfry. In that moment, his mind made a U-turn. From the hero of the hardwoods with his head held high, he slumped into a boy full of doubts. He suddenly remembered he could not have been more alone than if Middletown had been through the blitz the night before with bombs raining down by the hundreds and he was the town's only survivor.

As Adam opened the basket lid, he smiled. The bird looked up at him then hopped up onto his finger the minute the chirper could move about.

"Well, hello, Little Fellow. I'm sorry I can't stay around and visit for a while—gotta run."

Adam replaced the hummer, closed the lid and darted out of the belfry and down the ladder in record time. However, speed would be his downfall if he didn't pay attention. He had forgotten his coat. He could not come into the church from the frigid outside without a snapped- up coat. He slipped back up, grabbed his school jacket then flew done the ladder as if the hummer had taught him to fly.

Moments later, Alfred came through the front door as Adam left the building, turned around, and came back in through the rear entrance. He removed the jacket he had just put on and hung it on a hanger in the cloak-room area.

"Mornin' young man," Gunderman beamed. "We have a lot to do today. Christmas is Tuesday and that makes tomorrow Christmas Sunday."

"It's just another Sunday for most people to sleep in." Adam looked away and reached for the broom Mr. G. held in his hand. He had to be careful or he would give himself away. These people were helping him because they assumed things about him. He imagined that they thought he would be excited about Christmas like some little kid. He was not a child any longer. He didn't have the time, patience or luxury for childhood anymore.

"Well, I know you'll be here for church tomorrow, Adam. I haven't been feelin' real good, and I need you to work the big crank that pulls up that heavy wooden door between the sanctuary and the Agnes Coffee Lounge. It operates like a big ol' roll top desk. Folks will be wantin' their punch and cookies don't ya know, and the ladies will serve those refreshments in the Lounge."

"Yes Sir, I'll be here. I will be glad to raise the partition." That was partly right. He was fascinated by the roll up wooden divider between the two rooms. For the other part however, he had no intention of attending church services before Alfred assumed he would. He planned to say he had a cold or any other made-up story that came to mind. He was getting good at lying.

"I know I can depend on you," Alfred smiled and handed Adam the list of the day's chores.

Wish he hadn't said that he could depend on me. He took a deep breath and put away thoughts of pretense. "You can count on me," he repeated and cringed.

"I'm sure I can." Alfred started toward the stairs and paused at the foot. He looked up the sixteen treads to the upper floor but didn't place his foot on the bottom step. "Need to go up and sweep the Sunday school classrooms. But—"

"You all right, Mr. Gunderman?" The boy began to worry. Alfred moved slowly and panted as he walked, like Gramps did before he had his heart attack. His breath was just as short and shallow. *Oh please, God, not again*. Grandpa

95

Shoemaker was nearly an invalid when he died, which accounted for his car accident. His body hadn't been able to respond fast enough to stop in time.

"I'm just fine," the old man assured him, but his steps were slow and labored.

Shaddy, help him. Then, sounds bombarded his ears, from within himself and without.

"Gotta get all this done—I know I'm doin' too much. I know. I'll slow down after Christmas—I promise. Just a little more today. Gotta keep goin'."

Why can I hear Mr. G.? He's going upstairs. Adam watched the old man from the foot of the steps. *It's like I can hear his mind working. How is that possible?*

"Those are his thoughts, Son," Shaddy assured him. "Listen, the old one wants to deceive himself as much as you do. He knows he will die if he doesn't slow down, but he lies to himself to keep on going. Live in truth, Adam—" Shaddy whispered as his voice trailed off like a finely tuned motor's hum.

Adam watched Mr. G. climb to the top of the steps just as Gramps had. The next day, Gramps had felt sick and his shoulders and arms were sore. Adam thought the aches and pains were from splitting wood that afternoon. But, they weren't. When his grandfather took Grandma to town, they didn't come back. A truck darted out of the bank parking lot and Gramps couldn't stop before the impact.

Adam knew what Mr. G. knew. His condition could be serious. But, the boy wasn't going to argue with the old man. Mr. Gunderman was the boss. Adam decided to review the list Mr. G. had given him and not give the man any trouble.

1. Sweep the floor.
2. Wash the windows in all the doors. Sticky peppermint fingers you know.
3. Fetch the Christ Child for the nativity scene. It's in a box marked "Baby Jesus" that's on a shelf in the back of the

storage room. We need to make sure the statue is okay and ready.

There were enough chores on the list to provide work for the entire day. He was glad he was going to be busy.

"Hi working man," Fritzy called as she hurried in and stomped her snowy feet on the entry mat.

"Well, are my eyes playing tricks on me? You look like Fritzy Breman," Adam smiled.

"What are you doing today?" She bubbled as she reached for his broom.

"I'm going to wash windows, clean, and get out the statue of the baby for the crèche."

"Baby Jesus—on Saturday?"

"I guess they want him out for the Sunday before Christmas," he offered.

"They usually don't put the baby in the manger until the Christmas Eve services."

"I don't know. Mr. G. mentioned something about checking on it. I just do what I'm told."

"Every time?" She teased as she handed back the broom handle. "Then, this must be yours."

"Well—maybe not every time," he smiled an honest smile.

"I know where the carving is." She motioned for Adam to follow. Together they went downstairs to the Fellowship hall, crossed the painted gray floor and approached the storage room's double doors on the wall opposite the furnace room. With a jerk, she swung them open together with a flare and fanfare, like a scene from a movie Adam had seen.

Once inside the large closet, Adam was surprised by everything. There were extra folded up tables, chairs, costumes from an Easter pageant, and boxes of stuff probably no one remembered any longer what they contained.

"Over this way," Fritzy directed.

Adam followed behind and surveyed all the boxes. One was full of Sunday school literature and stacks of pictures that showed Bible scenes. There were wooden folding chairs with the church's name stenciled on the back. If he had known all of those supplies were in the huge closet, he would have rummaged through it all, just to break the monotony of the empty nights. There were no windows in the room so he would not have been seen.

"It's just over here," she said.

"No," the shadows hissed as they surrounded her. "Stay away from the carving, Boy. We will not look at it."

Adam could hear the dark ones clearly. Fritzy said nothing but then she stopped abruptly just before they reached the box.

"No!" The shadows ordered again as the air grew thick with the stench of them.

Fritzy didn't say anything about the smell. She just froze in place, and Adam nearly ran into her. He involuntarily reached out and grabbed her waist to steady himself. His face contorted with embarrassment. *What if she gets the wrong idea? What if she thinks —*

Fritzy turned and nearly ran into Adam. She wasn't angry. She seemed more mischievous than mad.

Adam didn't understand her expression but he liked her new sparkle. Their eyes met just as Alfred came into the storage room. He was out of breath and grabbed onto one of the shelves. Adam and Fritzy smiled sheepishly at each other and turned their infectious grins away from Gunderman's sight.

"Got him?" The older man asked as he leaned against a stack of boxes by the door.

"What?" Fritzy asked.

Adam controlled a laugh. "He means the statue."

"Not yet, Mr. Gunderman," she answered. "We were almost there before you came in."

"That's okay," Alfred glanced around and then started to walk out. As he moved, new orders were chattered over his shoulder. "Mrs. Gunderman is coming in. Should be here in a minute. Adam, she needs help with some boxes of decorations."

"Mrs. Gunderman?" Adam mumbled.

Fritzy snickered softly behind him. "Alfred often calls his wife Mrs. Gunderman to younger people. He is a strong believer in showing respect."

"So is my family," Adam agreed.

"Why are they getting the Christ Child out so early, Mr. G.?" Fritzy quizzed the old man as she followed the little procession out of the storeroom. "That's not the way we do it."

"You one of those, it-ain't-been-done-like-that-beforers?" Mr. G. chuckled and shook his head. "Don't know why. I just do what the pastor asks, and Adam here does what I ask. And you, well, I guess you do what any proper young lady wants to do."

"I do what Daddy says I can do," she protested.

"And you, Adam, who besides me, gives you marching orders?" Alfred quizzed. His expression was more that of knowing than asking. "God?" he chanced a guess.

"God? How could he . . ." Adam's gaze fell as the pain of disappointment came over him like a chill. "I haven't heard anything from God in a long time."

"God still speaks, My Boy but he's outside of our time. He answers in his time, but he always hears, and he always cares."

"But, maybe I don't," Adam spit out with a taunt jaw.

"Adam, you don't mean that!" Fritzy gasped.

"I'm just telling the truth as I see it."

"Expressing your pain is never wrong. We can't heal when we can't find the spot that hurts." Alfred patted Adam's shoulder.

"Well . . ." Adam looked at Fritzy. She seemed to trust him so much. He had a strange impulse to just explode with the whole truth, and then he remembered what his grandfather had said. *A man is only worth the truth of his words, Adam.*

What could he do? How could anyone trust him if he told them everything? He had told so many lies. "Well, I don't always feel that way. It's been . . ."

"What, Son?" Alfred was ready to listen.

"Nothing, not really. I was just asked to join the basketball team but had no shoes. Fritzy's parents solved that for me. Things are looking better all the time." He tried to cover his dark feelings with more of the same colorful fabrications.

That was not a lie, but he wasn't telling the whole story either. He was living a masquerade. No one knew him deep down.

Adam could not resist the need to talk about his world as if it were loving and normal. "We—are all looking forward to a great Christmas."

The lies rolled like marbles into every corner and filled the room that was his world.

Chapter 13

Christmas Sunday

Sunday, December 23, 1949

"Hi there, Little One," Adam smiled at the hummingbird as he opened the basket on the Sunday before Christmas. The belfry was filled with the happy sounds of the little bird in the makeshift cage that sat on the floor beside his palette. That Sunday morning broke like any other day, except for the chirping of the little hummer.

"Looks like you're dressed in Christmas colors. At least one of us is celebrating." He stroked the soft feathers with the downy undergrowth and smiled. The hummer's water-nectar was prepared as usual and placed in the basket-purse.

Adam watched the bird celebrate the morning. But, instead of joining in the jubilee, suddenly Adam became overwhelmed. He felt so empty he couldn't breathe. The bird was brightly adorned in a beautiful suit, and Adam had nothing but two pair of jeans, one too short and one okay, and three shirts. He had also found a flannel shirt in the box of items donated to the poor. You couldn't get much poorer than Adam. At least, he couldn't see how. His Sunday had started with promise until reality and truth found him. Strangely, he could feel his anger turn on the hummer. He didn't know why.

Dark, foreboding shadows crept up through the cracks in the floor. Their stench sucked the air out of the room. "The bird is mocking you, Boy. Why is he so happy?"

Adam wanted to turn away, but what the shadows said was true. He turned on his little companion and took his anger out on him. "If I could take that Christmas sweater off you, I would," Adam started to grumble at the tiny bird. The hummer retreated to a corner of the basket.

Adam could see that the little bird had pulled away. He felt worse. The more he saw the Christmas spirit around him, the more the joy left his heart. The hummer's green and red feathers did not help Adam's twisted celebration of the season. Everywhere he looked in recent days, he saw happy families that only reminded him of how alone and unhappy he was.

"How do you stay safe out there in the world, all blaring green and red and flitting about?" Adam slammed the lid down. "I don't have to look at you."

He started to leave the bell tower, when he heard a chirp again. The loud growling of his stomach made him think of his own hunger. He would have to wait to eat until after church services when platters of cookies would be laid out. Thoughts of the sweet treats still couldn't drive out the struggle he was having with his feelings. He knew the shadows were near.

"Get out of my home," he commanded the shadows.

"Maybe I'm not feeling hungry at all. Maybe this emptiness is guilt." Adam opened the basket-cage and attempted to smile at the bird.

As he watched, the little fellow sucked up the nectar in his usual haste, but seemed to be slow in other motions. The hummer made no attempt to fly away.

"Did you forget how to fly?" He wondered if trapping the little guy in the cage had made him sick. That thought gripped his heart. With the shadows gone, he could feel again. He reached out his finger for the bird to ride on and lifted the tiny fellow from the cage. He slowly raised and lowered his hand, waved it to and fro and gave the little guy a ride. The movement fluttered the bird's feathers. He gradually moved around. Adam's heart soared.

"I know what I'll do today. I'll leave the basket lid off. If you want to fly around the room, you can. Maybe you'll feel better if you get some exercise. Little fellow, you can't be hurt. You just have to be able to fly. We're both stuck up here together. This place is more like a prison than a belfry for both of us. But, you would freeze if I let you go." Adam's own arms began to ache as he thought about flying with broken wings. He wondered if his own feathers had gotten clipped the minute he moved into the belfry.

"By the way," Adam added as he pointed to his blanket, "that is my bed. Fly anywhere you want to, except over my space. You could drop little gifts around for me to clean up. I have no way to wash a blanket." He watched the little bird peer over the edge of his finger then beat his wings in rapid flutter. The hummer took to the air and flew around Adam's head, then returned to the basket and the food. Adam laughed and hurried to the corner of the belfry and hustled down the ladder before anyone came into the church.

"Good morning Mrs. Brubaker." Adam forced a smile as his English teacher entered the narthex just as he came around the corner. He carried his coat across his arm and hung it in the cloak room as Mrs. Brubaker did hers. Her coat was covered with snow. He brushed off all the fresh white powder from her shoulders so when his dry coat hung beside hers, it didn't give away the secret that Adam had not come in from the outside.

"Adam Shoemaker, it is good to see you here. We have a glorious, bodacious day, don't we?" Mrs. Brubaker always used the full depth of her vocabulary, acquired from years of reading every night before going to sleep, or so she told her classes. "I tell you, read, read, read," she would drone.

"Yes Ma'am, bodacious. However, the ubiquitous little man in red is beginning to tire me." Adam's words had an edge of sarcasm as he exercised his own knowledge of words.

Amanda Brubaker eyed the boy with a narrow gaze. "You are much too smart to have such a pessimistic attitude, Mr. Schumacher," she whispered. "Change your name if you want to Adam, but I knew your father and your father's father."

There was the connection he had dreaded. He had changed his name when he started ninth grade. He thought he could call himself anything he wanted to in the new high school. But, Mrs. Brubaker had linked him to the deserter with the foreign name. He was as big a failure as his father. As far as Adam was concerned, Pops had been absent from his life for a long time.

The great World War had tarnished the name of Schumacher beyond anything Adam believed he could polish. *You are known by your name,* Gramps used to say. And, his name was Schumacher not Shoemaker. But, Schumacher is German and Shoemaker is American.

"There's more to me than that name," Adam scoffed.

"Adam, no, I didn't mean—.Your father was one of my best students. He—"

"Hi Adam," Fritzy buzzed the minute she came in the door. "Oh, I'm sorry, Mrs. Brubaker. Did I interrupt?"

"Well, yes, Frederica, you did. But, that is all right. Mr. Shoemaker and I will talk again another time." She smiled and patted Adam on the shoulder. "There is joy in the Season if you accept the Spirit of Christmas as a gift, Adam."

That will be my only gift, he angrily reminded himself. *And, I have nothing for Moms.*

"Adam, do you want to sit with Daddy and Mother, Jim and me?" Fritzy started to pull Adam in the direction of the sanctuary that opened in front of them like a large, sparkling Christmas box.

"I don't know if I can. I'm supposed to crank up the dividing wall after church. Mr. Gunderman isn't feeling well."

"That's okay. We usually sit on that side of the sanctuary anyway." Fritzy linked her arm in his as she led him into the music filled room "Come on."

Adam smiled. He was amazed that Fritzy didn't seem to be afraid for people to see them together. Their friendship was real. It wasn't just another lie.

In the sanctuary, Christmas–tree–green, red and gold were everywhere, in the garland swags that draped across the front of the balcony, to the ten-foot Christmas tree adorned with fancy bulbs, white doves, large red–velvet ribbons and hundreds of lights.

They walked halfway up the right aisle and joined the rest of the Breman family. As they sat down, Adam studied the manger scene that was up near the altar. The crude crib was obviously empty except for the straw.

Fritzy saw him look over the entire scene. "The carving will be there on Christmas Eve," she whispered just as the service began. "The Christ Child hasn't come yet so the manger is empty."

Adam smiled faintly as the songs of Christmas swelled. Memories of Christmases past flooded his mind, images he had blocked out a long time ago. He wanted to be happy but he thought happiness was not possible for him. He hadn't been to his own country church since Moms went into the hospital. Their pastor visited her there, but when the minister got sick too, Adam had been forgotten. Some were told that he lived in town with his uncle.

"Joy to the world," the congregation sang, and Adam wondered what world they were singing about. He joined in, only because Fritzy would expect him to, not because he wanted to. He wasn't a baby. He was a man, yet he felt like crying. *Only women and little kids cry. Men with powers from Shaddy definitely do not.*

"Good Christmas Sunday morn," Pastor Silverman began as he stood at the open Bible. "And it came to pass in those days," he read from scripture.

Adam swallowed a yawn. A gaping mouth would not impress Fritzy at all. He would seem to be bored with the pastor's message.

His stomach growled again and Adam resisted the temptation to slump down farther in the pew. Everyone in the church that morning would go home to a hot meal of roast beef with potatoes and carrots, the usual Sunday meal in Middletown.

Adam's meal would not be anything special. He would dine on crackers and the macaroni he had found in the kitchen cabinets. Yesterday, four cans of soup showed up on the kitchen counter. There was a note attached, "For the needy." He believed more and more that the needy included him.

"A hymn that is often sung during the Christmas holidays is *Good King Wenceslas*," Pastor Silverman said. "The hymn was important for two reasons. First, the words spoke of the goodness of a leader king. It was one of the first references to a benevolent monarch."

Adam resisted the urge to laugh out loud. *A benevolent king?* He could not believe the two words went together. In 1945 the world had been torn apart by leaders who were so vile that the entire globe had erupted in flames. Families were ripped apart.

"Point two," Silverman continued, "the amazing words, written by John Mason Neale nearly a hundred years ago, tell us of the way through difficult times, a way to stay warm in a world grown cold, a way to survive through the stormy blasts of our lives. The way? We are to walk in the footsteps of the Master."

Like that would do any good, Adam mocked silently. *My world has grown cold, and God is not walking through it with me.*

Adam heard the pastor's words. He understood their meaning. But, life was not that easy. *Besides, all that love isn't for me, not anymore. Love never came home.*

But, there was a part of Adam that wished it were true. He felt just as caged as the bird had been. Then he thought of the green feathered wings as they lifted the little bird off his fingers. He closed his eyes and wondered if he, too, would ever take flight again.

"Adam?" Fritzy shook his arm gently. "Did you fall asleep? The service is over."

"Of course I'm not asleep, Fritzy. I was still thinking about what Pastor said," he fabricated.

Adam jumped up and opened the narrow closet that housed the crank to the roll-up door. It was a little hard to turn. He understood why Mr. G. had asked him to raise the massive wooden door. Slowly the wall raised up and out of sight, tucked away into the pocket of two crossbeams above the entrance. The members of the congregation stepped into the Agnes Coffee Lounge that was now open to the sanctuary. Couches covered in gold fabric created a conversation area near another Christmas tree which was more whimsically decorated than the one near the altar.

"What will you do for dinner today, Adam?" Mrs. Breman questioned as she made her way toward the refreshment table following the service.

"Dinner?"

"Yes, will your uncle have a hot meal for you today?"

"He wasn't able to get home yesterday. He travels, you know."

"You're all alone today?" Fritzy interrupted. "But, this is Christmas Sunday."

"Well, you are not alone today if you don't want to be. Frederica's grandparents are coming for dinner, and I'm setting a place for you," Mrs. Breman stated absolutely.

"I wouldn't want to—"

"I wasn't asking. I was stating a fact. I would not be able to look your dear mother in the eye if I allowed you to eat alone on Christmas Sunday. Besides, Frederica's sister, Sarah Jane, is in a friend's wedding today and won't be here. You will balance out the table. It's settled." Mrs. Breman took a cookie from the plate and smiled at him. "Help yourself."

"Yes, Ma'am," Adam smiled. He was waiting for an opportunity to have a few, or more.

"Take some with you. It's alright," she assured him as she pulled her gloves from her pocket, then turned to Reverend Silverman and shook his hand. "Wonderful sermon Pastor. Now relax the rest of the day and enjoy your time with your wife."

"Thank you. It looks like you're going to have a full house for dinner today."

"And it will be wonderful." Then she turned back to Adam. "You can ride with us if you want to. My husband can take you home later, after the Philharmonic's performance on the radio this afternoon—on CBS."

"A radio concert?" Adam had not heard a radio for so long even the Philharmonic sounded good to him.

The plan for the day was all settled. They all grabbed their coats from the cloak-room and went out into the crisp winter air. He piled in the back of the Bremans' station wagon just like a member of the family. But, Adam knew he wasn't.

Chapter 14

A Warm Fire and Warm Friends

Christmas Sunday dinner was with a real family. Fritzy's home was beginning to feel familiar to Adam, safe and welcoming. The house looked beautiful, with a loaded Christmas tree in the front window and lit candles around the room. Adam was drawn to the dining room table by the most amazing aroma. It was a mixture of browned roast, homemade dinner rolls, and assorted pies on the side board.

Coach Breman sat at the head of the table with Adam to his right. Fritzy sat between Adam and her brother, Jim. Mrs. Bremen was at the foot of the table and her parents balanced out the other side. Adam had just finished the last bite of food from his plate when Coach asked, "Would you like more baked steak?" He passed the meat platter to Adam.

"No thank you, Sir." The boy resisted the temptation to eat everything he could possibly fit onto Mrs. Breman's fine china plate.

"Well, I know you'll have more mashed potatoes and bread and butter," Fritzy smiled. "You seem to have enjoyed them a lot."

"Just a little, thank you." He placed two large spoonsful of potato on his plate, smashed them with his fork and spooned a little gravy over the top. He could not believe how wonderful every bite tasted.

"I am so glad you could come, Young Man," Fritzy's Grandmother Stafford smiled. "I'm always pleased to meet my grandchildren's friends."

"Yes, Ma'am. I'm pleased to meet you as well."

"I understand you had a good night on the basketball court," Grandpa Stafford smiled.

Adam's face lit up with a grin. "Yes, Sir. It was a good night."

"He did a great job. And, the game was his first—ever." Coach Breman's smile revealed an acceptance Adam had only dreamed of.

"I'm sure the luck was in the shoes," Jim joined in with big-brother style joking.

"Thank you for out-growing them," Adam smiled as he wiped his lips on Mrs. Breman's fancy cloth napkin. He was careful to leave as small a smudge as possible on the linen.

"Enough basketball you guys. Adam and I get the game table in living room. We're going to play dominos while you all listen to the Philharmonic. Or, while some of you sleep, Grandpa."

"Here now, I'll have you know I just rest my eyes."

"Right, Grandpa, and you only make the strange snoring sound to keep us guessing," Jim teased.

"I am simply part of the percussion section of the orchestra," Grandpa Stafford boasted.

"Okay," Coach agreed. "However you want it."

"If you decide to turn that game into Texas 42, Fritzy, just let me know. I'll be the third of the four needed." Mr. Stafford stood and stretched out his stiff legs before he walked. Then he took his official spot in the overstuffed chair beside the up-right radio that stood beside the fireplace.

Adam entered the living room quietly. He felt like he should whisper in the warmth of the firelight. The mantel of the white fireplace supported five stockings hung from decorative hooks. There was a thick oval carpet that covered the hardwood floors, and white sheer curtains graced the huge bay window. A widow seat provided one space at the old game table and a small antique Windsor chair flanked the other side.

Fritzy turned the domino box upside down and shuffled the white ivory tiles. Mr. Breman adjusted the radio to the CBS station and the concert began. Grandpa Stafford fell asleep before the orchestra completed their first movement in sonata form. Mrs. Breman had her knitting in her lap and the needles flew, almost in rhythm to the music. Grandma Stafford pulled the stereopticon and slides from one of the white cabinets beside the fireplace and settled down on the sofa for a quiet afternoon of picture viewing.

"I'm going to go up and get some reading done for class," Jim smiled as he looked around the comfortable room. "Nice meeting you, Adam."

"You, too," Adam said as Fritzy played the first tile. He breathed in all the family time he could possibly inhale. He felt like the hummer as it sucked in the sweet nectar. If a picture could be perfect, he was living inside the frame.

When the philharmonic finished the concert, he and Fritzy went out to the kitchen to make taffy. She pulled the recipe from a file box in the cupboard. Then she put the sugar and cornstarch in a saucepan, added salt, corn syrup and water and mixed all the ingredients together.

"Bring to a boil—" she talked mostly to herself as she read the recipe. To Adam she added, "You can stir in the butter. That would be a good job for a man with basketball muscles."

"How long do I stir?" He took the wooden spoon and began slowly.

"We'll drop a little bit from a spoon to see if the syrup will form a hard thread. Then, you can stir in the vanilla and pour the mixture into Mom's square Pyrex dish. When the taffy is cool enough, we'll pull it until it isn't shinny anymore and the texture becomes stiff. The last step is, we'll cut the candy into pieces and wrap them in waxed paper."

"How about now?" He raised the spoon out of the mixture and tested the consistency for the hard thread. "Looks ready to me."

"While the taffy cools, we can find some tree pictures for our Biology project. The assignment will be due by the middle of January."

"How do you know when the tree project will be due? It hasn't been assigned yet." Adam asked then glanced back into the living room at Coach Breman. "Oh, I get it— inside information."

"Mother has collected *Better Homes and Gardens* magazines for years. They're up in the attic."

Adam followed her up to the second floor and felt the smooth wood of the banister all the way to the top. The attic stairs were behind a door that went up from the second floor hallway. Those steps led to the completely surfaced third story, a treasure land of old trunks and spinning wheels. From the moment Adam set foot on the attic floor, memories flooded his mind that he had completely forgotten.

The memory that came to mind was of the room off Granny O'Hara's upper sleeping loft above her cabin. A red door with a wrought iron latch led to the rafter eaves. The two summers Adam and Moms had spent with Granny were full of mystery and unanswered questions.

"Granny, what are the black forms that move around in the attic? They scare me but seem to want to be friendly too," Adam had asked the last time he was there.

"Adam, I told you never to look at them. How do you know they want to be your friend?" Adam could feel that Granny was alarmed, and he didn't know why.

"They talked to me—well, not with sounds. I heard them in my head," Adam had explained.

"Oh, Adam, no," Granny O'Hara screamed. "You let them in?"

"Who? Adam, you let who in?" Moms had heard the shout. Adam knew that Moms had grown up in the valley and knew all about the old beliefs there.

"The shadows—Bridget, Adam has spoken to the darkness." Tears ran down Granny's fear gripped face. Adam didn't understand why.

"Mother," Moms had yelled, "I warned you. Will said if you fill the boy with those Gypsy lies, we have to come home and we cannot come back—ever."

"Bridget O'Hara you know they are not lies," Granny had argued.

"That argument is over. Will was adamant." Moms packed their clothes, got a ride to town, and Adam and his mother were out of the valley on the next train.

"What did you do on a rainy day, Adam?" Fritzy asked.

Adam was jarred back into Middletown, almost against his will. He always wished he could have found out what Granny and Moms were so frightened about. He was amazed that he had forgotten some of the secrets of the valley. "I haven't thought about that for a long time."

"A long time—Adam, you're not old enough for anything to be a long time past."

"It feels like a very long time ago," Adam's voice drifted off as he looked around the dusty attic. Over in the corner, he pulled an old rug back from a wooden cobbler's bench. "Gramps had one of these. I remember seeing the bench up in our attic."

"An old cobbler's bench? Did he teach you how to make shoes?"

"Yes . . ." Adam's memory wandered into the space above his parents' bedroom. "You had to pull down some steps to get up through the attic entrance. The old bench had a drawer with several lasts—those wooden, foot-shaped molds

113

that shoes are formed over. Those lasts had square toes. You know, that's where our name came from—Shoemaker. There is even a barrel full of small wooden pegs that they used to hold the shoes together."

"That's amazing Adam."

"That was one thing I did on a rainy day. I had forgotten. Funny, when we try to forget something bad in our lives, we forget everything about that time. I do remember one thing. Gramps would give me a piece of leather and I would use the lasts to sew moccasins to use as house slippers. I made some for Moms and Pops as well as my grandparents."

"What a great way to spend a day."

"I also went out in the barn where Grandma had an old potter's wheel in an empty stall. Why did I forget all of that? I would spend hours throwing pots, and then Pops would help me fire them in the kiln."

"Do you still have any of the pottery left?" She paused from her task of leafing through magazines for tree pictures. "That sounds like a lot of fun."

"Fun? Yes," Adam said as he picked up a magazine and earmarked several pages. "You know the great thing about throwing pots? If you make a mistake, no one ever has to see the messed up vase or bowl. You can just start again. That's not like life, right? You make a mistake, and everyone sees it."

"Who cares who's watching, Adam?"

"I do." Adam slammed a book closed and stared at the floor.

"Well, I don't care who looks at me and what I'm doing. I try to do my best. If I make a mistake, it is just that—a mistake. If I were going to deliberately do something wrong, I would make a grand falderal of it all. I would do my very best at that too. So see, the flub is still not a mistake. It's a deliberate act." She kept talking and seemed to ignore Adam's anger, or she was just a good diplomat.

"I hadn't thought about flaws and mistakes like that." Adam watched as Fritzy tore the pictures from the magazines. "Your mother won't care if we just tear them out?"

"Of course not. Mother said she had been saving these magazines for an assignment like this. She just didn't know what pictures would be needed or what they'd be used for." Fritzy tore several more pages from the book. "Where did you say the pottery is?"

"I didn't. How could I have forgotten about those pots? It feels like I've been walking in a dream world. I can't remember where I've been and have no idea where I'm going." Adam focused on his homework and clipped a few more tree pictures. "Pops took the pots to the Capitol and sold them in an arts and crafts store there. They sold for a lot of money. I got ten dollars for some of them." He looked over at Fritzy like he had not seen her before. "Why didn't I know that Fritzy? Why didn't I remember? Pops set up a savings account for me at a bank. I can't remember which bank. I think it was at the Capitol so I wouldn't be tempted to withdraw money on a whim like I might if the cash were here in town."

"That is wonderful. You're an artist, a real artist. You've earned money from your craft." She bubbled over with enthusiasm. "Just think—I know a famous artist."

"Well, I don't know about the famous part. Not famous enough for me to even remember any of it until you and this place and this great day, reminded me."

"Well, I am impressed," she insisted.

"You don't have to be. My art isn't memorable enough for me to remember it, let alone someone else."

They both laughed.

"What are these magazines over here?" Adam asked when he spied an open box.

"Those are Daddy's. You can look at them but we can't tear them up."

He rummaged through the ones on top and saw they were all *Time* and *Life* magazines. "Wow," he whispered, "I haven't seen these."

Adam placed a few of the older ones on the rough floor and fished through the stack in the box for more recent issues mixed in with the rest. "January 1944," he mumbled as he turned the paper covers that were preserved as though they were new.

"Ah," his breath caught in his throat as he turned the pages.

"What's wrong?" Fritzy asked when she saw the stunned expression on his face.

"These are pictures of the Battle of the Bulge," he gasped as his hands trembled. "All these guys, they all look like Pops—the living, the dead, the injured—every one of them. They all look the same to me. They all look like my dad." Maybe it was easier to think that Pops was a deserter, rather than find out he was dead or maimed, but it made him ache all the way down to his stomach.

"Let me see," Fritzy said as she reached for the magazine in Adam's hand.

"No," he demanded sharply. He stood up and paced over to the window where the light made the pictures glare at him more dramatically from the paper. He fanned the pages one after the other then slammed it closed. "We need to get back to the trees," he said hoarsely.

As he stood at the window at the front of the house, where the snow-covered road was clearly visible, Adam's heart sank. The same blue car was parked out front. No exhaust came from the pipe, so he knew the man inside had parked there to watch the house.

As he slipped to the side of the glass where he could watch but the man couldn't see him, he saw Coach Breman walk causally from the front of the house over to the car. Still dressed in his Sunday dress shirt, he leaned on the window the man had rolled down. Then he walked back in the house.

"Sorry," he called from the sidewalk a few minutes later. His voice carried to the attic on the clear, icy air. "I can't find him."

"Well, if you see him, please tell him I'd like to talk to him. I'll be around town for a few more days."

"Sure will," Coach said and hurried back into the warm house.

The man looked at the house again, started the engine and moved on.

Adam replaced the magazines in the box and closed the lid with an over and under pattern. He was mad and frightened at the same time. He had led the man to Fritzy's house when he let him drop her off after having been at the farm. Why was the man stalking him right out in the open?

"Let's get this job done," he snapped.

"What's going on with you?" Fritzy questioned.

"Nothing," he said sharply.

"It doesn't sound like nothing."

"How many more pictures do we need?" he asked as he changed the subject.

Well, let's see," Fritzy said as she looked over the project selections, with one eye on Adam. "We have two small piles of pictures stacked up, yours and mine. Without having a list of required specimens, this could be okay for now," she announced. "Let's go see if the taffy is ready to pull."

They gathered up their pictures of Maple, Ash and a multitude of other trees and rattled back down the wooden steps into the upstairs hall. "We'll lay them here on the hall table and I'll get them later. Now let's go down and pull that stuff into candy."

"There you are," Fritzy's dad said as they came down the main staircase. "Adam, there was a man here looking for you, but I couldn't find you two."

117

"It's your fault, Daddy," Fritzy teased. "We were in the attic tearing tree pictures from Mother's stash of magazines."

"Oh, I hadn't thought of looking there." He patted Adam on the shoulder. "Besides, Middletown folks don't like to have their Sunday disturbed. To be honest, I didn't look very hard for you two. He said he'd be around town for a few more days. There'll be plenty of time to talk to you on another day."

"Okay, thanks," Adam replied. "I've seen him all over town. He never did get around to telling me what he wanted. I'll see him again, I'm sure." And, Adam was sure, but he wished he weren't.

When they got to the kitchen, they washed and buttered their hands, then collected the taffy from the dish. With Adam on one end and Fritzy on the other, they pulled and played with the sweet candy until the sticky goo lost its sheen and was stiff enough to hold its shape. Then they cut and wrapped each piece of taffy in waxed paper.

The taffy and the fun they had pulling it into shape lifted Adam's spirits, and he soon forgot the war pictures and the man in the car. "This has been the best day of my life, or at least for the portion of my life I can remember, considering my recent memory lapses." They both laughed as he put on his jacket.

"Let Daddy drive you home. He said he would be happy to."

"No, that's all right. It isn't a long walk and the cold air might clear up my thinking. But, I do appreciate it. I enjoyed the whole day." Adam pulled his hat over his ears and started to leave when Fritzy ran, grabbed up some taffy, and stuffed them into his jacket pockets.

"Here Adam," Mrs. Breman called out. "Wait a minute." She came back with something wrapped in more waxed paper. "It's a nice roast beef sandwich. I believe I saw you put some catsup on your meat at dinner."

"Yes, Ma'am, catsup of course."

118

"A staple of life isn't it?" she joked as she handed over what would be Adam's Sunday evening supper.

He said his good byes and when back out into what seemed like a never-ending winter. He walked along the snowy streets and looked back once at the house to see if the magic was still there. It was. Fritzy stood in the bay window and waved. The corner of the Christmas tree could be seen through the glass. To Adam, the scene looked like a Christmas card, a perfect picture of family and home. There were no shadows in the whole house.

Once back at the church on Cranberry Street, Adam went up to the tower-room and found the belfry cold and empty. There was no warm fire, no laughing family, only a little hummingbird to chirp and twitter, "Hey, look at me."

Could the rest of the night have seemed even darker? Could the silence have been any louder? Ice droplets slipped down the window pane like frozen tears. There were no tears left in Adam.

Chapter 15

Night Intruders

Very early on Monday, December 24, 1945

Now what? Adam wondered and grumbled. The night was too black for shadows to loom in the corners that Monday morning or very late Sunday, whatever you call the middle of the night. Christmas Eve services would be later that same evening.

Adam had awakened with a start. Not by Charlie Baker's car horn but, Adam was startled by something. He sat up and listened—he heard nothing but the wind and silence. He pulled the covers around his ears, rolled over and tried to go back to sleep.

Screech. *That was the storage closet door. I can tell by the sound of the squeak.*

Adam slipped off his pallet, eased himself across the belfry floor and down the ladder in his stocking feet. On the main floor, he heard another sound, so he inched toward the stairway to the Fellowship Hall, and silently floated down, tread by tread.

Shaddy, make me silent. Not a sound was heard as he swooped on Shaddy's promises across the floor in the direction of the storeroom closet. *Why would someone be here at this hour?*

Icy sleet lightly peppered the windows. It wasn't a real blizzard, just a reminder of the stinging cold outside.

He almost called out Pastor Silverman's name, but remained silent. *The night intruder might not be him?*

Since Adam had no more business in the church at that hour than a common thief, he stayed in the darkest places and crept along the wall that led to where the sound seemed to come.

"Shaddy," he whispered, "let me see."

The wall outside the storeroom burst forth with light that penetrated the studs and lath. The surface of the plaster glowed with promise. Adam was stunned. He could see through the wall with his eyes, or his heart, he couldn't tell which. Whatever Shaddy had done, Adam didn't know, but he saw and heard the boys in the room beyond the thick walls. Their open jackets flapped and banged into nearly everything in the room.

"Quiet Freddy," a young male voice ordered from inside the huge, walk-in closet.

"Who are you afraid of waking, Buddy—God? Who would be here at this hour?"

"I don't know, but it is Christmas Eve day."

"You think Santa Clause will come through this place driving a sleigh?" Freddie jabbed his partner-in-crime in the ribs. "Are you sixteen or six?"

"Never mind that," Buddy smacked at the other boy. "Keep your hands off me, Freddy Boy. I'll have to clean your clock if you don't stop."

"You think you can stop me?" Freddy glared.

"I'll show you," Buddy barked and grabbed the other boy around the neck.

Freddy pushed Buddy off and together they stumbled into the storage room shelves. The shelves rocked and teetered but Buddy and Freddy kept brawling and rolling around the room. With no care to what was around them, they shoved and tackled and fell from one side of the store room to the other. Boxes fell to the floor. Easter Pageant costumes were pulled and ripped from their hangers. They continued their assault on each other as they neared the valuable Christ Child carving.

What should I do, Shaddy? Adam struggled with the responsibility he could feel. *No one can know I'm here. How do I stop them and still make sure no one finds out I live here?*

"Watch out Buddy," Freddy shouted as he wiped a trickle of blood from the corner of his mouth onto his jacket sleeve. "We came here to steal the carving, not destroy the thing."

Steal the Christ Child? Adam's heart pounded with anger, mixed with the fear of being caught. *Fritzy would never forgive me if I let them take the Baby Jesus statue.*

"We were lucky the kitchen window wasn't locked," Freddy snickered and pushed back.

Adam squeezed his eyes and hung his head. He had left the window unlocked.

"Do you think that guy will still want to buy a precious carving if it isn't so precious anymore?" Buddy asked. "Quit shoving."

Knock him over. Knock him out. Whatever it takes to get these guys out of here, Adam pleaded with Shaddy.

"I don't know if he'll want it or not, but there's been no damage yet. And, if you'll quit horsing around, this hunk of carved out wood won't get broke." Buddy was firm. "The guy came driving into town the other day and started asking my dad about a carving by some famous artist." Buddy brushed himself off and grabbed Freddy's collar. "Now, get yourself together. I heard Dad and the art lover talking, and later I found the guy at the filling station." He looked Freddy squarely in the eye. "You didn't tell anybody about him did ya?"

Adam thought of the man in the blue car. *I had never seen him around town before. Maybe he's the guy Buddy's talking about?*

"No, no . . . I didn't tell nobody. What's the matter with you? Let me go." Freddy pulled Buddy's fingers from his collar and staggered back.

"Well, you'd better not breathe a word about any of this. No one else knows this guy. No one will think to look for the statue with someone they ain't even heard of. You got that?"

"I got it," Freddy agreed. "Now leave me be," he pushed Buddy off him. "We'd better hurry and get out of here. You don't want to be wandering around in this building when the minister gets here."

"I ain't afraid of any soft, old Bible Thumper," Buddy boasted.

"Well, this Thumper was a Golden Gloves winner a long time ago, Dummy. My dad told me."

Pastor Silverman—was a boxer? Adam nearly blurted out loud. Thankfully, his surprise didn't knock-out his control.

"I could take him," Freddy puffed out his chest and hitched up his pants. "I'm a pretty good boxer myself."

"Boxer? Fred you're a street brawler, and a bad one at that."

"You want to test my strength? You ready for that? Huh?" Freddy got right up in Buddy's face and crowded him into a corner.

I can't step in between them. I could take them, probably both at the same time. But, everyone would know I was here. Adam's heart pounded harder. *I hate hiding here in the dark like a coward. I can't do anything.*

The furnace room was next to the storage closet. Adam knew that, but the two hoodlums didn't. When the coal, wet from the recent snow, popped in the huge firebox, the two new-to-crime thieves screamed out like little girls. "What was that?"

The furnace you idiots, Adam responded in silence from the darkness.

The two intruders jerked and flapped about, ran into each other and bounced off more shelves.

Adam had to hold in his laughter. He was so happy to see the two inept thieves get a small taste of the revenge he held in his heart, he bubbled with jeering glee.

The shadows, not seen in the dark but obvious in the light of the store room, rose up like the phantoms of anger and fear that they were, with piercing dagger-sharp eyes. "We will destroy them for you," they seethed.

Suddenly, Gertrude jumped out from nowhere, her long sharp toenails exposed, and landed on top of Freddy's shoulders.

"What the—? What is this thing?" He screamed in a pitch no longer heard in boys his age.

"It's a cat, Dumbbell," Buddy laughed.

"Well, get him off me!"

"A cat? Thought you could handle a Golden Gloves champion, Freddy Boy." Buddy laughed until he doubled at the waist. "Or, are you Freddy the Wild One?"

"Get him off of me, now!" He demanded.

Her—the cat is a her. "Get her off of me," you Ding-a-ling, Adam smirked.

Buddy reached up to the underbelly of the cat to lift her off his frantically screaming accomplice. Gertrude turned in the direction of the shadows. With glaring green eyes, she arched her back, switched targets and jumped from Freddy onto Buddy's hat. Buddy reached up and brushed the cat from his head like a large pesky fly. Gertrude flew through the air with all feet spraddled out.

Adam nearly gasped from his dark corner. *She better not be hurt,* he boiled with anger.

125

Gertrude hit the floor on all fours. She simply turned and walked off. Apparently her fun had passed and she would move on to church mice.

"Get the Christ kid and let's get out of here," Buddy demanded.

Freddy rummaged quickly through the boxes on the shelves. He knocked off more decorations and small containers than he left stacked. Old hymnals, Vacation Bible School materials, and children's choir vestments lay scattered all over the floor. Then, there it was. There could be no mistake about what they had found. The statue was amazing. A beautiful carving of the Baby Jesus was crudely pulled from its box and jammed into a duffle bag the boys had brought with them.

Oh no, Adam moaned internally. There was nothing he could do but stand in the dark and watch the boys run out of the church with the carving, while the vicious, howling laughter of dark spirits still hissed in his ears. *Tsss.*

As the boys passed, Adam etched their faces in his memory. He recognized them but didn't really know them.

School's not that big. I've seen them. They don't want to be close to anyone. They want to slink around the edges, Adam sneered.

He stayed against the wall after the two had run away like the sneak thieves they were. To Adam's thinking, hiding in the same darkness that let the two get away, made him no better than the thieves. The carving was still gone. The desperate desperados had stolen the joy of Christmas from the Cranberry Street Church, and Adam had remained silent.

Chapter 16

Christmas Eve in the Morning

The next morning, Adam felt just as guilty as he had the night before. Those boys had stolen the Baby Jesus statue and he had only watched. *What on earth should I do?*

He awakened with the same heavy heart and the same question weighing him down that he had when he went to sleep. *I'm the only one who knows that the Christ Child carving has been stolen and I know who took the masterpiece away. But, I can't do anything about it. If I tell anyone, they are going to want an explanation.*

"And, just why were you in the church in the middle of the night, Young Man?" *I can hear the questions now. But, I can't hear my explanation.*

The day belonged to Adam, not Principal Sparrow or any of the other classroom birds, so he took his time rolling out of bed. The hummer was in full chirp with one of his long "Watch me!" songs warbling forth. Adam opened the bird purse and smiled. "Good morning my friend, my roommate I guess."

With the basket lid open, the hummer jumped onto Adam's extended index finger and lapsed into his little short, quiet chirp that was to say, "I'm out of food."

127

"I know, I know—breakfast," Adam agreed as he checked for sounds in the rooms below. Then, he transferred the little bird feet to the top of the basket before he opened the trap door. He eased himself through the opening, closed the door again, and slipped down the ladder.

With school on Christmas recess he would have few hot lunches, except at Fritzy's home yesterday on Sunday. In the fall, he had signed his mother's name on a form that allowed him to work in the school cafeteria. He usually operated the dishwasher. He didn't mind the work. He exchanged water-shrunk, old-man hands for a warm meal. Now, Adam had to find food on his own. He thought about the baked beef sandwich Mrs. Breman sent home that was still in his coat pocket.

Adam went down and prepared the brightly colored sugar water for the hummer and looked around the kitchen. What would Pops say if he knew he had stolen food? The boy preferred to think of food acquisition as "local charity." Even a small packet of saltine crackers could be a banquet if nothing else was on the table. Then a thought came to him. He remembered a half-quart of milk that had been in the refrigerator for over a week. He knew that milk would spoil, so he would do the ladies a favor and drink every drop. That would save them the disgusting chore of emptying stinky, spoiled, lumpy-curdled milk a few days later.

He opened the glass jar and up-ended the entire pint of cold milk in a few gulps. "Um, a little cream is still in the bottle. That doesn't happen very often. The ladies usually pour off the cream to beat for whipping cream or put in their coffee."

Adam took the saucer of nectar back up to the belfry and looked for the bird. The little one was perched on the top of Adam's school notebook. The tiny hummer fanned its wings in a blur of motion and fluttered over to Adam's finger that was still holding the saucer. The bird attached its skinny feet to the edge of the dish and looked at the sugar water and back up at Adam.

"Little one, you are a survivor." He put the hummer and his breakfast in the basket-cage then got dressed. He was going out.

Adam had one thought in mind. The robbery. His silence in it was a puzzle with no solution. He had to get out of the church for a while or he would get island fever. At least, that's what they called his closed-in feeling in the movies down at the Dabell Neighborhood Theater. But, there was nowhere for him to go. If he went into stores, he was afraid they would think he was loitering. Still, he had to go somewhere.

He grabbed his jacket and cap from the corner of the room, opened the trap door and listened. No one seemed to be in the church that early in the morning. He hustled down the ladder and out the back door.

Outside, the wind had picked up during the early morning hours. Adam pulled his jacket around him as he tried to fold the wool and make a double thickness. Beneath the fabric, he could feel his own ribs. Unstopped, he kept his head down and started off toward town a few blocks away.

"Oh no!" a female voice screamed from an adjacent yard as he passed.

"Are you all right?" Adam called over the fence to the woman who stood there bent over.

"I think I sprained or twisted my ankle," she gasped in frustration. "I have been trying to get ready for company. My family is coming for our annual Christmas Eve Party. I have to get this sidewalk shoveled off. There's ice from the doorway to the edge of the garden fence." She rubbed her hands together rapidly and blew into them.

"Yes Ma'am, I can see."

"I don't know if I dare finish this job—or even if I can." It was obvious that her ankle hurt as she began to use the shovel as a crutch. Her eyes welled up with tears.

Adam could easily see she was upset. "I would be happy to clean the walk off for you, Ma'am—in exchange for a jelly sandwich." That was all Adam could think of with which to barter. Most women had home-make jams and jellies in their pantry.

"I am Francine Bisque, young man. Who are you?" Her question was quick but friendly.

"Adam Shoemaker, Mrs. Bisque. I'm the part-time janitor over at the church on Cranberry Street."

"Oh yes, my boy, I know many of the people there." She paused for a moment, then added, "If you can help me into the house, then clear all the ice off the sidewalk, I will be happy to make you a strawberry preserves sandwich. You're not allergic to strawberries are you?"

"No Ma'am," Adam smiled at her thoughtfulness.

"And, a nice dollar bill to go with that sandwich. A glass of milk or apple cider too," she added, like someone who had just summed up a major transaction.

Food and money? "Yes, Ma'am," he pronounced with eager determination. *I need speed and strength this morning Shaddy. Fill me with might and power, like the comic book heroes.*

With Shaddy's help, Adam's arms wound up like a whirligig in a windstorm. He shoveled and scraped and had the ice and snow off the sidewalk in record time. *A whole dollar!* Adam could not believe his luck. *A dollar for Moms' present.*

He quickly finished the sidewalk and leaned the shovel on the house near the back door. Mrs. Bisque provided the sweet sandwich, the cider and the dollar. "The drink is in one of my good pint jars. Just set the glass by the back door when you're finished."

Adam downed the cider. The special apple juice was sweet and tangy at the same time. It touched him in that spot usually reserved for Grandma Schumacher's apple concoction.

He tucked the sandwich inside his jacket, the dollar in his pocket, and started off in the direction of the Woolworth store.

I'll save the sandwich for later. But now, I have money to spend. I'll have every right to be in the store. I'm not a vagrant today. He rounded the corner and came out on the main street of town.

The double glass doors easily opened with one pull and Adam entered the dime store in search of a Christmas present. Holiday decorations hung from the ceiling and large evergreen wreaths with bright ribbons hung on the walls. Red and green lights were draped around the candy counter and checkout desk in celebration of the holy time of year.

"May I help you?" the sales clerk smiled from behind the u-shaped display of glass bens filled with candy.

"Um," Adam closed his eyes and inhaled the fragrances just inside the store. "I never can decide which is better, the salty smell of the peanuts, the sweetness of the chocolate clusters, or the combined flavors of the caramel corn."

"Well, I'll be happy to get you anything you want," the sales clerk offered.

"Thank you, no. I'm going to look around before I decide," Adam said proudly, like a regular shopper.

"If I can help, just let me know," she smiled.

Adam walked slowly through the store as the narrow boards of the hardwood floors squeaked beneath his feet. He was a customer—a real customer. The broad table-like shelves with clear glass dividers provided small cubbies to perfectly display each item type—tea towels in one, dish rags in others. He touched everything but could not decide on anything. He didn't stop until he came to a stack of linen handkerchiefs. They were beautiful.

"Aren't those a little too frilly for you," Fritzy teased when she came up behind him as he debated his find.

"Hi, Fritzy." He was surprised. He had not even thought of Fritzy being anywhere but at school, church and home.

Adam hadn't been out in the world for so many months, except to school, the thought never occur to him that others were out and about every day.

"Who's the hanky for?" She reached for one of the delicate, lace-bordered soft cloths.

"You smell good." Adam blurted.

"Thanks. The fragrance is called Chantilly." She smiled and waved her hand near Adam's face. "You just put a little on your wrist. The pulse is close to the skin there, and the warmth brings out the scent."

"It's great." Adam looked back at the handkerchiefs. Just then, he and Fritzy were jostled by two boys who shoved each other, and anyone else around them, in the main aisle. They were nearly bowled over as the boys pushed their way through the store.

"Watch out, Freddy," Buddy whispered hoarsely. "The idea is to not get noticed and not knock over everything in the store."

Adam could hear him clearly. *Wow, Shaddy, super hearing! Thanks.*

"Quit bossing me around." Freddy pushed again and a comic book fell from under his jacket.

"That's just fine. You want to drop the others too?" Buddy jabbed Freddy in the arm.

"I know them . . ." Adam finally realized who the two were. He had just seen them during the night, and he recognized their voices.

"Who," Fritzy questioned and looked past the boys to see who, of any account, Adam could be referring to.

"Never mind," Adam whispered. He looked back and saw a clerk watching the boys. He had to do something this time. Adam turned and ran into Freddy again and this time there was a zap, a charge like Adam felt when he helped Gramps with the old truck and crossed some wires that should have been left uncrossed.

"Yow!" Freddy yelped and shook his arm. Two more comics fell from beneath Freddy's coat and lay on the floor.

Adam simply pretended he had been knocked off balance by Freddy during the boys' rough horseplay. He raised both hands, *No foul,* he gestured.

"Are these yours?" Adam asked as he grabbed the comics off the floor before either of the two could touch them again.

"No, no they aren't mine," Freddy threw up both hands in denial as he looked back at the clerk who continued to watch him.

Everyone turned to Buddy. "Hey, they're not mine." He thrust his hands as far into his pockets as he could jam them. The contrived innocence on his face was comical—or stupid.

"What's the matter with you two?" Fritzy yelled. "You dropped them," she accused the boy named Freddy.

"Let it go, Fritzy," Adam whispered as he saw the expression on the clerk's face.

"They are mine, I believe," the clerk said as she reached for the comics. She winked at Adam and took the magazines from him. "Thank you," she whispered.

Adam handed them over without giving any acknowledgment to the boys. He didn't even look in their direction.

Freddy and Buddy pulled their hats lower, darted out of the store and didn't look back.

"Same school, different circles," Fritzy mumbled as the two darted off.

"They are definitely not my friends." Adam was adamant without explaining why he felt as he did. Their behavior was explanation enough.

"You are so brave, Adam," Fritzy admired, "so honest."

The praise stabbed him like a dart in a bull's eye. "I'm not so—"

"Thank you, Young Man," the clerk repeated. "You have to be commended for your honesty."

"But," Adam stopped. There weren't any words for what could not be said. "Thank you," was all he could say.

"Now, tell me about the handkerchief," Fritzy demanded.

"I earned a little money this morning shoveling a walk. I want to get Moms a Christmas present." He held up the two handkerchiefs he admired. "Which one do you like?"

"Well—that would depend on how much money you earned. The pretty one with the tatting on the edge is fifty cents and the one with the tatting and the crocheted flower in the corner is one dollar. Which one can you buy with your money?" She held them up. "They are both pretty."

"I just have a dollar and tax on the expensive one would make the cost about three cents more."

The clerk with the comic books was near them. "Well, you should get some reward for having caught the shoplifters. Let's make the fancy one a dollar even, if that's the one you want. How's that?"

"Are you sure?" Adam gasped.

"Of course—you earned a special price."

He stepped up to pay for his purchase at the front counter.

The checkout girl smiled. "I believe Charlotte may have been wrong on that price. I think the ticket should read seventy-five cents—total."

Adam could say nothing at first. "But—"

"I'll hear no more about my decision. I'll begin to doubt myself," the cashier stated as she handed him the thin box that contained the cherished Christmas present.

"Thank you," he said, but in his mind he calculated: *a hamburger for lunch would be fifteen cents and a glass of milk would be a nickel*. He smiled. He could save the jelly sandwich for supper and actually have lunch as well. He would survive another day.

"What do we do now?" Fritzy looked around the store. "Everything is so bright and colorful in here, I don't want to leave. Christmas decorations are everywhere."

The saleslady at the music counter along the west side of the Woolworth store sat at an upright piano and sang as she played. "I'm dreaming of a white Christmas—"

"I love it when they demonstrate the music."

"I didn't know they did that."

"Have you been living in the basement for the past year?"

Adam actually smiled at that description. "No place near the basement," he laughed. "What do we do now? I don't really know." He wanted to eat but didn't have enough money to treat Fritzy, so he said nothing more.

"I am going to get a malted," Fritzy giggled as she headed toward the lunch counter. "Do you want half?"

"I think I'll get a hamburger. I'll share half my burger with you if you want to divide the malt with me."

"Well," she edged toward the fountain and pulled Adam by the hand, "I don't want any of the hamburger, 'cause Mom would kill me if I spoiled my lunch and . . . I wouldn't be able to drink the entire malt by myself. I was hoping you would take the other half of the malt so I could have some and not get Mom's bun in a tangle at the same time."

"Okay," Adam thought. *I'll be money ahead and have a full stomach at the same time.*

They found two seats at the lunch counter. The year was 1945, but the Woolworth and the fountain had been there long before that. The black marble counter was even worn in a few of the more favorite eating spots.

"You've talked about your grandfather but not your dad, Adam." Fritzy removed her coat and placed it over one of the empty stools and sat down without giving much thought to what she was saying.

Her comment was harmless enough but Adam didn't know what to do with it. He didn't want to talk about his father. He didn't know what to say. "He went overseas a couple years ago."

"When does he get discharged? Is he part of the clean up?"

The waitress sat the malt on the counter, along with the metal mixing can and a second glass. Fritzy poured the malted milk from the tin into the spare glass and slid the full one over to Adam as the waitress sat the sizzling hamburger in front of him. The bun smelled like it had been buttered and grilled. It looked delicious and smelled even better.

"He . . ." Adam bit into the burger as he stalled for time. "We haven't heard from him in a long time."

"I imagine that's kinda scary."

"Sort of."

"Where was he the last you heard?"

"Um, he had been shot down over Germany. A pilot in another fighter saw him go down."

"Adam, I am so sorry. If you don't want to talk about it—"

He didn't know what to dream up next. The whole thing was a lie. Pops was not a pilot.

He was a sergeant in charge of some troops who were part of the thousands of men who fought in the Ardennes Counteroffensive. It began December 16, 1944, in the mountain region of Wallonia in Belgium, known as the Battle of the Bulge. But, no one knew what had happened. So many men had died. The rest of his men had already come home. No one knew where Sergeant Schumacher was. Adam finished the rest of his sandwich and pretended to have his mouth too full to talk.

Fritzy laughed and pushed the malt closer to his reach. "You had better wash some of that down. Didn't Mother feed you enough food yesterday?" She chuckled again.

"Too long ago, can't remember," he teased. "Besides, I kinda like to eat every day."

She laughed again. "I guess you're right. As thin as you are, you probably want to eat about six or eight times a day."

"Are you sayin' I'm skinny?"

"I'm not saying any more—at least not now." Fritzy giggled again.

A wide mirror that stretched above the full length of the lunch counter, allowed diners to enjoy the activity of the store behind them while they ate. Half of the fun of being in the Woolworth was seeing other patrons as they bustled about.

Adam's eyes suddenly snapped to attention. His heart began to pound and he felt trapped. The man with the blue car came into the store and stopped. He looked around, mostly toward the back of the store. Adam put his hands over his face like he was yawning or tired and needed to keep his face from falling off. Fritzy was focused on her ice cream.

"Are you sleepy already? It's only 11AM."

"Sorry," Adam yawned and peeked at the man through his fingers. "I guess I'm more tired than I thought."

"The services are tonight. Maybe you need a nap." She finished her malt and wiped her mouth. "So decadent, yet, so yummy."

Adam used the large mirror to watch the Smith guy walk to the back of the store. He decided to use the man's presence in the store as a cue to leave while blue-car man was at the back. Adam chugged down the last few swallows of the thick malt and grabbed up his mother's present. "I think I'll catch a few winks. Let me walk you home."

As Smith walked to the back of the store, Adam and Fritzy walked out the front. Even outside in the crystal clear air,

Adam didn't feel safe until they had rounded the corner, out of sight of the door in case the man came out. He felt crowded, fearful, and had no idea why he felt that way.

Adam was almost dizzy. His world was whirling around him and he couldn't find the center. What was happening? It wasn't enough that he lived in a birdcage with a hummingbird? Now, he felt stalked. Would the man follow them? Would he find the church on Cranberry Street?

Chapter 17

A Crime Discovered

Adam really didn't want to nap. He was back in the church to hide from blue-car man, not to rest. *The people will be coming for the Christmas Eve service in a while. I'd better look busy.* He took the broom from the supply closet and swept the entry again.

Later that day, Adam picked up some leaves from a red poinsettia plant that Polly Graham had brought in. There would be a blanket of red at the foot of the altar, formed by the close placement of many Christmas flowers.

Everyone who stopped by the church that afternoon stomped their feet and shook as much snow from their boots and coat as possible. Adam kept the floors cleared and mopped. The folks cared about their church and wanted to be part of its blessing by each small thing they did.

People began coming to the church at six PM. The folks in Middletown were much too practical for a midnight service. Wives had to get up early the next morning to start their Christmas dinner. Adam guessed that God ought to have just about enough practical people by now, with all the ones he had seen in town.

"Mr. and Mrs. Brumble, it's good to see you this evening." Pastor Silverman stood near the West entrance and greeted parishioners as they came in. Bee Bee was carrying a new, expensive looking leather purse. She must have struck a pretty good bargain with Mr. Brumble when she got rid of the birdcage, basket-purse.

"Good evening, Pastor. You too, Adam," Mr. Brumble smiled. He seemed to stand a little taller since the birdcage no longer dangled from his wife's arm.

Adam had become an accepted member of the congregation and he had only been in church one Sunday. It helped that the Bremans and Gundermans vouched for him with their friendship. The fact that he was the church's newest employee didn't hurt either. The thought of building a good name with his hard work at the church didn't get past him.

"Hi, Adam." Fritzy came up from behind and startled him. He had been watching the people as they came in and his thoughts were lost in the daydreams he had formed. He was still in transition, between his imagination and circulating with friendly people.

"I'm going to run down to the kitchen and see if they need any help. We'll have punch and the cookies we made, after this evening's service." She pulled on Adam's sleeve.

There wasn't anything he needed to do for Mr. G. at the moment, so Adam followed in mocked protest. "Cookies? Who can eat cookies at this hour?"

"You can, Adam Shoemaker, that's who." Fritzy continued to lead the way down to the church kitchen. The room was bright and warm and full of women dressed in their Christmas best.

The bustle and swish of red and green taffeta, fancy hats with veils and small Christmas pins attached to the brim, hurried around the kitchen. Small glasses were out of the upper cabinets and fancy Christmas napkins were stacked near the corner of the counter.

"Ah, Frederica." Grandma Stafford threw out her arms and hugged her granddaughter. "I'm glad to see you again too, Adam. Please come over after services with Frederica for some wassail, non-alcoholic of course. The holiday drink is a tradition of ours."

"Oh yes, please," Fritzy grabbed hold of that same shirt sleeve.

"That sounds nice, Ma'am."

"Unless you have your own family traditions. I wouldn't want to interfere with your family's Christmas plans." Mrs. Stafford beamed with holiday joy.

"No Ma'am. Not this year."

"Adam's mother has been sick, Grandma. Remember, we talked about that."

"Oh, yes, Dear. Your mother thought she knew her."

"Yes, Ma'am, Bridget is her name." Adam felt uneasy. He did not like talking about his family. They lived on a farm with no running water. Pops was a deserter, and Moms was in a sanitarium. Most people were afraid of TB. The disease was very contagious. Recently, Moms had been treated with new antibiotics; Adam, however, still had a feeling of shame about the disease. He wished the new medicine would help, but Moms had said not to wish for things. She said, wishes that come true leave no satisfaction. The wisher feels more and more empty.

When Moms was real sick and Adam was afraid she would die, he had thought he would strike a bargain with the shadows. A deal with evil wouldn't make anyone feel empty or unhappy. Because, once the person struck the bargain, they would never feel guilty or lonely again. They would not be able to feel anything anymore.

But, Granny O'Hara had warned against making eye contact with the shadows. "They will offer comfort, even healing, but they are evil. Once they have you, they won't let you go."

The old grandmother's words haunted him as he struggled to turn off the bad feelings that gnawed at him. He wanted to hide from all the Christmas cheer. He withdrew inside himself, far from the happy people all around him.

"Here Adam, eat a cookie. You're falling asleep here." She popped a cookie into his mouth and watched him chew. "Okay, your motor is primed again. Let's go up and take our seats in the sanctuary." Fritzy led Adam out of the kitchen.

As they walked out of the kitchen, Adam touched her shoulder. "Fritzy, I don't want to walk behind you. I want to walk with you."

Fritzy laughed. Adam had taken a stand and it was a good move. He didn't want to be led around. They walked together up each step.

Upstairs, the sanctuary was full of Christmas music as Adam and Fritzy approached the doors. The large, horseshoe shaped room was beautiful. There was a huge gathering of poinsettias at the base of the altar that resembled a red coverlet that had been tucked in at the base. Red tapers glowed on the altar and additional ones lit the aisles from candelabras that stood like sentries at the end of each pew. The whole scene was a flickering masterpiece of flame and fire. It smelled like fine beeswax at a slow burn.

"It's not there," Adam heard Pastor Silverman whisper to Alfred as they stood just outside the sanctuary door.

"Not there?" Alfred repeated. "That cannot be."

"What?" Fritzy interjected herself into the conversation.

"The Christ Child carving. You and Adam went down to the storeroom and got the statue out. Right?"

"No, Sir," Adam interrupted. "Remember, you came in and asked us to help your wife? We left the carving in the storeroom." Adam knew the figure was not still in storage because he was there, in the dark, when the Christ Child was stolen.

"Yes, yes," Alfred spoke softly, but Adam could tell from his tone that he was worried.

"The carving just isn't in the storeroom anywhere. I looked through every box myself." The pastor was concerned but restrained. "And, there was stuff strewn all over the floor."

"That's not how the storage room was when we were in there the other day," Alfred shook his head in confusion.

Adam could not meet their gaze. His eyes searched the floor for a hole to crawl in. He knew what happened to the Christ Child, but he couldn't tell them. What could he say? Nothing.

"Pastor, there's a doll in the nursery. I played with it when I was a kid," Fritzy offered. "Let me wrap Baby Bubbles in a blanket. Maybe no one will notice the bundle isn't our carving."

"Well, all right. It's too late to do anything else tonight." The pastor's voice showed his disappointment. "But, remember, Fritzy, even the work of art is just a carving. The real child of Christmas is in our hearts."

Adam turned away and walked to the windows in the front doors. He had to think, to sort out his stories, his lies. As he stood there with his eyes fixed through the window on the snow covered street outside, Fritzy hurried to the nursery for the doll.

In our heart? The real child of Christmas is in our heart? Most of the time, my heart feels empty. No one lives there anymore, not even me.

Two dark shadowy figures appeared beside him. He was tempted to ask them for help. He didn't. He followed them with his eyes until he remembered Granny's warning and turned away.

Fritzy hurried back with Baby Bubbles wrapped in a blanket. "The babe doesn't look too bad. The doll will be okay this time," she smiled weakly. "With the carving, we always carried it with the blanket underneath so both of the child's hands and arms could be open, reaching up to his father. Mary will have to carry the infant differently this year." Adam could see by Fritzy's expression that she was upset.

Adam's eyes darted away from hers. He could see her sorrow, which made him equally sad. He knew what had happened to the Christ Child, yet he stood there, cowering in the front entrance.

Fritzy handed the doll over to the *Mary* for that year's nativity scene. Silently, Fritzy and Adam walked into the sanctuary and took their seats.

Adam finally relaxed a little. He knew the shadows would not dare go into a worship area.

Just before the service started, Mrs. Silverman handed her husband a piece of paper. The pastor read the note, closed the yellow lined sheet and bowed his head.

The chancel choir and cherubs sang *Away in a Manger* while the entire congregation seemed focused on the doll in Mary's arms. Adam's stomach felt heavy. It nearly fell to his knees when he saw Buddy and Freddy walk into the sanctuary with their parents.

Those guys come here to church? They pretend to worship in the very place they just robbed? Adam watched as the boys climbed the stairs to the balcony and sat in the section on the right side, above the pulpit. *Great, I'm going to see them out of the corner of my eye through the whole service.*

"My friends," Pastor Silverman began his sermon, "some of you may have noticed that our carving is not in the manger this year. I know how hard that is for all of us. My wife found this note attached to the front door of the parsonage when she left. It reads: 'We have your carving.'"

The congregation gasped. Mrs. Brumble mouthed, "What? How?"

Adam thought he was going to be sick. Nauseous waves rose and sank within him. To add to his misery, he saw Freddy elbow Buddy in the ribs and both boys stifled childish giggles.

The pastor continued. "That's all that the note said. My friends, we have to believe that someone is playing some sort of prank on us, and they will return the statue. Maybe not before Christmas, but perhaps we will have the carving back for next year's celebrations. The note doesn't say more. So, I can only assume that they think this is a funny trick, and we will get the carving back soon."

They have no intention of returning that statue. They already have a buyer! Adam screamed inside and thought his head would burst right out the top.

"Good friends, we are not going to let this loss spoil our Christmas Eve service. As much as we have loved having the carving over the years, a wooden Christ is not whom we worship. We don't value the representation. We worship the real thing. Only truth is worthy of our praise. They were probably just children playing a childish game."

Adam heard the boys gasp and wondered who else may have heard them. *Go ahead, wise guys, get loud enough and you will give yourselves away*. Adam actually hoped they would do just that, and then he wouldn't have to do anything. But, deep down, he knew he wouldn't speak up. He didn't last night when the carving was stolen, and he wouldn't say anything now.

The pastor said no more about the Christ Child carving. He said that love came to earth a long time ago and remained here for those who would accept that love.

The whole service touched Adam. He marveled at the beauty of everything, the warm candle light, the music, and even a doll with straggly hair that substituted for the son of God.

He didn't talk about the doll either. He was afraid if he opened his mouth the whole story would pour out, including the fact that he had been living a complete lie.

Only truth is worthy of our praise. The words echoed in Adam's ears like a bully's taunt. But, he knew that silence contributes to a lie, not clears up the mystery. Adam had done nothing wrong but hid himself from those who tried to care for him.

Shaddy, what should I do? But, the wind was silent. In the void, dark shadows howled from the outer hallway. They could not come into the room of worship but Adam heard them and knew how easy it would be to let them help him. To call on the forces of darkness to find the Christ Child carving was wrong. That partnership would be like two opposing worlds colliding in space. Adam didn't want to be under that great cloud of wrath when the junk rained down.

Chapter 18

A Christmas Eve Truth

"Over here," Fritzy directed Adam after the Christmas Eve service. "You are joining us, right?" She grabbed her coat from the cloak room, scooped up Adam's jacket and hurried him to the church door.

"Yes, I guess, sure." He put on his jacket as he stepped out onto the freshly shoveled sidewalk. The snow fell gently but had not corrupted his hard work. He smiled with pride.

The Breman's hustled Adam into their station wagon and followed the Stafford sedan out of the church parking lot. He looked out the back window of the wagon at a long procession of other friends that joined in the fun.

"They're all coming." Fritzy smiled when she saw Adam count each vehicle. "The church is a family and a family celebrates Christmas together."

"It has been a long time since I've experienced this much 'family' all in one week. It's a little mind-storming."

"Boy, you can say that again. I know I find my family overwhelming sometimes," Jim Breman joked.

"All right now, Jimmy," his mother reminded him. "Adam is talking about feeling a little smothered about having so many family members around at one time. He didn't say that he doesn't appreciate his family."

"Yes, Mother dear," Jim mocked. "You'll have to excuse me, Adam. I am trying to figure out if I'm the man my college expects me to be, or the little boy my parents want."

"Trust me, Son," Coach laughed, "for what college costs, there had better be a man coming out the other side of graduation, not a perpetual little boy."

I'm fifteen and I'm on my own. Adam smiled inside. *I'm growing up for free.*

"The biggest decisions at Grandma and Grandpa's house will be, which cookie didn't I get to taste at the church and, do I want a cinnamon stick in my wassail?" Fritzy giggled.

Jim jumped out of the car as the wheels stopped in his Grandparents' driveway. The other visitors parked on the street.

The house was Victorian in design and lit with the glow from hundreds of Christmas lights. A decorated tree was positioned in the middle of a large, round window and even the front yard had just enough snow to create a storybook picture.

Adam stopped on the front sidewalk and tried to take in all he could see. He wanted every light and every ornament to be a memory for him to carry back up to the dark belfry.

"Come on in, Adam. The winter wind is cold out here," Fritzy started to pull on his coat sleeve, then paused and gently put her hand in his.

"If I forget to tell you later, Merry Christmas, Frederica Breman."

"And a very Merry Christmas to you, Adam Shoemaker." As snowflakes lit on her nose and lips, she giggled, stuck out her tongue and tried to catch a few crystals of the icy fluff as they fell.

"You are always happy," Adam marveled.

"Of course, why not?"

"Why not? We just went through a war that wrapped around the whole world."

"My point exactly. You put that statement in the past tense. The war is over."

"Not for me," Adam mumbled, surprised he heard his own words out loud.

"Sorry, Mr. Negative. The war is over for everyone. That doesn't mean that every problem has been solved for everyone." She said nothing for a second as they walked into the house. "I am sorry your father is still missing, Adam. But, until you know what happened to him, it might be better to believe he is well, and he's on the long way home."

Adam said no more. People from the church and neighborhood pushed in and around them. Laughter was everywhere. Smiling faces were reflected back wherever he looked.

"Come on in," Mabel Thornton called as she sat at the piano and began to play. "*Silent night, Holy night,*" the people sang. And, "*Chestnuts Roasting on an Open Fire*" was a reflection of the scene around the marble fireplace in the Stafford living room.

"*Have yourself a merry little Christmas, let your heart be light,*" people sang through the evening.

Fritzy led Adam into the large kitchen that smelled sweet and wonderful. The linoleum on the floor resembled multi shades of red bricks and looked new and shiny. The cabinets were white and circled the room. Adam couldn't help but compare the room to the farm kitchen he left behind.

"The kitchen looks happy," Adam observed. Flashes of the farm kitchen flooded his memory. "All Moms had is a black Home Comfort Range, and that huge thing sure wasn't electric." He laughed. "I remember the story about the day the salesman came by in his horse and buggy and convinced Grandma that she simply had to have that stove. That range was the best that could be bought for a non-electric kitchen.

Moms is still using the same range. She'd check the wood in the firebox and if there wasn't enough, I'd go out back and bring some in to fill the wood bucket."

"Adam, that sounds wonderful!"

"Wonderful? It is primitive, Fritzy!" Adam nearly laughed at the thought that all that work could somehow be praised.

"Sure. My Grandma and Grandpa Breman live on a farm, and they have the same kind of stove. Jimmy and I used to argue over who got to bring in the wood for Grandma. Sarah was usually setting the table." She looked at Adam with a look of surprise. "How can honest work be anything but beautiful—and fun too?"

"I hadn't looked at it that way," Adam admitted.

"I'm a teacher because I wanted to work with kids." Coach Breman added to the conversation as he came in to get a fresh pitcher of wassail. "I had a favorite teacher I admired—Mr. Anderson. So, I worked hard and went to college," the coach added. "I don't mean to interrupt you kids, but a college education is just a degree, not a pedigree. Education doesn't make you smarter or better. College makes you prepared to choose the work you would love to do and not have to do the work you can find."

"I guess," Adam blushed.

"My brother, George, was two years behind me. He graduated from the same college I did, with highest honors, and he farms our parents' farm. Why? Because he loves farming. Working the land is honest work and you have no boss but God."

"Honest work?" There was that word again—honesty.

"There aren't special jobs that are worthy. A day of work is a day of work." Coach smiled and filled his cup with wassail.

An honest day's work. Adam thought about those four words.

"Come on," Fritzy coaxed again. "I want you to meet Grandpa Breman."

Chapter 19

Memories Remembered

Tuesday, Christmas Day 1945

"Yikes!"Adam bolted out of bed the next morning. From the singing of Christmas Eve carols the previous evening, to the tolling of belfry bells that morning, Adam was propelled into Christmas Day by a loud and continuous deep-throated *bong*.

The bells in the bell tower pealed forth the news that Christmas Day 1945 had arrived. Adam slapped his hands over his ears and bent in acoustic torture. The bells hadn't rung since Adam had taken over the small room directly below the open tower loft. He had no idea that the sound, which was majestic out on the streets, would reverberate in the tower like a blacksmith's anvil on his ear drums. It had been so many years since the bells had chimed, he would not have remembered the experience in the same intensity as that particular Christmas morning.

The little hummingbird scratched and chirped in pain. The little one would have flown out of the tower if it had been free.

"Sorry, sorry," Adam laughed while he held an ear with one hand and opened the cage with the other. "Do what you have to do."

The little hummer hopped up onto Adam's extended index finger and seemed to pace up and down between the knuckles. The tiny guy was obviously being tortured by the chimes.

Adam smiled at the little bird, and then he opened the tower window. In recent days, he had let the bird out of the cage but not out of the belfry. The window had remained closed for the winter. Adam didn't know what else to do. The sound of the bells was too much for him as a human. He knew that birds usually fly out of a tower when the bells begin to chime.

"*Joy to the World,*" the melody rang out and the bells in the belfry hit every note with perfect ting on the high ones and deep tonal vibrations in the lower register. Adam hated to see the bird take to the air beyond the tower, but he knew he had no other choice.

No one would be around. It was Christmas. People would be at home with their families, drinking cocoa and opening presents around a brightly lit tree. At least, that was how Adam remembered Christmas morning to be.

He took his time dressing, even though the wind blew through the cracks around the belfry windows and chilled the room even more. Once he laced up his last clodhopper, he stepped slowly down the ladder. He put on his jacket, cap and the gloves he had brought from the farm house, and tucked Moms' present under his coat.

Outside, the streets and sidewalks were deserted. He searched, but he couldn't see his hummingbird in the adjacent trees. *His* hummingbird—the little guy had been *his* hummingbird, but now he was gone.

The weather was bitter cold. Fine, icy snow swirled along the sidewalk in small whirlwinds of frost. Adam worried about the hummer and his heart ached. *Hummingbirds aren't winter birds.*

He had to get himself together. He didn't want to think about the bird, and he definitely was not going to think about how lonely the tower would feel when he got back.

Adam lowered his head and started to walk toward the sanitarium. He arrived in good time, owing partly to the wind at his back that pushed him along, and partly to the same wind at his back that froze him to the bone. A fast pace was the only way to build up body heat. He let the harsh weather push him to the sanitarium until he staggered into the hospital on a bumpy blast of north wind.

"Let me get you some blankets and hot tea," a nurse offered as she hurried over.

"Thank you." He shivered through chattering teeth while ice dripped from his eyebrows.

The nurse handed him a blanket from a cart in the hallway. He wrapped himself in the dark blue wool like an Indian chief. As he warmed, he redirected his thoughts to his mother.

"Is Bridget Schumacher doing well today?" Adam asked. He had to say something, but hoped he knew the answer. Moms had promised to be up and about by Christmas Day.

"Bridget?" She pointed to the large gathering room with open stairway and soft lights. "You're in luck. You can visit her and warm yourself by the fire at the same time." She pointed again. "Go on in."

Adam pulled the blanket even tighter and walked into the open space. "Hi, Moms," he smiled and entered the room which was full of Holiday music and Christmas peace.

"Adam," she stood up and reached out her arms. "You got a ride."

"I walked, Moms."

"Walked? Adam, you could have caught your death of cold." Bridget put her arms around her son and rubbed some warmth into his back.

"I'm fine." He chuckled with a twinkle, "But the back rub sure feels good. It feels like you have gained some strength, Moms." When she stopped, Adam held out the present he had brought. "I kept the comics section of the Sunday newspaper someone had left on a chair at church the other evening and used it for the wrapping paper. There aren't any Christmas scenes, but the paper is colorful. I wrapped the box in my favorite strip, with Dick Tracy square in the middle, found a piece of string and tied the whole package together. I don't think the wrapping looks too bad."

"Son, it is wonderful!" Bridget took the present and pressed the gift to her chest.

"The comics aren't the gift, Moms. What's inside is the present." Adam enjoyed the fun of making his mother smile.

Bridget Schumacher carefully opened the wrappings and lifted out the linen square with the lace border he had selected at the five and dime. "Adam, the handkerchief is lovely. Where did you get the money?"

Adam's chest puffed out a little. "I earned it, Moms. I shoveled some ice and snow for a lady. . . . And—"

"You have a job? That is wonderful, Adam."

"The sidewalk only took a few minutes to shovel off. But, Moms, I do have another job—"

"You didn't quit school, did you, Son? If you did, when school starts again after Christmas break, you march yourself right back in there and—"

"No, no, Moms. I'm still in school. I work on Saturdays and for a few hours after school. This will please you. Mr. Gunderman said I could have the job as long as I can keep my grades up. Also, I have Fridays off because—" He paused and studied her face. He didn't want her to think he was shirking work for play. "Because, I am on the basketball team at school."

"Basketball? You're on the team? Oh, how I loved to play basketball in high school."

"You, Moms, you played basketball?"

"You think all I've ever done is garden, cook and clean?"

Luckily for Adam, his mother was chuckling through her litany of chores.

"No, Moms. It's just that you have never talked about playing sports before."

"Well then, for that I am sorry. I loved every position of basketball. I was a little short for center. We wore a middy with a string necktie and bloomer shorts."

"I can just see you running up and down the basketball court."

"Okay, okay," she chuckled. "Now—I'm hungry. I've made a reservation for you to join me for dinner. They are serving turkey and dressing." She sized up his arms and face. "Are you eating all right?"

"Yes, Ma'am."

"Mrs. Crammer feeding you well? You look so thin."

"I'm not staying with the Crammers, Moms." Then, before she could ask any questions, he changed the subject. "Speaking of the Crammers, I saw Sidney Crammer yesterday."

"Dinner is being served," a nurse interrupted. "Bridget, you can take your visitor into the large dining room with you."

"This is my son, Adam."

"Good to meet you, Adam," the nurse said.

The dining room was full of flowers and the wonderful aroma of hot food. They could have been serving squirrel for all Adam cared. The food was warm and the plates were served on a white table cloth. That Christmas dinner was his third hot meal in a row.

"Like I said, I saw Sidney Crammer. He said something about Pops telling him he would sell the creek and bottom land. That doesn't sound like Pops. Did he ever tell you about selling any land, let alone the land down by the creek?"

"Sell the creek?" Bridget unfolded her napkin and placed the cloth slowly in her lap. "Your father never spoke to me about selling off any land, and I wouldn't think the land he would consider would be the creek, if he considered any at all."

Adam put his fork down. "I think it is all a trick to cheat us out of valuable land. Crammer didn't farm the land last spring like we all agreed he'd do. That way, with no money from the crop, we would be forced into selling some land, maybe the whole farm."

"Adam, do you think so? There's nothing I can do about it. I'm in here. I'll have to ask you to handle all of this," Moms whispered as she looked around the room.

"I'll take care of Crammer. Gramps said, 'A good farm has good soil. A great farm has great soil and water.' That farm is ours."

Adam lifted off a biscuit as the plate was passed. He inhaled the aroma of the golden flaky quick bread. "They should bottle this biscuit smell and spray the school right before it starts. That would get everybody inside fast."

"Adam," Bridget put her knife and fork down, "you come up with some unusual ideas."

"One thing that is not unusual is indoor plumbing. How are you going to get to come home any time soon if we don't have an indoor bathroom?"

"I've wondered about that myself. I just don't know what we will do."

"The money Mr. Crammer would pay for the land would put in a new bathroom." Adam couldn't believe he was bringing up the farm sale again. He didn't want to sell off one foot of the land that had been in Pops' family since President John Quincy Adams first deeded the parcel over to the Schumacher ancestors.

"You know, the fireplace in the farm parlor is the same one your dad's great-grandmother cooked over when they first moved into the valley. The cabin was just two rooms with a loft above. As the farm prospered and the family grew, the cabin was enlarged, until the house was as we know it today." Bridget's eyes shone.

Adam guessed that old scenes danced in his mother's head just as they did in his. "Can you imagine baking a pie or cooking Thanksgiving dinner like that? That would be hard." Adam marveled.

"Probably, but I doubt they thought it was. That was the way farm life was back then." She smiled. "That life sounds wonderful to me. My people moved into the eastern hills in much the same way. They cooked over open, outdoor fires and gathered berries. Most of the clan moved on. They never stayed in one place very long."

"You never told me much about them, Moms. We only visited Granny those two summers. Were they farmers? I don't remember seeing any farm equipment."

"Not exactly—they were tinkers. They dealt in tin—but they traveled all the time."

"Why? And, why don't you ever talk about them?"

"The clan has traveled for centuries. That was, and is, who they are."

"They sound like gypsies," Adam joked.

"Your father forbids me to use that word. We haven't talked about them since your dad put a stop to our visits. But, they are travelers, Irish travelers." Bridget cut strips of her turkey and took a bite. "Um, this is good."

"I would think that life could have been fun, hunting all the time, working with tin—to make what?"

"Oh, I don't know. I guess my great-grandfather loved moving about as a boy. Grandpa would tell stories about how his father used to play with the Indian children from a nearby village." Bridget sipped her coffee as she retold the family tale that had been told before, but she never grew tired of the telling.

"They came into that valley a long time ago, didn't they?"

"Our settlers were among the first. They made friends with the Indians, and Morningstar, an Indian woman, taught my Great-grandmother how to weave."

"Did Morningstar teach any of them how to make pots? Pottery, you know—pots."

"Why yes, of course, Adam. And what is interesting, your Grandpa Schumacher, out at the farm, also taught you how to throw pots on a wheel. The potter's wheel is still out in the barn. Your dad glazed and fired them in the kiln for you. Don't you remember?"

"I didn't, but someone reminded me." He put his fork in the potatoes and ate a bite while he thought. Could his memory have been right?

"I don't see how you could forget it. The curator at the art gallery said your talent was amazing. He sold a lot of your pots there at the gallery. He even shipped some to Boston and New York where they were sold in fine stores."

"How is that possible? I didn't fall and hit my head. Why didn't I remember?"

"I've noticed that memories have been hard for you to come by in the last six months. I asked my doctor about you. He said that you must be taking all of this very hard, so you hide inside yourself and forget the past that is painful. You can't just forget the day Pops left. You forget the whole thing, the whole year and maybe a few of those years before." Bridget's voice cracked as she tried to talk. "I haven't been able to be much of a mother for you," she whispered.

"Moms," Adam felt a big lump in his throat and couldn't swallow, "you have been sick. I know that."

"Is everything all right?" One of the nursing attendants asked as she came near their table.

"Yes, thanks," Adam smiled. "We're just happy." And, that was not a lie. Adam was beginning to remember.

"Grandpa would take me with him out to the barn. While he cleaned out stalls, I would offer to help, but he would say, 'No, you're an artist. You make some more pots.' And, I did. One time Pops came out to the barn, and I thought I'd get in trouble for not helping with the chores. But no, he said he was amazed by my creations and was very proud of me."

"Can you make pots fast enough to bring in some money?" Moms was so excited her voice wobbled as she whispered the family business in the public dining hall. "I don't want to sell any of the farm."

"Me neither. Selling any of our land would feel like we were betraying the family. I don't want to sell even a foot of that land." Adam whispered.

"I know, but we need the money so fast. Oh, I wish your father would come home. I cannot make a decision like this on my own."

"Moms, don't you think he would have been home by now, if he was alive or if he hadn't been a deserter."

"Deserter?" Bridget's voice sounded both shocked and angry. She lowered her tone and her chin, as if she were preparing herself for a fight. "Don't you ever say that again. Never call your father a deserter. How can you even think such a thing?"

"I don't know. But—" Adam's head and heart were banging into each other. He had been utterly alone for months. He had lied to his mother throughout the entire autumn. If Pops wasn't dead, why didn't he come home and make everything right? If he was alive and would not come home— Adam was beginning to hate him.

"Wait a minute," Bridget gasped. "What about the bank account? I know that money is yours, and Pops was saving it for your college. But, maybe we could use a little of it now. Adam—"

"The bank account?" He dropped his fork on the plate and the metal made an awful clatter on the china.

"What's wrong?"

"Then, there is a bank account? That wasn't a dream or just a wish?"

"A dream? Of course not, Honey. And, your dad had forbidden you to wish for things. Those are the clan ways."

"What do you mean? A wish is just a wish."

"Not to the clan. Wishes come true and they always require a price to be paid. The old ways are not our ways. If the shadows grant the wish, the price is irrevocably everything you hold dear. If wishes that come true are responsible, the prize is empty and does not satisfy. It only makes us wish for more. The old clan ways are not for us."

"But Moms—wait. Granny talked about wishes coming true because our family is lucky. I haven't seen any luck but—"

"Adam, don't talk about luck," she cautioned through clenched teeth.

"Moms," he was stunned. "What are you afraid of? Why can't I make a little wish for the good of the family?"

"Because wishing and the Luck of the Irish will only trick you, deceive you. Even if you get the money, the cash won't be for free. The price you will pay will be more than anyone could ever imagine. There will be an unquenchable aching for more, always more that will never be satisfied."

"Granny said the only that I was not to look at the dark shadows. I was not to look at them at all."

"I know. When you told her the shadows talked to you, she was terrified—and so was I. Your father insisted that we come home if Granny filled your head with tales of the travelers. We packed and left on the next bus." Bridget put her hand to her mouth. "Did the shadows actually talk to you?"

"Yes, I guess. I could hear their words in my head. Granny only said I wasn't to look at them."

"Have they—have you seen or heard them here?"

"Yes . . . sure. You have seen them too. I've seen your eyes follow them as they move around."

"That is enough, Adam. Pops always protected you from the gypsy ways." She sipped her coffee and went on. "No more of that. Let's talk about something else. Your daddy opened an account for you at a bank over near the gallery in the Capital." Bridget threw her hands in the air in silent affirmation of a memory once lost but now found.

"What bank?" Adam jumped on the excitement. He would skip the questions about the O'Hara side of the family— for now.

"Don't you know?" Moms dropped her hands in her lap.

"Did I go with Pops?"

"Yes, I'm pretty sure you did. You said to me, 'Pops and I went to the bank on the way home.' I remember." She watched Adam's expression. "Now, just relax." She reached out and patted his hand. "Relax, relax. Focus on one of the pots you created if you can."

"Okay," He tried to empty his mind of the possibilities that might be there. He didn't see a pot, but he could feel a soft matte glaze on his fingers tips. Then, he saw Pops and a sunny day—and paintings.

"Can you see you and Pops talking to the man at the art gallery?"

"Yes." Adam was surprised. He had not thought about that scene for years, not since Pops left. "The man said something like, 'You're gifted young man.' I didn't know what he meant but he smiled a lot. He touched my pottery very gently."

"He was saying that God has given you a gift, a talent for doing something special."

Adam opened his eyes and grinned. "I like that." He closed his eyes again. "Pops and I celebrated by getting a cola at the drug store nearby, across from the National Bank." His

163

eyes flew open. "The National Bank, that's the one, Moms. It was the National Bank in the Capital. I know it was."

"Great!" She cheered him along. "We'll have to have the account number."

"Maybe the number is in my room at the farm." He finished his bread and folded his napkin. "I wonder how much is in the account."

"You don't remember?"

"I was about twelve. I would have been excited if the guy had flipped me a quarter," he chuckled.

"I am sure he paid you much more than that or your father would not have opened an account for you. I'll bet you had your name on the Savings passbook but Pops would have had to sign too since you're a minor."

Pops—again. We need him, and he's nowhere around. "If I still have money in that bank account I should be able to get it out. With Pops gone and the government not knowing where he is, you should be able to sign for me as my only parent."

Nothing more was said about the farm or the land or the creek. There was nothing that could be said. Adam was not old enough to sell any land even if he wanted to, and Moms was obviously not strong enough to make that decision by herself. If they were going to get a bathroom at the farm, the savings account would have to pay for it.

They talked no more of the shadows, Pops, or Irish Luck. The day was good, full of mystery, and a puzzle that fascinated Adam for the first time in months.

He walked back to town a few hours later with not a single present to distinguish this day from any other. He wasn't a baby. He understood his mother had no way to shop, even if she had the money for a gift. If there was a God in heaven, he had not made his presence known to Adam Shoemaker.

But, there was something else. In the silence of the icy air, he began to think through his options. *That money in the bank is mine. I can spend every dollar—if I can get the information to open the account. There has to be a way. Perhaps one wish wouldn't hurt. I wouldn't be asking to get rich. I just need help getting at my own money. So far, Shaddy, you have helped with powers but not hard cash. Shaddy, what do I do?"* The late afternoon wind was silent as he walked back to town.

Alone on the road with fear and doubt, Adam still felt hope began to stir within him. There was money—his own money—somewhere. He felt the pride of work and accomplishment. How long would the good feelings last? They rose and fell like the road that stretched out before him. Somehow, everything was different. Was it really true? Was an artist's heart buried beneath all the rubble of his life?

Could it really be? Had life taken a turn for the better? Adam continued his walk into town and a rekindled hope went with him.

Chapter 20

Police Questions – No Answers

Back in town, a young boy called from a front yard lit with multicolored Christmas lights. "Hi, Adam." Then the boy mimicked a jump shot and yelled, "Are you going to play in the next game too?"

"Sure am," Adam answered but didn't slow down. The long walk from Moms' hospital had chilled him to the bone. He was too cold to stop moving. It was late in the afternoon on Christmas Day.

He saw the boy set up a target for what appeared to be new BB gun. At another house, two other children bounded out onto their concrete driveway and returned volley for volley with new tennis rackets. It had been snowing all Christmas Day but the never-ending out-pouring of frozen white flakes didn't seem to keep neighborhood kids from enjoying their new Christmas presents. Adam thrust his hands into his empty pockets to brace himself from the cold then turned the corner onto Cranberry Street.

"Adam," Fritzy giggled, "where are you going?"

"Fritzy, what are you doing over here? Thought you'd be at home in your nice warm house on a cold day like this. You live blocks away from here."

"Today is Christmas, Adam. And, I live just three blocks from here. You know that. I was out for a walk. What's wrong?"

"Oh—nothing, sorry. It's just that—never mind." Adam threw his hands up over his head, frustrated. He started to walk past the church. He had to lead Fritzy away from the corner. She could not discover his hiding place, his only sanctuary. His heart raced. Was this the moment all his secrets would come tumbled down around him?

"Are you Adam Shoemaker?" A Middletown policeman pulled his squad car to the corner and leaned out of the window.

"Yes."

"What's wrong officer?" Fritzy asked.

"We'd like to talk to young Mr. Shoemaker. Sorry Miss." The officer got out of the car and came around to the sidewalk. "You'll have to come with me."

"Why?" Fritzy quizzed.

"Mr. Shoemaker just started working at the church on Cranberry Street, right?"

"So?" Fritzy tone was puzzled.

"The Christ Child carving, Miss. The statue came up missing just after Mr. Shoemaker started working there. He's the only outsider."

"Outsider?" The bottom fell out of Adam's heart. *How can I be an outsider in God's house? If that were true, I don't belong anywhere.*

"I'd like for you to come to the station and answer a few questions." The officer stepped a little closer and took Adam by the sleeve.

Adam was dazed and confused as the officer put him in the squad car. He said nothing. He could feel Fritzy watching him from the curb. At first, he couldn't even look at her. Before they pulled away he was finally brave enough to catch her gaze.

Was she disappointed in him? Was she angry?

"Officer, you have no right—" Fritzy barked as she put her hands on her hips, while the policeman walked around to the driver's side of the car. "He doesn't have to answer your questions."

"Yes, Miss—he does," the officer returned.

Fritzy stomped her foot and clung to the side of the squad care. "Call me when you get back," Fritzy said frantically.

Adam was stunned. Nothing made any sense. He sat slumped forward in the back of the police car. He would jump out but there were no handles on the inside of the doors. What strange world did he live in?

• • •

The squad car pulled up to the Middletown Police Department. Adam recognized it. He had been passed it many times. But, this time, it was different. He was being ushered from the car, up the steps and into the squad room by a large, burly man he didn't know.

"Sit down, Son." The officer pointed to a chair beside an old wooden table in one of the interview rooms at headquarters.

The police station was nothing like Adam would have imagined—if he had ever thought about it.

The room was dingy and drab. Gray-green paint peeled from the walls. There weren't any bars on the windows but there might as well have been. The window frames looked like they had been painted closed, over and over, year after year. A whiff of fresh air had not blown through that room in a very long time.

Adam did what he was told. He couldn't make sense out of anything anymore. The people who had shown him love and acceptance, the people of the Cranberry Street Church, had turned his name into the police as a likely suspect in the robbery of the Christ Child figure.

"That statue was hand carved, Boy, by a very famous artist. Now, I'm no art expert, but it seems to me, if a fellow were to steal something of any value, he would want to sell it."

Adam said nothing. Not that he was trying to be secretive. He didn't know the answers to anything anymore. He did, however, know who took the carving, but he couldn't say a word. He wasn't protecting those stupid boys. He was making sure his secret sleeping place was not found.

"You tell me where you hid the carving, and I'll call your dad so he can come pick you up. No questions. No blame."

My Dad? Lots of luck with that. Pops is nowhere. Let me know when he gets to town.

"Where do you live, Son? Does your family have a phone?" Detective Frank Overton didn't look at Adam. He studied the paper he was going to write on. That kept him distant, in charge, in control.

Son? I'm nobody's son. Bitter tears started to stream down his face.

"Look, Kid, this doesn't have to be a problem. The church doesn't want to press charges. They just want the carving back." The detective stifled a yawn.

Adam closed his eyes. He felt beaten. No one believed him. His name was ruined. He couldn't tell anyone where he lived. He felt like he had been running a race for four months. He had finally reached the finish line and he had come in last. There was no one to cheer him on or welcome a triumphant winner. He had lost.

"Today is Christmas, Adam. I would like to get back home to my family. If you will not tell me where you live or how to contact your folks, I'll have to call the County Agency. However," he paused and Adam found the silence deafening, "nobody will be there today. So, you will have to sit in this jail overnight. I'm not charging you with anything, not yet. We haven't found the statue in your possession. But, I cannot let a boy, with no way to contact his parents, out on the streets alone."

Adam just stared at the table. There were several coffee rings on the surface. On the left, a sticky substance covered a spot about the size of a deck of cards. He studied every dot and blotch as he tried to control his fear and disappointment.

If I don't look at Detective Overton, if I can focus on something else, he will not be in my world. If he's not in my world, he can't hurt me.

You will not intimidate me, Overton. The muscles in Adam's back tightened as he pulled himself up to his full, seated posture and looked squarely at the detective. He said nothing. *A night in jail will probably be the warmest I've spent in weeks,* he thought, but no words were spoken.

Detective Overton stared at Adam for a moment, shrugged his shoulders and stood up. "Well then, come along with me, Son."

The detective didn't handcuff him. "I'm sorry you've chosen this path, Adam. No one wants you to spend the night in jail, but—" He motioned for the boy to walk ahead of him as he ushered him through the outer office and into the holding area. He pointed to Adam's belt and gestured for him to remove it.

Adam turned his empty pockets inside out and walked into the cell. The door slammed closed. Night had gathered within him regardless of the time of day. Darkness crowded out all hope that had just started to stir inside him. He knew the shadows would come unless he fought the despair. But, he had a bank account that could not be opened, a talent that had been forgotten, a cherished farm that could to be traded for the price of a bathroom and friends who had turned him in like a bitter foe. He lay down on the bunk and waited for life to completely go out.

Adam closed his eyes and pleaded, *Shaddy, why? What can I do? Spring the lock and set me free.*

Chapter 21

Sprung

Wednesday, December 26, 1945

"Well, well, the pretty boy finally woke up," a scruffy man with yellow teeth mocked from the large holding cell down the hall.

Adam Shoemaker woke up in a jail cell, just yards away from Big Willy, or whatever the guy's name was. Actually, Adam hadn't slept too badly. He had a real bed, even if the room was three walls and bars. He had tossed and turned at first, then finally fell asleep. He was used to sleeping on the hard floor. The jail bunk was much too soft when it was compared to the splintery floorboards of the belfry.

He woke up hungry and exhausted. All around him was silence, with an occasional interruption by the clank of a jail cell door and a verbal jab from Mr. Sunny Teeth. The detective had put Adam in a single cell, away from the rabble that had sought a warm place to sleep off their holiday cheer and chose Club Blue.

"Did the little prince sleep well?" The decayed tooth felon mocked again.

"Leave him alone," scolded a man wearing a pin stripped suit that had seen better days, and a dirty white shirt that hung out of his waistband. "He's just a kid."

"Hey, Kid, did ya drink too much spiked eggnog on Christmas yesterday?"

Yesterday? Adam tried to pull together all that had happened in the last few days. He had learned there was yet another obstacle to Moms' coming home—a bathroom for the farmhouse. The money for that extravagance could come from the sale of a major part of the family farm. The problem was that would include the sale of the farm's water supply.

For a few days he had allowed himself to feel hopeful. Maybe they should sell the bottom land.

There was the bank account, but he couldn't remember the number. Pops could solve it all, but he wasn't there.

For months he had no spending money for anything. Then, the part-time job at the church solved that. But, that was the same church that accused him of stealing a valuable carving. *With every blessing comes a curse,* he moaned as he rolled over on the bunk.

"Shoemaker," a policeman called out Adam's name as the officer entered the hall.

"Yeah," a horrible looking bloke with stringy hair piped in from the drunk-tank.

"Not you," the officer dismissed. "Mr. Adam Shoemaker."

Adam got off the bunk and stretched a little as he tried to understand his surroundings. "Yes, that's me." He walked over and leaned on the cell door. To his surprise, it swung open.

Shaddy? Shocked, he stood there for a moment then stared at the officer.

"You are absolutely right, Mr. Shoemaker. The door hadn't been locked all night. You weren't arrested you know, not at this time. Our problem was that we couldn't determine where you live or who your folks are."

Adam still said nothing.

"There's somebody here to vouch for you," the officer explained.

"Who?" Adam's voice was barely a whisper. *Who would ever vouch for me after all of this? Even Fritzy knows I was hauled off to jail. What does she think of me now?*

"Come on," the officer ordered. A measure of sympathy was heard in his voice.

Adam walked into the outer office. He squinted and shook his head, confused yet curious.

"My boy," Alfred Gunderman called out from the other side of the Desk Sergeant's area. "Are you okay? What on earth happened?"

"Yes, Sir, I'm fine. What are you doing here?" Adam couldn't believe his eyes.

"I saw Fritzy at the Corner Market this morning," Alfred explained. "She told me she was with you when you were put in the back of a squad car yesterday. She said she hadn't seen you around this morning. So, since the police were the last people you were seen with, I came here."

"Thanks, Merry Christmas," the boy mumbled with disdain. "It was merry indeed. I was entertained by a guy who yelled drunken carols until about midnight. I feel blessed," he complained with sarcasm.

"Oh horse feathers. We will just see about that. I'm taking you home."

"Wait a minute, Mr. Gunderman," Detective Overton interjected. "This boy is not old enough to live on his own, and he won't tell us where he's living. We can't just release him to the streets."

"He won't be on the streets, Detective. His ma's been sick, and he has been staying with me," Mr. G. announced with a firm set to his jaw.

"He's staying with you, Alfred?" Overton turned to the boy and studied him slowly. "Then why in blue blazes didn't you tell me that last evening? That information would have saved you a night in the jail."

"It was warm in here," Adam smiled sheepishly.

"You keep the heat pretty cool at your house, do you Gunderman?" The officer joked.

"Somethin' like that," Alfred grinned, took the boy by the arm and started to leave. "He okay to leave?" he shouted back over his shoulder as he neared the door.

"Sure, take him home."

On the street, Adam stopped before getting into Mr. Gunderman's black 1937 Ford pickup. "Mr. G., I do thank you for picking me up from that place, but—I don't live with you. You lied to the police."

"No, now Son, that wasn't a lie," Gunderman reasoned. "I work at the church, and I'm there every day, aren't I?"

"Sure, I guess—"

"Well, you live in the bell tower of the church, my church, so you live with me, right?"

Adam stumbled back. "How did you know?"

"I didn't—not 'til this morning. I have looked everywhere for the Baby Jesus, and I even thought about the bell tower. I put things up there from time to time. So, there I am, up on the ladder, when I see Mrs. Simington's tied and knotted quilt all made up into a comfortable pallet on the floor. You know, she made that quilt from some of Sam's shirt. I had seen him wear the blue striped one many times."

"I didn't steal that quilt, Mr. G. She put the blanket in the rummage box. She gave the quilt away to anyone who could use it."

"Oh, I know that, Adam. I'm not saying you did. I'm just saying how I knowed where you was livin'."

"How did you know Moms was sick?"

"The Shoemakers, or Schumachers, aren't spooks in this town, Adam. I knowed your grandfather for many years, God rest his soul. I asked my misses if she knowed your mother. She said she knew that Bridget Schumacher has been sick for a long time, months even."

"More than four months now, Mr. Gunderman." Adam stopped and pulled at the back of his neck. He was confused and felt overwhelmed. He had been alone for so long. No one seemed to notice that he was living by himself until yesterday. "Why are you doing all this for me?"

"Didn't you listen to Pastor last Sunday, my Boy? This is the Day of Stephen, the day after Christmas. A day to remember. If Christmas was yesterday, what are you going to do about it today? Remember: 'Ye who now will bless the poor shall yourselves find blessings.'"

The hair on Adam's neck bristled. "I am not poor. I have a home. It's just that—"

"I know, I know. But, you'll have to admit, when a boy lives in a tower with the pigeons, it's not his best day."

Adam laughed. Mr. Gunderman was right, almost. "It wasn't pigeons. He was a hummingbird."

Chapter 22

A Turn of Events

Once they left the police station, Adam and Mr. G. started for "home." The sky was a brilliant blue and that made the cold tolerable.

"You had anything to eat?" Gunderman quizzed.

"Not since yesterday noon." Adam ran his fingers over the leather on the front seat. "This is a great truck, Mr. Gunderman."

"Thanks. I've had the little workhorse for a long time." Alfred smiled broadly and went back to his question. "Christmas dinner? Adam, was your last meal yesterday's Christmas dinner?"

"I guess yesterday was Christmas." Adam said no more. He just watched the buildings pass. He appreciated what Mr. G. had done for him, but his mind was numb. He had grown tired of caring, tired of feeling.

They drove down a few roads Adam hadn't been on before. They wandered around through tree lined streets with nice, new brick ranch style homes. Fancy dogs, the kind that come with official papers, romped in some of the yards. Adam thought of Big Jake, the German shepherd with mixed pedigree

179

that woke him every morning on the farm with a slobbery kiss and hot dog breath. He smiled to himself.

"They have been putting up these houses as fast as they can get the foundations dug. Lots of former military men need homes since they got home from the war," Mr. Gunderman scanned both sides of the street as they passed.

"Lots of families that were left behind are trying to put their lives back together too," Adam whispered.

Alfred heard him. "I know, Son. Lots of families have been torn apart. But, now, you will have to admit, these are nice homes for those who are starting again."

"Yes, Sir," Adam smiled. Mr. G. was right. "They—" Adam stopped and slunk down in the seat.

"What's wrong with you?" Alfred questioned.

"I see some kids from school."

"Not your best friends I take it."

"Not hardly," Adam found that statement funny. Buddy and Freddy were definitely not friends of his. He had never seen the pair with anyone, except each other. Not at school or anywhere else.

"Then why'd ya duck?"

"I don't want to tangle with either of them, Mr. G."

"Adam, by now, they're a block behind us. You're safe."

"I'm not worried about my safety. They are bad guys. I don't want to be near them when everyone else finds out what kind of people they are."

Adam turned and watched the pair through the back window. Dark, ugly shadows followed the pair of thieves and stalked up behind them so close it was hard to tell where darkness left off and the boys began. Adam turned and faced forward as they rode through the neighborhood and emerged in a more settled part of town.

"Well, I hope that made more sense to you than it did to me, 'cause it made no sense to me at all," Mr. G. said.

"Good, I mean, yes, it does make sense to me," Adam insisted.

A few miles on the other side of town, Alfred slowed the truck as they passed a few houses with large trees in the yards. "Well, come on in then," Alfred pointed as he pulled into the driveway of a great craftsman style home. The house was not large—medium in size by the standards of Middletown. Small wreaths with electrically let candle-lights in the center hung from every window.

"Where are we?"

"My house, Boy. We're going to find you some breakfast."

Outside, twin sets of columns accented the entrance and the roof was dramatically pitched in keeping with the popular style. The scent of pine was everywhere and came from the three large evergreen trees close to the house.

Alfred led the way onto the front porch and opened the door. Inside the house, the ceilings were high with plaster medallions in the center from which hung artful glass chandeliers. There was a homey elegance.

"The French doors are nice. I bet the side porch is great in the summertime." Adam's eyes darted to the white built-in bookcases that flanked the fireplace. "You read all those books Mr. G.?"

"Me and the Mrs.," Alfred admitted. The house looked comfortable. "I'm not sure I like all of these flowery pillows. Mrs. Gunderman calls them throw pillows. She has them thrown around on every piece of furniture in here," Alfred's chuckle gave away his true feelings.

"You might not like the pillows, but I think you like Mrs. G.," Adam smiled.

"You gotta know that, My Boy."

In the dining room, a lace table cloth covered the maple wood. On through the house, the kitchen was big enough to eat in. To Adam's mind, the house was just the right size.

"You sit right here, Adam," Arletta Gunderman patted the back of one of the kitchen chairs. She got out her favorite cast iron skillet and rubbed a piece of the bacon across the bottom. The fat made the surface shine.

She laid out six pieces of the bacon on a piece of wax paper and turned on the gas. Once they met the hot surface, the strips quickly began to sizzle. "Can you eat three eggs with this bacon, Adam?"

Alfred chuckled as he poured himself a cup of coffee. "He can probably eat half a dozen eggs."

"Oh no, Ma'am, three would be great."

"Then I'll help fill out the chinks in your belly by dropping down a few pieces of toast for ya. I'll butter them, and you can add any jelly you might want." Alfred took a loaf of bread from the bread box and dropped two slices in the toaster.

He started with the toast and piled mounts of Mrs. G.'s grape jelly on each slice. "This is wonderful!" Adam was amazed. He hadn't realized how hungry he was until he started eating. Then she served the eggs and bacon—it was a real break-of-day feast. He ate every bite.

"Thanks Mrs. Gunderman." He smiled and stretched.

"You are most welcome." She smiled and added, "Are you sure you've had enough food. Looks like you could hold a bit more."

"Thank you, Ma'am, no. I'm full." He patted his stomach and smiled. He hadn't been full in a long time.

"Al says you're a good worker, a good boy," she began and nodded at Alfred. "I wonder Adam, if you could use another little job." Arletta Gunderman smoothed her apron and took her handkerchief from the pocket and dabbed at her nose.

"Sure . . . I guess. School doesn't start again until January 7." He looked at Alfred, "What about it Mr. G.? With church responsibilities, do I have the time?"

"When the Mrs. needs help, we find the time. What did you have in mind, my Dear?"

"We had that addition built onto the house when your mother came to live with us." She poured herself and Alfred more coffee. "The apartment hasn't been cleaned in ages. No one has been in there since Mother Gunderman died. I was looking for a place to stretch out all my sewing materials and not have to put the things away. Then I thought—that little apartment would be perfect."

"Sounds good to me," Alfred agreed. "Sure would be nice to be able to sit down without runnin' straight pins in my hands where you've used the arm of the chair as a pin cushion."

"Now, Al, you always said the pins toughened you up," Arletta smiled and winked at Adam.

"We'll be done cleanin' the church by lunch time. You can have lunch here with us, Adam." To Arletta he interjected, "That's okay isn't it?"

"Land sakes, yes. I'm just going to fix homemade vegetable beef soup. Is that all right, Adam?" Mrs. G. pointed to the pot of beef cubes she had been cooking for the soup stock.

The plan was settled. Adam had another chance to earn some money and get a good home cooked meal at the same time. Money was coming his way from every direction. Most of the opportunities just landed in his lap. He felt lighter than he had felt in months, like Grandpa's mule had been sitting on his chest and decided to stand up. But he had to wonder, when would Old Blue sit down again?

Adam went into the living room and picked up his coat from the chair where he had placed it. "I'm going to start back to the church."

"Okay, I'll help Arletta move the living room furniture back into place. We had to make room for everyone at our family Christmas party yesterday. I'll be there in short order," Alfred said.

The winter sun peeked back out from behind gray clouds as Adam neared the church and the sky returned to a brilliant blue. If Adam didn't know better, he might have thought the day could turn out to be great.

"Adam, wait up," Fritzy called after him.

"Hi, Fritzy." Adam felt a little giddy seeing her again. Then he saw her face and the feeling dropped to his toes, like that old mule had sat down.

"Adam . . . I don't know what to say to you. I'm so upset."

"Why? Did I do something wrong?"

"No, you didn't do anything. It's what you did not do, Adam that hurt me."

"I don't know what you mean." Adam didn't know what Fritzy was talking about, but he feared the other shoe was about to drop, the flip side of happiness—the curse.

"Mr. Gunderman said you have been living in the church's bell tower—for months." Tears welled up in her eyes as she whispered the words that had to be said.

"So what? Now I'm not good enough for you?" Adam was hurt and angry. What he had tried to hide for so long was coming out into the open despite his efforts. He wasn't acceptable. Their farm had no bathroom so Moms couldn't come home unless they sold off valuable land and water. And, the most painful, Pops was a deserter. Adam turned his back and started to walk off. His name was still ruined.

Fritzy didn't follow him. She started to walk back home, then she turned. "I did not say that, Adam," she called after him. "I thought we were friends, special friends, and you didn't trust me enough to tell me."

Adam called out without turning around. He didn't want to see her face. "I couldn't tell you. I couldn't tell anyone."

Adam kept on walking. Snow had started to fall again, so he pulled his collar up around his neck. What had been a happy moment just minutes before was another defeat. *With every blessing comes a curse. Shaddy, hide me from everyone.*

Chapter 23

A Ransom Note – A Fallen Friend

Adam kept on walking. *That's okay. I don't need her. I don't need anybody. Let her turn her back and walk away from me.*

Once inside the church, Adam yanked the sweeper across the hall floor. The heavy vacuum cleaner banged into the wall and he winced. *Great, that's all I need. Scuff marks on the walls.*

As he pulled and pushed his way around the church, the smell of the carpet reminded him to be thankful for the work. It felt good to clean. Maybe he could scour some of the dirt of the jail cell off himself. With every elbow bending rub of the polishing cloth, Adam released more anger. He could feel the anger flow from his body when Mr. G. walked in.

"Looks like you're doin' just fine," Mr. Gunderman said after he stomped his feet on the entry mat.

"Thanks, Sir. I've dusted the pews and started to sweep."

"I'm going downstairs and get you another sweeper bag. I think you'll need one." Alfred's speech was slow and labored.

"I'll go down," Adam offered. "Just tell me where they are. You don't look like you're feeling too good Mr. G."

187

""No, I'm fine. Just feeling tired today."

"Please, I'll get the bag," Adam dropped the sweeper and started after the old gentleman.

"I need for you to fold up all those extra tables and chairs. Just stack them neatly in the storeroom. They're too heavy for me today."

"But—"

"Now, never you mind, Adam," Alfred waved him off as he started down the stairs.

Adam waited until he heard Mr. G. get to the bottom. There were fourteen steps and he listened, thirteen—fourteen.

Why didn't I stop him? He shouldn't have walked down those stairs. What will happen when he tries to come back up? I didn't stop Mr. G. any more than I stopped those boys. What's wrong with me?

Adam hurried into the Agnes Coffee Lounge and grabbed the first table. There were four extra tables on that floor. They had been set up for those who couldn't get down the steps after the Christmas Eve service. No one would want to miss out on holiday cookies and punch. Adam had the chairs and tables down in no time and hurried back into the foyer.

"You okay Mr. G?" Adam hollered down the stairs.

"Of course. Did ya think I would explode from too many Christmas sweets?"

"No, Sir. Just thought I could help." Adam started down the stairs.

"Now Adam, quit your fussin'. I need you to put up that large candle stand, with the big green candle on top. Place it to the right of the altar. Pastor says green represents new plant life, and we have a whole new year ahead of us. Says symbolism is his thing, but I like it."

"Sure, Mr. G. Where are the stand and candle?"

"In that tall narrow closet next to the crank for the roll-up door."

Adam hated to leave the stairwell. He was afraid Mr. Gunderman would need him, and he might not hear him if he were in the Lounge. But, Mr. G. was his boss. He would follow through as told. He quickly took the candle and its stand from the closet and placed them exactly where he was told. He stepped back and looked at the arrangement.

"Sure would look better placed a little farther forward than this," Adam mumbled out loud. "But, I do as I am told." He took another glance. "I still think—" He stopped when he heard the door open to the narthex.

"Morning, Adam. Where's Alfred? He'll want to hear this." Pastor Silverman came in excited, waving a scrap of paper.

"Hi, Pastor." Adam tried to be friendly, but he didn't feel pleasant deep down.

"That Smeltzer family makes a mess don't they." Pastor noticed the paper and crumbs Adam was sweeping up.

"I guess they're a big family. If you have a hundred cousins and kinfolks, all unwrapping presents, you're going to leave some paper around," Adam said.

"Well, I'm not complaining. We're always pleased when the church is in use. What better place to celebrate family at Christmas time, than in the church?" Silverman turned as footsteps approached on the hard wood floor. "There you are Alfred."

"Pastor," Gunderman acknowledged. "Here's the sweeper bag, Adam." Alfred's hand was shaky as he handed the bag to Adam.

"Mr. G?" Adam was worried about the man. Gunderman was out of breath and he looked pale.

Pastor Silverman was too excited to notice. "We have good news and bad news about the Christ Child."

"What?" Alfred was excited before he even heard the note. He had caught Pastor's enthusiasm and leaned one hand on Adam's shoulder as if including him in the good news.

189

Adam could feel a different message from the man. He could feel Mr. G's tremor through his own flannel shirt.

Pastor Silverman unfolded the piece of paper. "This note was put between the door and the storm door over at the parsonage. We were in the kitchen. We heard the doorbell ring and the sound of boots." He smoothed the paper with his fingers.

"Dear Pastor Silverman, I know the church likes the statue of Jesus. I'll bring it back if $25.00 is put in an envelope and left at the bottom of the slide in Jefferson Park. No one better be around when I pick up the ransom. If the money's there, and no people, I'll put the statue in a brown paper bag and leave the sack on the front steps of the church."

"A ransom note?" Adam was shocked. "Who would do such a thing?" Yet, he already knew. He just could not believe those boys would try to ransom the carving and plan to sell it too.

"Wait a minute. Did you say twenty-five dollars?" Alfred turned to Adam. "That's the amount you said you needed." His face grew white and drained. Suddenly, Mr. Gunderman grabbed his chest and fell over onto Adam who steadied him before he fell.

"No, Mr. G. No! It wasn't me—I didn't—" Gunderman couldn't hear him. He had collapsed on the floor at Adam's feet.

Shaddy, save him. Touch his heart and make him well, Adam begged. But all he heard was the sound of labored breathing.

Adam bent down and tried to gather the old man in his arms. How could he make him hear?

"Touch him, my Son. I will send him back." Shaddy whispered in his ear.

190

I can't save him, Shaddy, Adam cried inside.

"I didn't say you would heal him, Son. I said, touch him and I will send him back."

Adam knew no one else heard Shaddy's words, but he knew he had to obey. The boy frantically touched Alfred's chest and immediately felt the static shock he had felt when he touched Buddy. What could touch possibly do?

Chapter 24

We Can Depend on You

Alfred Gunderman was on the floor where he had fallen after grabbing his chest. Adam was stunned. He had knelt on the floor, touched him as Shaddy had instructed and held Mr. G.'s head in his lap.

Pastor Silverman ran into his office, grabbed the phone and quickly dialed the hospital. "Yes, good." Pastor was excited and shouted so loudly Adam could hear him from the hall, away from the conversation. "You have an ambulance at Russell Franklin's home? Would you have room? Oh, okay. The church on Cranberry Street." He relocked the door and quickly returned to the two in the hall.

"Sounds like they're close," Adam tried to reassure Mr. G., although the old man had not regained consciousness.

"They're close, yes, Adam," Pastor said. "The hospital dispatcher said our neighbor, Russell Franklin, fell and his wife had called the hospital. When the ambulance got there, just minutes ago, Russell refused to ride in the thing. He said, 'I am not going anywhere lying down. An ambulance is too much like the last ride I'll take—in a hearse. If I decide to go to the hospital, and mind you, I have not decided that, my Louise can take me. She can drive ya know.'"

Adam smiled faintly. *Not the curse again—with every blessing comes a curse.*

"Snow's coming down," Pastor spoke mechanically as he watched out the front door windows for the ambulance to come. Then he walked over and knelt down beside the two, the stricken in body and the stricken in heart.

Adam looked through the window and watched the snow float down in giant clumps. He felt a chill inside.

"Alfred, I am going to assume you can hear me. I know God can." Pastor prayed for Alfred's health, his strength, and his peace. He prayed that God would work his wonders in Alfred's life as he went to the hospital to heal.

Adam's hand rested near Mr. G's chest. The boy could feel the warmth increase beneath his hand. Adam's fingers floated just a hair's width above the gruff-spoken, dear old man.

As the ambulance slid to a stop out front, Silverman tossed Adam a large key ring loaded with keys of various shapes and metals. "Adam, here are my keys," he began to bark orders. "Please, go back to my office and call Mrs. Gunderman. Tell her what happened. Then, call my wife and let her know that I'm going to ride with Alfred in the ambulance. Ask her to please bring the car to the hospital to pick me up. Just lock up when you're done."

The driver and his attendant rushed in with the stretcher, lifted Alfred onto the canvas and carried him out. Pastor ran after the stretcher that carried his friend.

"Okay," Adam answered mechanically. His mind was rattled as the impact of Mr. G.'s collapse hit him hard. He looked down at the keys. Then his eyes followed the rescuers all the way out to the ambulance door.

"I didn't take that carving, Pastor," he called after them as they started to enter the ambulance. Adam was worried for

Mr. Gunderman and afraid for himself. Then he felt guilt for his own self-pity.

"Of course not," Pastor Silverman turned back to Adam and smiled broadly. "You think I would give you the keys to my office if I thought you had stolen the carving?"

Again Adam stared at the ring of keys in his hand. One looked like the key to the pastor's car. One was probably the key to the front door of the parsonage. The brass key he recognized as the one that unlocked the church door. That left the skeleton key. *That has to be the one to the study.*

Adam walked around the corner, unlocked the door, and stepped into a world of books and leather that aroused a strange feeling within him. The room was warm and elegant at the same time. He felt strangely at home. *Will I ever belong in an office like this?*

He took the receiver from the phone's cradle and hesitated. Then he put it to his ear and listened.

"Well, I don't know Maud," he heard through the receiver. "You were there when I reminded Harold that I wanted a blue housecoat for Christmas. He deliberately bought me a new coffee pot so he could enjoy *my* gift too." Party-line patron number one complained to someone named Maud about her husband's choice of Christmas present.

"Oh Shirley, you don't think he—"

"Ladies," Adam butted in, "I hate to interrupt you but—"

"Well then don't, young man," Shirley ordered. "Hang up and go away. Say . . . who are you? You aren't on our party-line."

What should he do? He couldn't convince anyone of anything. *Shaddy, give me the gift of persuasion. Let me be a convincer.*

"Please . . . Shirley . . . Ma'am, I have to use the phone for an emergency," Adam stammered.

"Mrs. Bartoni to you." Then her tone lightened with party-line interest. "An emergency?"

"Yes, Mrs. Bartoni. I'm sorry. I have to place a phone call."

"Well of course, if you have to make an emergency call, it would be a phone call."

"Mrs. Bartoni, you sound like a very nice lady." Adam lied again. She had actually been very snippy with him. Adam began to think he would die from choking on a lie someday. "I have to call Mrs. Gunderman to tell her that her husband has just been taken to the hospital."

"Alfred?" The Shirley-line-mate questioned.

"Yes, Ma'am."

"Get off the phone Maud so this boy can make an important call. I'll talk to you later."

"Thank you, ladies." When he heard the two lines click and the dial tone hummed in his ear, he made the hardest call of his life.

"Mrs. Gunderman, this is Adam."

"Well hello, dear."

"Mrs. Gunderman, Mr. G. collapsed here at the church a few minutes ago and was taken to the hospital."

"What? The hospital? Is he alright?"

"I don't know how he is, Ma'am. They just took him away. The sign on the side of the ambulance said Middletown Community Hospital. Pastor Silverman was here and rode along with him in the back."

"Oh thank the Lord. And, thank you, Adam. I will go right over. You'll say a prayer for Al, won't you?"

"Of course," was his answer but inside his thoughts were different. As he dialed the Silverman home, he thought, *Prayer? I don't know how to pray. God, just help Mr. G. please. Amen.*

"Young man, you said you were just calling Arletta Gunderman," Shirley Bartoni scolded as Adam dialed again.

"Mrs. Bartoni? Where you listening in?"

"Indeed I was not? I just picked up the phone and heard you dial again."

"How did you know that wasn't my first call?"

"Never mind that," she protested.

"Hello?" Mrs. Silverman answered.

"This is Adam Shoemaker . . . and Mrs. Bartoni is just hanging up," Adam announced more boldly.

"Well, I never!" Shirley Bartoni announced with disgust and embarrassment.

I doubt that you "never." Adam was wise enough to not say it out loud. "Pastor Silverman asked me to call you. Mr. Gunderman collapsed and was taken to the hospital by ambulance. Pastor went along to stay with him until his wife gets there. Pastor would like for you to pick him up there at the Middletown Hospital."

"Yes, Adam, of course. Thank you so much. What would we do without you?"

What would you do without me? I haven't heard that kind of talk in a long time. Now, I've heard it again. "I still have Pastor's keys. Do you want me to bring them over before you leave?"

"No, that's all right. He can get them tomorrow. I know they are safe with you," Mrs. Silverman answered, then hung up.

I know I can trust you; Adam repeated as he tried to bury the thought in his heart where the shadows couldn't take it away. *What would we do without you, Adam? I can trust you.*

Chapter 25

Work Soothes the Mind

Alfred Gunderman had collapsed at the church and Adam was in charge. He could not believe all that had happened but it was gradually sinking in. "What would we do without you, Adam? We trust you," echoed in his head.

Better lock up the pastor's study, Adam thought as he slowly walked around in the room of books and paintings and art before he left. He breathed in all the sweet smells of a man who knows who he is and why he is. *Was Pops ever like this?* Adam's question hung in the air with no answer.

Adam ran his fingers across the back of the deep maroon leather chair that sat at the desk, and drank in the perfume of the hide. He carefully picked up a brass figurine of a small child with his curly head laid in the lap of Christ. The piece was amazing and aroused the artist within him. He longed for his home, his family, and he grieved for the loss of who he could have become.

I trust you, Adam, he heard Pastor Silverman say again. *What would we ever do without you?*

Adam looked around the room once more. "I do belong in an office like this." Regardless of all that had happened, there was one thing he always believed in. It was something

199

Pops had said. "Tomorrow is always better if you live fully in today."

Pops also said, "Hard work never hurt anyone, Son. Laziness destroys the body, the mind, the spirit, and the future."

Pops? Why do I remember words of wisdom from him? I haven't cared what Pops had to say for a long time. Why am I thinking about him now all of a sudden? He left us and won't ever come back.

"I have loosed your memory, My Son," Shaddy spoke in his ear. "Remember more."

Moms' words as Adam left the sanitarium on Christmas rattled around in his head. "Be fair, Adam. Your daddy did not leave us. He was drafted. Your father was . . . no . . . he is a quiet man. But, just because he doesn't talk very much, that does not define his character. He loved us both . . . loves us both. He would never desert his country or his family."

"Truth is the only present I have for you today," she had said as she kissed him goodbye. "But, if you will accept the gift, truth will be the most valuable present you will ever receive. Make your peace with the memory of your father, Adam. Only you will suffer if you don't."

A gift is it? The "truth" she called it. Tears filled his eyes and that made him angry too. He didn't want to cry over anything. *But, what if Moms was right?*

Adam locked the office door and ran his fingers over the panels in the dark, heavy wooden door. *Now I have to get busy. If I don't, this day will drag on and turn into all the others, full of nothing. Fritzy doesn't believe me anymore. Mr. G. is probably in the hospital because he thinks I'm a thief. But— maybe things can be different. I know some people believe in me.*

He grabbed the sweeper off the floor where he had dropped it, and put in the new filter Alfred had nearly died over. *Why didn't I stop him?* He cleaned the carpets vigorously, then the mop boards, the window sills, and the furniture. He put a clean cloth over the end of a dust mop and carefully ran the extended dust rag over the surface of all the stained glass windows. With the furniture polish he found in the utility closet, he rubbed the pulpit, lectern, and pews until they shone.

As he worked, he could feel anger and tension flow from his muscles, mind and heart—out through his hands and arms as he polished and cleaned. He laughed out loud. *Pops was right!* As impossible as that would have been to admit a few days ago, he was living proof Pops' wisdom was true. *Hard work cleanses the mind, the soul, and the body.*

Then why do I still feel so confused all the time? Why am I always on the washboard road of life? Why are things so rough? Why does every face of joy have to wear a dark mask? Will life always be this way?

Chapter 26

A Turn for the Better

Thursday, December 27, 1945

The next day after Mr. G. collapsed, Adam awakened again in the belfry on Cranberry Street. *I cannot drag myself out of bed. I don't want to face anything.* Adam rolled over and stared at the empty room. The hummingbird was still gone, and he was still alone. *I have to see Mr. G., not because I must, because I want to want to.*

Adam was surprised. He was not stiff or sore as he thought he would be after the previous day's hard work. He smiled to himself when he thought about all he had accomplished. *Amazing how a good day's work makes me feel so great.*

The wind had blown hard and cold during the night. Icy air howled through the old rafters and made the room seem even colder than the temperature would have revealed. He heard limbs crack from tall tree trunks and wondered when one would come through the roof.

Adam certainly didn't look forward to the hike across town in the steady snow fall, especially with such a heavy heart. How could he look Mr. Gunderman in the eye when Mr.

G. thought he was a thief? He had never even seen the carving of the Christ Child and he would never have taken the carving that was so precious to everyone. The strange fact that both he and the thieves needed twenty-five dollars was just a coincidence.

"I don't know why those guys need the money," Adam mumbled to the cold room. "My cause is noble, well sort of. I needed twenty-five dollars to buy some coal for the farm and to take Fritzy to the party, but now she thinks I'm a liar." He stumbled around as he looked for his left clodhopper. "I did not lie. I just didn't tell her about my life. Why would I? She wouldn't have wanted to be around me if she knew." The more he thought about the whole situation, the madder he got.

"Wait 'til she finds out Pops might be a deserter." His feelings about his father were a carnival ride. Why was Pops okay one day and totally unacceptable the next?

He shoved his foot into the shoe that was half buried under his bedding. As he bent over to tie the laces, he spied the little saucer in the corner of the tower and thought of the hummer.

"Just another deserter." He felt his heart harden with the cement of bitterness. "At least a stone-cold heart will be harder to break."

I can't put it off any more. If I'm going to visit Mr. G., I had better get started. He put on his coat, hat and gloves and started out on foot. His first stop was at Pastor Silverman's home.

"Good morning, Adam," Mrs. Silverman greeted when she opened the door.

"I need to return Pastor's keys, Ma'am."

"Hi, Adam," Pastor Silverman chimed in.

"Yes, Sir, good morning. I'm returning your keys." Adam handed over the ring with the fob in the shape of a cross.

"Thank you, Adam," Pastor said with enthusiasm. "We are so lucky to have someone like you covering for all of us when things happen. We can depend on you."

"Thank you, Sir." *There's that flattery again. Does he mean what he says or is he just being happy, happy, happy like a lot of other church people?*

"Can we get you some coffee or hot chocolate, Adam?" Mrs. Silverman offered.

"No thank you. I have to be on my way." He didn't tell them where he was going. *They'd probably want to drive me over. I can't be beholding to everyone in town.* He had never minded walking anyway. He was used to being on foot.

He walked through familiar streets he had trudged along every day. This time, the snow made it both fun and tiring. He would have to hurry before the freezing wind would play a rick on his mind and make him want to stay in the cold.

An hour later, covered with icy snow, both on the inside and the out, Adam arrived at Middletown Community Hospital. "I would like to see Alfred Gunderman," he whispered.

"Are you all right?" The receptionist at the Information Desk asked when she saw the tall young boy with bright red cheeks. "You don't have enough spek on your bones to keep you warm."

"Yes, Ma'am." Adam blew on his hands through his gloves but his lungs were so full of cold air, little warmth came forth. "I would like to see Alfred Gunderman, please," he repeated. "What room is he in?"

"Are you family?"

"Sort of like family." *Shaddy what do I say*? Then he remembered what Alfred had told Overton. "I live with him."

While the receptionist looked up the room number, Adam turned his back to the desk. He took off his gloves and blew again on his frozen fingers, this time with the warm breath heated by the presence of Shaddy.

"That's fine, Young Man." The reception said as she looked down at her notebook. "Let's see—he is in room 204, at least for a while. He'll go home this afternoon."

"Great!" Adam started down the hall toward the elevator. He got on and road up to the second floor.

"Two-hundred . . ." he started to mark off the room numbers from the end of the hall. "Two-hundred two, two-hundred four," he ticked them off and stopped. Adam took a deep breath, squared his shoulders, and walked in.

"Adam," Mrs. Gunderman hurried over and gave the boy a big grandma-hug. "Tell me you didn't walk."

"I can't, 'cause I did."

"Well, I will run you back to town when you're ready to go. I have to pick up some pills at the pharmacy for Al. Then, I'll come back here this afternoon and take him home."

"How are you doing?" Adam approached the bedside cautiously. Mr. Gunderman looked weak to him, and Adam was worried.

"Adam, what a surprise. You didn't have to walk all the way over here. I'm fine. Some little pills the doc ordered are going to fix me up real good. They started them already." Mr. Gunderman reached out his hand and took Adam's in his.

"I thought your heart attack was my fault—"

"Your fault? No, no, no. My ticker just complains a little sometimes. Doc said I was really lucky this time. He said something caused it to start up again after it stopped. Like it had been jolted by God himself. That's why I need you at the church to help me, to take a little of the load off."

Adam heard what Alfred had said and he knew what had happened. Shaddy had told Adam to touch the old man and he would bring him back. But, that wasn't what he worried about right then. "Mr. Gunderman, I did not take that Christ Child carving." Adam was emphatic.

206

"My goodness, Boy, I know that." He was not ready to let go of Adam's hand. "I didn't get to finish what I was sayin' yesterday. I have worried about that for the past few hours."

"Don't worry because of me, Mr. G."

"And why not?"

"I have lived a lie—for months now. I didn't expect you to believe the truth."

"We shook hands on the truth, Adam." He smiled with a caring smile. "Now you let me finish. I just meant that it was interesting that both you and the thief said you need the same amount of money, twenty-five dollars. I figured he might be a young person, like you." He looked at Adam thoughtfully. "Now, what is all this talk about lies?"

"I just make up things that make me look better than I am. I like nice stories, make believe, rather than the real stuff that's so hard. Like hummingbirds flying south on the wings of Northern geese. Nice tale, but not true, just made up to make things sound miraculous." Adam hung his head, his voice was a whisper.

"But the hummingbird story is a miracle, Adam. No, they don't piggyback on larger birds. But, those tiny hummers, who have to eat nectar all of the time, manage to fly all the way across our southern states to Mexico or Central America with only God as their strength. Some fly through the eastern two thirds of Texas and others through Florida and Cuba. Some little birds fly right across the Gulf of Mexico. If you don't think that's a miracle, you don't recognize the miracles that are all around you."

Adam smiled and thought about what Mr. Gunderman was saying, but said nothing.

"You shouldn't live a lie, Son. If a tiny bird can fly hundreds of miles, Adam, you can endure what you are dealt. I know you have the strength."

"I'm afraid, Mr. G. If people knew me, they wouldn't like me. I don't like me." He was silent a minute while fear boiled inside him.

The corners of the hospital room grew dark. Maybe a cloud passed in front of the sun, but Adam didn't think so. He felt the presence of the shadows, but he didn't see them or smell their repulsive odor. He chose to disavow them. In his mind, they were not there.

"Does anyone still think I stole the statue," Adam asked cautiously. He wanted to know, but he didn't want to hear the answer. "Like the Bremans—or maybe Fritzy?" Adam could not stand the thought that his name may have been ruined.

"I don't know, Son. I've been in here."

"I do," Adam admitted. "She was mad."

"I'm glad you're still here, Adam," Mrs. Gunderman said as she breezed back into the room. "Could I get you to do me a favor?"

"Now a boy can always use a good cheese sandwich and a bowl of tomato soup," Gunderman suggested.

"All right then, for a sandwich and a bowl of soup, would you please help me take down the Christmas tree at our house and move the living room furniture around so Alfred can see out the window this afternoon when he gets home?"

"Sure."

"Arletta, I can move that furniture." Alfred insisted as he rose up on his elbow.

"No!" Arletta and Adam responded in unison.

• • •

At the Gunderman home, Adam came around the side of the car and helped her. "Watch yourself. It's really icy here in the driveway. Before I leave, I'll put some salt out here if you have some."

"Thank you. Alfred keeps salt in the garage, in the bucket just inside the side door." They slipped a little as they tiptoed across the drive. Even the grass was covered with ice.

"We would have done better with ice skates," Adam smiled.

"Not me. I can't skate," Arletta laughed as she stepped onto the porch and unlocked the door. "Now you come right in here, Adam. We'll get lunch around first." Mrs. Gunderman threw her coat over the back of Alfred's chair and led the way to the kitchen where handmade Christmas curtains and Santa-face tea towels greeted them. "I haven't had anything to eat since yesterday noon either. I stayed at the hospital with Al last evening."

"You must be hungry too, Mrs. G."

"I hadn't thought about food. I had made the broth for soup yesterday then got your call. I covered the beef stock and put it on the open back porch. It made a good refrigerator. I am hungry, but—oh my! Adam, look at this!" Arletta stood at the kitchen sink and looked out over the back yard.

"I heard the wind blowing last night as I sat with Alfred in the hospital, but I never thought—"

Outside the Gundermans' kitchen window the view was a jumble of twisted, broken branches. The entire half of Gunderman's large maple tree that faced the house lay on the ground and the small top branches draped over the back porch rail.

"A few more inches and that tree would be sitting at the kitchen table, Mrs. G."

"Well, now," Arletta rolled up her sleeves and got out a soup pan, "I believe I have several jobs for you, if you want them."

"Okay," he didn't know yet what she had in mind, but he didn't want to go back to the cold, windy bell tower—not yet.

"I'll show you where to put Al's chair, and you can move the other furniture too while I fix lunch. As to the Christmas tree, if you'll please put all the bulbs and decorations on the couch and haul the tree out to the curb, the trash man will take it away tomorrow. Then, if you want to make some money after we eat, you can get the ax out of the shed," she paused and looked at Adam carefully. "Have you ever used an ax?"

"Sure."

"Now don't story to me, Adam. Don't stretch the truth. Holding an ax is not the same as using one. Do you know how to swing an ax and not chop your foot off? I can't send you home to your ma with half a foot."

"Yes, Ma'am, I mean, no Ma'am." He stammered a little but he was telling the truth. He had helped his grandfather chop wood many times, even as a ten-year-old. "You want me to clear that tree away from the house for you?"

"Well, yes, I do. I want you to chop the whole thing up for firewood. In fact, you can add the Christmas tree trunk to your stack of wood if you want to. If you can get all that done, I'll give you the four dollars I have in my purse and you can keep all the wood you chop. How is that for a creative barter?"

"That would be great!"

Of course! He nearly shouted out loud. He hadn't thought about heating the farmhouse with wood in the fireplaces. "I think that is how the farmhouse had been heated when the home was first built. That would be great."

"Families have done that for centuries," she agreed.

After lunch, the weather was still bitter cold, but Adam jumped right into the job, thankful for the hard work, for being able to help Mr. G., for the money and especially for the wood. Besides, the hard work kept him warm in spite of the unrelenting winter. With every swing of the ax, he thought of Moms.

When Moms gets home, we'll have a family again. His mind raced through the empty rooms of the farmhouse and turned on every light. But, with the new illumination came the bold truth that Pops wasn't part of the picture, not now, maybe not ever.

Shaddy, give me super strength. Adam swung the ax high. He used the full stretch of his arms and brought the blade down swift and hard onto the downed trunk. The work went fast, strike upon strike, blow upon blow. He envisioned the rapid, jerky movements of an old time movie, with Charlie Chaplin toddling down the road in record time.

He worked for hours and when Adam finished all the chopping, he used a maul and wedges to wrestle the largest logs into firewood size pieces. Mrs. G. had told him to pile up the split wood by the shed until he was able to have the logs transported out to the farm. He stood back and looked at the stack of firewood with pride.

Mrs. G. opened the storm door. "It looks great, Adam."

"It's a fourth of a cord. I'm sure of it," he puffed with pride. "I know that a cord of wood measures four feet wide by four feet high and eight feet long when the logs are lined up in tightly stacked rows of the same size pieces." He stood back and eyed the work he had just done. "Leaning against the shed, I know that stack is a fourth of a cord."

"Wonderful!" she called out as she started to close the door against the winter day. You've done a fine job."

As Adam stood admiring his hard, muscle-building work, he realized a truth. With all of the talk about honesty, he still preferred the lie. He knew that wood needs a whole year to cure before it can be burned in the fireplace, but he could not face that fact, that truth. All he could see in his homey, imagined scene was Moms and him sitting in front of a nice warm fire at home.

"Adam, come in here please," Mrs. G. called from the house.

He put away all of the tools he had used and went back into the warmth of the kitchen.

"I have been thinking," Arletta began and patted the kitchen chair beside her. "Would you like a cup of cocoa? I'll make you some."

"Yes, Ma'am, that would be great. It sure is cold out there." He rubbed his hands together to generate some heat and blew on them with Shaddy's help.

Mrs. G. passed him the cup, and he wrapped his hands around the mug for the warmth. He even thought of putting his fingers in the hot drink. Then he thought of a better idea and blew across the surface of the warm chocolate so the steam could rise and warm his face.

"I'll pour you another cup when you finish that one. And, I put two cheese sandwiches and a nice roast beef in your jacket pocket for later."

"You didn't have to do that, Ma'am," he protested politely but was grateful she had thought of him.

"Of course I did, Adam. A man has to have food to work as hard as you did today." She got her own mug and sat down across the table from him. "I have been thinking," Mrs. G. began again. "We still haven't gotten to the guest area yet, but that's okay for today. The tree interrupted us."

"Yes, Ma'am."

"That little guest space has a bedroom, a small sitting room and a bathroom. The apartment is very comfortable. There's even a little kitchenette. I wonder—now please, don't take this the wrong way. I know you have a home and family but—I understand from Alfred that your mother has been in the TB Sanitarium and is ready to be released as soon as your home is ready for her. Is that right?"

"Yes," Adam spoke slowly and wondered what she was getting at. Did everybody in town know his business, that he was homeless, that Moms was sick, and that Pops a gone?

"I wonder if you and your mother would be willing to move into the guest house for a few months while your house is readied for your mother's return. When school starts again, after this Christmas break, I'll have to go back to work. I'm a cook in the elementary school cafeteria. I know Alfred will not stop working at the church, but Pastor will be around every day to remind him to slow down. And, you will be there after school to help lighten his workload. I sure would feel more at peace if your mother was around here at my home, so she could check on him on Al's days off. Not do anything, mind ya. I know she's been sick. I wouldn't expect her to do a lick of work, but if she sees him flat on the ground in the back yard, I would feel better if someone was here to call for help."

"Well—" Adam didn't know what to say.

"Al said the place where you are now living is too small for both you and your mother."

"Small, yes, too small—among other things." He tried to make sense of all that had happened. Thoughts and doubts ricocheted around in his head. *Why would anyone do anything that big for me? She doesn't know I've been homeless?*

"How much would the rent be?" Adam asked. *Nothing's ever free. What else will happen? With every blessing comes a curse.*

"Oh, there would be no rent, Adam. You would be doing me a favor. I couldn't pay you and your mother very much, maybe $5.00 a week?"

"Pay us?"

"Yes, dear, of course—for keeping your eye out after Alfred and you could keep the sidewalk shoveled. School will be over in May, and then I'll be home all day through the summer. I can keep my eye on that scamp myself then. What do you think?"

"I haven't seen the space, but if you think the apartment will work, then I guess the place will be okay." Adam's head was in a spin. Having a place for Moms to come home to, was a good thing, he knew that. But, he still didn't want to accept help from others.

"Don't be takin' handouts from anyone," Gramps had always warned.

Adam felt poorer than poor. He had no money, no warm home, no running water, no electricity, and no father to make things right. Was he now the man in the family?

Chapter 27

Escape From the Stalker

Adam declined Mrs. G.'s offer to drive him back to the church. Mr. Gunderman might already know that he lives in the bell tower and not try to rescue him, but he knew Mrs. G. didn't know. If she knew, she might say, "A boy should not live alone."

Ordinarily, a long walk would have cleared away fuzzy thinking and self-pity. But, not today. Adam was too tired. He had walked all the way across town to visit Mr. G. in the hospital. Then, he moved furniture and chopped up a tree for Mrs. G. When he started back to the church, the walk brought on a weariness he had never experienced before. He was tired to the bone.

He hurried past the Norman Avenue corner. That was where he would turn if he were going to Fritzy's house. He didn't want to see her.

A few doors down, a group of children were gathered on Tony Hammond's concrete driveway. They turned two long ropes in double-dutch. With a rope in each hand, the ropes whipped around so children could jump in double time.

Cousins, Adam guessed, and secretly envied the size of their family. *Cousins are always around, if you have some. In*

215

the O'Hara family, there were more cousins in the clan than I could count. But, that was then. Nothing is the same now.

Two girls passed him on the sidewalk, giggled and moved on. *They are laughing at me*, he thought and anger rose up again. *They know I'm a Schumacher and that I spent the night in a jail cell.* He hung his head in shame.

As he hurried along, the sleet and snow began again. *Great, it's not enough that I'm cold. I have to be freezing cold.*

He started to cross the street when that same blue car from the farm road, pulled up beside him. He was afraid. Was the man following him? If he was—why?

The man rolled down his window and leaned out. "Shoemaker—right?"

Adam kept on walking. He felt very uncomfortable around Mr. Blue Car. He didn't know why, but that was the problem. He didn't know the man.

"Some families changed the spelling and pronunciation of their name when they came to this country," the man smiled.

"I suppose." Adam kept on walking and said no more.

"Sometimes, the Immigration Officers at Ellis Island took in more information than they could handle. They gathered passenger arrival records, border crossings, emigration records, and passports, but they sometimes got the emigrant's name spelled wrong—like Shoemaker for Schumacher."

"So."

"You said you don't know any Schumachers in town, Son?"

I'm not your son. I'm nobody's son. Adam decided he'd better not pick a fight with the stranger.

Suddenly, Adam could hear the man's thoughts race through his own head. *How is that possible? How can I hear him thinking?*

"Gotta get this kid to believe me. His whole life depends on it." Adam heard the words as the man thought them.

To Adam, the man's thoughts were terrifying. But, his spoken words were calm and reassuring.

"Look," the man said, "I'm just trying to find the Schumacher family and since your name is an Americanization of that old-country name, I have to believe you may know them."

Again, the man's unspoken message was heard. "How do I make him believe me? What I have to tell him could change his life."

Adam looked neither right nor left. He kept his head down and continued to walk. A biting sleet had started and it stung his face.

"At least let me take you home," the man offered as he slowly followed the boy.

"No, thank you." Adam's teeth chattered as he tried to sound strong and brave. The icy rain came down so fast the roads and sidewalks got worse with each step he walked.

"Ah, come on. I know you're cold. Just look at you. You're shaking." The man in the blue car continued to coast along beside the boy. He shifted gears every once in a while.

Maybe his car will stall out, Adam hoped.

"Watch out," the man warned as Adam nearly stepped onto a frozen puddle. Again, the man's inner thoughts escaped. "Gotta make this kid believe me or the whole thing won't work."

I can take care of myself. Adam's heart felt like it would pound out of his chest until it broke free.

"See, I told you," the man mocked as Adam slipped on the glassy ice. "You need to let me drive you home. Come on. The heater is warm and I'm a friendly guy." He smiled broadly at Adam as he continued to coast beside him.

Why am I getting such scary feelings from this man? The boy was afraid the car's bumper would brush his legs if he slowed in his steps. He felt stalked. Fear rose higher within him, and he started to run.

Adam slipped with every step. He stumbled and slid his way along the streets toward the church. The blue car kept up with him as he passed every driveway and yard.

"Let us push him off road," the shadows groaned from the dark side of a tree. "We will obey your feelings."

Adam refused to acknowledge the evil ones, even though he desperately needed help. When he got to Jefferson Park near the church, he turned abruptly and sprinted past the swings into a small woods.

Let that guy try to follow me through the park. Then he feared, *Maybe he'll get out of his car and chase me on foot.*

Adam trembled as he stood behind the trunk of a large tree. He had to catch his breath in the thin air that filled his lungs with ice until his chest ached. He waited, but had to stand guard too. He had to know if the man was behind him.

Adam could see his breath hang in the air like a cloud of steam around him. He wished he could stop breathing. If the guy was behind him, he might be able to see the icy mist. *What should I do? Is he there? Will he drive around and be there when I come out on the other side of the park?*

Cautiously, he peered around the hickory tree and searched the space behind him. The darkness was coming on faster than he thought it would. He was grateful for the cover of gray that came before the night. In the dim light, he could see no one. All was quiet. All was still.

He tried to catch his breath by filling his lungs with slow, deliberate gulps of air. His lungs couldn't expand any further and yet he could barely breathe. He was exhausted and thought he was going to be sick. He waited in the darkness and rubbed his hands over his chest. He hoped to feel warmth return to his body. Adam cupped his hands and blew the warmth of Shaddy into them, then placed them palms down on his chest. Once his head was clear enough and his lungs began to fill again, he made a plan.

Shaddy, place the cloak of invisibility over me. He began to feel safe and strong.

He decided to leave the woods on a path at a different angle to his entrance. If the man tried to continue to look for him, he might believe that Adam would have run straight through the park and come out on the opposite side, not at a right angle to his entrance.

Adam checked one more time before he left the safety of the tree. He could see no one. His heart pounded hard and fast when he reached the church. With the key Mr. G. had given him, he unlocked the door then leaned against it in the dark entry. The only sound was that of his rapidly beating heart. Beyond the door, he heard nothing on the street.

Adam's face was so cold, his little smile felt frozen in place. As he stood just inside the church door, he was glad he was finally home. He didn't, however, thank God.

I got myself home, he boasted to himself. *Home,* he laughed sarcastically. *Pastor talks about the church being our home. Little does he know. This may be God's house on Sunday but it is mine tonight and I don't want to share.*

Chapter 28

Wrestling Rats

Friday, December 28, 1945

Adam spent the next morning at the church. Yesterday had been a full day. He had worked hard for Mrs. Gunderman and then cleverly escaped from the man in the blue car. That morning, he ate one of the sandwiches Mrs. G. had put in his pocket for supper last evening, one was for breakfast and the third one would be his lunch. Goodness knows the belfry was cold enough to serve as his refrigerator.

That morning, he buffed the floor in the entry and wide hallway until the hardwood shone. He swept the carpet in the sanctuary and picked up each knit-picky that he saw. He had to stay busy.

"Adam, I'm glad you're still here," Pastor Silverman said when he found the boy in the corner near the grand piano. "Are you about finished here?"

"I've been done for a while but I had to stay busy."

"You're going to wear out the carpet, sweeping it again and again." Pastor smiled.

"Sorry, Sir."

"I was teasing, Adam. Relax. I came over to ask if you could help Mr. and Mrs. Stafford this afternoon."

"Fritzy's grandparents?" He liked the idea of helping Fritzy through the Staffords. "Sure. What do they need?"

"They seem to have a rat problem. If you're not afraid of varmints," Pastor Silverman smiled, "they'll pay you for the job," he added quickly.

"Well, I hate rats, but I really do like that green stuff." He looked out the window for any sign of the stranger. "Sure, I'll do it." He would do almost anything to help Moms get home.

Adam put away the sweeper, got his jacket and cap from a hook in the hall and started to walk over to the Stafford home. He stayed off the sidewalks by walking through snow-covered yards in order to avoid the open spaces. Blue-car man could appear at any time. Adam searched the roads as he walked along. The man was nowhere.

Adam walked out of the alley behind the Stafford home, went around and rang the front doorbell. He shuffled from one cold foot to the other and turned his back to the house as he waited. He didn't want to feel vulnerable with his back to the street. He wanted to know if anyone passed by. Suddenly the door was jerked open.

"Oh, Adam, I am so glad you could come," Mrs. Stafford nearly pulled him into the house. "It's in this way. Follow me."

Adam followed Mrs. Stafford through the living room and hadn't even gotten to the dining room yet, when he smelled the odor. He didn't want to say anything that might embarrass her so he said nothing.

Mrs. Stafford stopped at the head of the table and spun around. "You mean to tell me, Adam Shoemaker, you can't smell that awful stench?" she laughed.

"Sure I can. I just didn't know that you could," Adam admitted.

"That is why you are here, my boy." She laughed again as she started into the kitchen.

"Tell me more," Adam said as he followed her slowly.

"We have a partial basement under the kitchen and dining room and a crawlspace under the living room." Rats have gotten into the crawlspace and seem to have—died there." Mrs. Stafford closed her eyes and held her breath.

"Wow," Adam whispered at the thought of how much he hated rats.

"My husband had to go to Lancaster today. He said he'd be home by supper and to pay you twenty-dollars if you'd take the job. It's nasty."

"Twenty-dollars?" Adam couldn't believe his good fortune. That would be two full days salary for a grown man. "I'll do it. It's all legal, right? There's no dead body down there except rats, is there?"

"None that I know of." Alma Stafford went to the kitchen sink and took a pair of rubber gloves from the cabinet beneath it. "I've had these since before the war. Here, use them. You won't have to touch anything. But, be careful with them. I can't buy rubber gloves yet, even though the war is over."

"Thanks. I'll be careful. I'm not real anxious to play with the ugly critters."

Adam cautiously crept down the basement steps. He looked for rats but hoped he wouldn't find any. He studied the area and spied cellar steps on the opposite wall that led up and out into the backyard. He approached that exit, walked up the cement steps and checked the deadbolt on the door. The latch was unlocked. He turned, and then had a better thought. For precaution, he opened the slanted wooden, double cellar doors wide.

Odd. It looks like the lock to this cellar door has been broken. I'll have to tell the Staffords before someone just walks in. He thought of the stranger in town.

Back down the steps, he faced the crawlspace opening again.

"Are you alright down there, Adam?" Mrs. S. hollered down the stairs.

"Yes, Ma'am. I'm just setting the stage for a quick and easy exit."

"Good thinking," she said.

There was something on the floor near the wall. The little blob was about the size of a baby kitten but Adam didn't want to cuddle it. He tiptoed over and leaned down to get a better look.

The thing twitched!

"Yuck!" He shuddered.

It twitched again.

Adam put on the rubber gloves and held his breath. The odor was horrible. He grabbed the rat by the tail, ran up the cement cellar steps and flung the beastly stench into the back yard.

"Hope that's it," he gaged as he went back down the out-door basement steps.

He approached the opening and something shinny was easily seen inside the narrow space. "Eyes?" he shuddered again.

He eased his hand hesitantly into the space. He felt something hard and jerked it back.

"I will do this," he insisted. "Shaddy, I can't stand any part of this job. But, I don't have to like what I'm doing; I just have to do it." A sense of determination filled him.

He reached again for the shiny object. In his mind, he saw eyes, hundreds of beady eyes. "Don't be silly, Shoemaker," he mocked himself out loud. "If a rat's dead, their eyes wouldn't shine." He cautiously reached out to the left. The mysterious piece was thin, cold and hard.

"A pocket knife?"

He withdrew the cold metal and studied the surface closely. "B. P." he said as he touched the initials. "Buddy Phillips," he nodded. "They are up to mischief again." He jammed the knife into his jeans pocket.

He heard, *eek scratch,* from deeper inside the crawl space and Adam knew what he had to do. He hoisted himself into the four foot tall crawlspace, head first and slithered on his stomach. The opening was tall enough for him to get on his knees, but he couldn't stand up. The putrid odor was stronger the farther he crawled. The space was dark but there was enough light to see two more rats a few inches from his left hand. He grabbed the ugly things by anything that stuck out, backed out of the space, and dashed up the cellar steps, violently retching as he went.

Hold it! Hold it! He commanded himself. At the top of the steps and into the backyard, he flung the rats and his lunch at the same time. He doubled over and threw up again.

"Shaddy," Adam pleaded, "you have given me super smell. Please, I beg of you, turn it off for a while." Adam felt a tingling numbness in his nose, then nothing. "Thanks."

Adam dragged himself back into the basement and stared at the opening again. He grabbed a flashlight from a table in the corner and maneuvered inside again. He flashed the beam right and left. Nothing but dirt.

He aimed the beam into the deeper recesses of the space. He saw no other rats—except. In the middle of the area was a heavy, thick cross beam that ran the full length of the house. Just beyond the beam he could see another filthy carcass. The stench was horrible, but, there was no way to reach the ugly critter.

He backed out for the last time, dashed up the steps, and commenced to throw up again. It felt like he had emptied everything down to his toenails.

"Adam?" Willard Stafford called down from the top of the basement steps.

"Coming." Adam raced back down the cellar steps from the yard and up the inside basement staircase. "Yes, Sir," he panted.

"You okay, Son?" The older man patted Adam on the shoulder as soon as he came up.

"Here, Adam," Mrs. Stafford offered. "Have a glass of ginger ale. You'll feel a whole lot better. I could hear your sacrifice."

"I'm so sorry," Mr. Stafford appeared to be embarrassed. "I had no idea there would be that many. Thank you so much."

"I'm afraid there's more," Adam said. "There is one trapped in the middle of the room above the crawlspace, and I can't get to it because of the cross beams."

"The middle of that room is the living room." Mrs. Stafford threw her apron up over her face. "Oh dear, our New Year's Eve party and wedding shower will have to be cancelled."

"The stench is pretty bad, Honey, but, maybe no one will notice," Willard Stafford stifled a laughed. He couldn't contain himself any longer. He dissolved into great gulps of laughter.

Alma stared at him, then smacked his shoulder and grinned. "Well, do you have another solution?"

"Adam, you pull the carpet back in the living room, and I'll go get the tools," Mr. S. said as he started through the kitchen for the tool shed out back.

"Willard Stafford, what are you going to do?" Alma hollered after her husband as she slumped onto a kitchen chair like a damp linen tea towel.

"Only what has to be done, Dear," he said. To Adam he added, "Please pull up the living room rug. I'll be right back." The door swung shut behind him

"I don't think I'm going to like any of this," she moaned.

Adam went into the sitting room and grabbed the large Persian carpet that spanned the center of the room. He moved all the furniture from the right side of the living room and piled it on the left. Then, he grabbed hold of one corner of the carpet and pulled it diagonally across the room in the direction of the stacked sofa and chairs.

Like an Army General prepared to stage an attack, Mr. Stafford marched back into the room. "I have only what I need."

"What can I do to help?" Adam offered.

"Thank you, Adam, but Mrs. Stafford will be as mad as a starving she-lion when I'm done. I don't want you to get in her path. I'll have to do this myself but please stand by in case I need to be resuscitated." Willard reached out his hand. "The gloves, please."

Alma joined them and sat with Adam on the remaining pieces of furniture and watched in disbelief.

Right in the middle of the living room floor, Willard took his brace and bit and drilled a small hole. Then, he placed the pointed end of a keyhole saw in the opening and gradually cut a crude circle in the middle of the polished oak hardwood.

Alma said nothing. She sat in stunned silence.

Willard put on the rubber gloves, lay on the floor, reached into the opening and fished around for the last beastly body. "It's in there." He touched the rat and his face turned white. "Oh no," he shuddered as he jumped to his feet and dashed outside. He gagged the whole way out the front door.

"I'll try to get it, Sir," Adam volunteered, but didn't want to. The last rat out was probably the first one in and the first to die. It could smell the worse.

Adam had no gloves. He had given them to Mr. Stafford. He closed his eyes and whispered one word, "Shaddy," and reached into the opening.

The slimy, decayed skin of the grotesque creature had dried in one spot of the underbelly. It was hard for Adam to

227

pull it loose; all the while he stifled his gag response. He slid his fingernails under the slippery body and popped the small stuck spot up.

He couldn't aim for the back yard, it was too far away. So, he pulled the rotted, diseased rat from under the living room floor of one of the most elegant homes in Middletown and ran out the front door were he jammed the indescribable rodent into a snow drift where it could remain on ice. Adam threw up whatever was left in his stomach, then rolled his bare hands in another snow pile and tried to wash off the slithery slim.

Mrs. Stafford followed them onto the porch and brought her apron up around her shoulders. "Thank you gentlemen. That is what I call bravery."

Adam walked back into the living room. It still smelled awful. "Shaddy," he whispered low, "give me super breath, sweet in smell but not too ooey-gooey sweet, just pleasant to the senses." Adam breathed in as deeply as possible. Then he gently let out a steady stream of cool, sweetly pleasant air that filled the space beneath the living room floor and spread to all the back recesses of the crawlspace.

As Mrs. Stafford came back into the house, she stopped just inside the door. "Oh my goodness, Adam, it smells wonderful in here. When you dug out the last rat, it removed the odor as well. How is that possible?"

"I don't' know Ma'am."

"Well, praise the Lord," she gasped as she threw her hands up.

"Praise the Lord, indeed," Adam echoed.

Chapter 29

Into the Thieves' Lair

Saturday, December 29, 1945

Adam woke up the next morning in the belfry, tired but determined. If he could evict smelly rats, he could do something else that had to be done. He had to. He had tossed and argued with himself all night. He was the only one who could, since he was the only one who had seen the boys take the carving. But, how? Daylight would break soon. There would be no shadows of night he could hide in. The shadows of day were always nearby but, he didn't want any part of them.

When Mr. Gunderman picked him up at the police station, the day after Christmas, they had passed through a section of town Adam hadn't been in before. It was a nice, new neighborhood with comfortable homes on friendly streets.

Adam certainly couldn't say anything to Mr. G. at the time. But, Adam had seen them. As he and Alfred passed, he had seen Freddy trudge across the snow in his front lawn and into the yard next door where Buddy, the leader of the pair of thieves, apparently lived. Slumped down in the car, where he could watch without being seen, Adam saw Buddy open the garage door. The two boys stood for a few seconds and jabbed at each other. Then Buddy poked around in the garage, under what appeared to be a work bench. Adam saw them pull out and open the same duffle he had seen them shove the carving into at the church. The bag was stamped with USN, United States Navy, on the front. Neither of the young felons looked very happy about their initiation into their lives as thieves as they punched and jabbed at each other. Adam didn't care what they did to each other. He had discovered where they lived and that's what he needed to know.

Now what do I do? He couldn't just walk up to their front door and say he was there to pick up the carving of the Christ Child. He didn't know how dangerous the boys could be. The two were loaners who poked each other and argued every time Adam had seen them, even in the church balcony on Christmas Eve.

Adam stalled around all morning as he tried to decide what to do. He was not a thief. Therefore, he could not bring himself to think like a thief. How could he take something that wasn't his, even though it was already stolen goods?

It was now nearly three in the afternoon. He wanted that Christ Child back where it belonged, in the manger, before Mrs. Gunderman brought Alfred to the church. Mr. G. had insisted that he would need to check on everything to make sure all would be ready for Sunday's service. Adam had cleaned in the morning, but he was only pushing a dust cloth around. Everything was spotless already. He still had a few hours to do something about the Christ Child carving. But, what?

If they're out of the house—maybe. But good ol' Buddy Boy and Freddy wouldn't be doing anything productive. They never do. Adam could not imagine that the pair would begin a life of virtue today. They were probably lying around doing nothing.

Shaddy, tell me what to do. As quickly as he asked, a full scene came to him, but to step into that reality, he would have to go where he didn't want to go. First, he had to walk over to

Fritzy's house, not to see her, but to talk to Coach Breman. Adam believed that he couldn't just show up at her house to talk to her. But, if he happened to see her while he was there talking to her father, that would be okay. He thought he was ready.

He put on his coat, cap and gloves and began to walk the few blocks to Fritzy's house. He had become accustomed to checking the road behind him almost as often as he watched the road in front. No one was out that afternoon except the mailman and an occasional shopper set on returning a Christmas gift of the wrong size.

When Adam got to the Breman's house, he hesitated before stepping onto the porch. What would he say if Fritzy came to the door? He hadn't rehearsed that because he had no idea what words would be believed.

"Adam, come in Son," Coach smiled his usual generous greeting.

"I had better not, Sir. I have a lot of snow on my shoes. I just stopped by to check on a job I heard about. They need people to help get ready for the party on Monday night, right?"

"Well now, Adam, I thought Fritzy and Alfred have been keeping you very busy lately."

"Yes, Sir, she is . . . they are . . . we are . . . we were." He studied the tips of his clodhoppers and watched the snow drip small dirty puddles on the Breman's front porch and was glad he had not gone in.

"Let me start over." Adam cleared his throat and looked Coach Breman in the eye. "I heard that they need a couple of people to set up tables and chairs over at the gym and prepare the room for the Holiday Celebration Party on Monday night."

"Yes, that's right."

"Well, I know two guys who I don't think are going to the party. I hadn't heard them talk about it. They might be interested in setting things up, especially if they could earn a few dollars. I don't have their phone numbers, but one is

Buddy Phillips and the other is his neighbor, Freddy something."

"Yes, Freddy Alexander lives next door to Buddy. You think they might be interested? Are you a friend of theirs?"

"No, Sir. I can't vouch for them. I happen to see them in church on Christmas Eve, and I thought you might know them or their families. Do you think you could call them? I would be happy to wait right here on the porch while you call. That way, if they can't or don't want to, I might be able to think of a couple other guys. I know there's not much time and everyone has been great about getting the party all put together."

"Well that sounds fine, but you must step in. If you stand on the entry mat, the floor will be just fine." Coach Breman stepped back so Adam could come in, then he went to the phone on the front hall table near the stairs. He took a phone book from the drawer in the phone table and read aloud.

"Here it is. Phillips on Maplecrest Avenue. Here's the number, Walnut 3321." He dialed the number, WA3321. "Hello, Buddy? This is Coach Breman." He paused, "Yes."

Adam began to add up the dangers involved if the two thieves were to find out who had recommended them. He didn't think the two culprits knew that he was alive; much less that he knew what they had done. But, he didn't want to take any chances. He gestured to himself with a negative hand signal, a sign that he didn't want his name used.

"Someone has recommended you and your neighbor, Freddy, for the job of set-up people before the school party. I don't know if you're interested but we could sure use you. It is a little after three now. You would need to be at the school by four. That's when they're going to work. You'll be paid. What do you think?"

Shaddy, he evoked.

"I am here," Shaddy whispered low.

Adam watched Coach as he talked on the phone. He only heard the coach's half of the conversation, but that was enough.

"You would?" Coach smiled. "Very good. You'll have to ask your friend. I don't have his phone number. If you could call me right back . . ." Mr. Breman paused again. "Really? He lets you speak for him does he?"

Adam rolled his eyes and agreed.

"Well, fine. Now, be sure to call back if your parents say—What?"

Adam sighed. *I'll bet he doesn't tell his parents anything.*

"Good, I'll call Principal Sparrow and tell him I have hired you two. You will both be there in less than an hour? Well, thank you."

Adam smiled and stuck out his hand. "Thanks, Coach. I don't know the guys, but they both seem to need money lately,"

"Thank you, Adam. That solves a big problem for me. I was going to have to go over to the school myself. Fritzy wanted me to see her new party dress, and her mother hasn't finished making it." He smiled and the two chuckled as Adam edged out the door. He wanted to see Fritzy, but he didn't want to see her disappointment again. He backed onto the porch and down the steps as quickly as he could.

He took one last look at the house before he got to the end of the sidewalk. To his surprise, Fritzy stood in the upstairs hall window and waved. *Well, at least she's smiling.* He smiled. His stomach felt giddy. He remembered he hadn't eaten much that morning. How could he have forgotten the peanut butter sandwiches Mrs. G. had given him?

As Adam walked, he pulled the wax paper back from one of the sandwiches and devoured it all. He shoved the empty paper into his jacket pocket and licked his lips.

Suddenly, Adam realized he was probably on the same path the two thieves will take when they walk to school to help set-up for the party. Even though the snow had fallen all night, the concrete in front of each house had been freshly shoved by the homeowner. Walking was safer than in recent days and he made good time.

The Middletown Public Library was just ahead in the next block, on the left. Adam hurried across the street and dashed into the building. Once inside, he turned and watched through the window in the door. Freddy and Buddy lived just two more blocks down on the other side of the street.

"Are you going out, Young Man?" A blue haired lady with a purple flowered head scarf tapped one goulashes-covered foot in Adam's direction.

"No, Ma'am. Here, let me get the door for you." He smiled broadly and held the door open for the woman. From his reconnaissance position, he could see the boys a few houses down as they walked along the sidewalk. Adam stepped behind the lady as he waited for her to pass.

"Thank you. It is nice to see polite young people again. I thought perhaps the war had wiped gallantry off the list of manly attributes."

"No, Ma'am. The list is still intact." Adam pulled the door closed as soon as she cleared the threshold. He stepped to the side of the door, peered around the wood frame window pane and watched.

Look at them, still hitting and punching at each other. They have a home and food and heat and lights, and they are the unhappiest pair I've ever seen. I never noticed them much before, and will try to ignore them when school starts again. You guys don't know it, but today I will become your very best friend.

After the boys passed the library, Adam stepped back out into the cold. What would he do? Then, he knew. The power of knowing had come over him.

Mrs. Phillips is probably in the kitchen fixing dinner. That feels right. The time is just a little past four o'clock. Mr. Phillips might be home from work, might not. If he is, he could be in the living room reading the newspaper or listening to the radio. Edward R Murrow isn't on yet, so maybe there would be no radio distraction. I've got to take the risk. I have to believe that what I am doing is right, and I won't get caught. Shaddy, cloak me in invisibility.

Adam crossed the street a few houses up from the Phillips' home. The sun was bright. He knew he couldn't hide in the center of a spotlight, and he couldn't just stand out in the street to look the situation over. He didn't try to understand any of it, but he felt safe.

Not too fast and not too slow, he warned himself as he walked past the Phillip's garage and studied the layout carefully.

The garage had a side entrance. Adam could casually walk up to the garage door. If anyone were to pass, he wouldn't draw attention to himself if he was relaxed and looked like he belonged there.

Shaddy cautioned quietly, "Move slowly and deliberately."

Adam would do his best to follow those orders. "Shaddy, give me x-ray vision," he whispered into the afternoon sun.

He was thankful the garage had a side entrance so he wouldn't have to open the larger, louder door. He knew Shaddy would follow through, so he focused his x-ray vision on the inside of the garage. Next to the side door was a long workbench. Adam knew he had remembered correctly.

He walked up to the door like he lived there. He didn't check over his shoulder or fumble with the knob. He simply opened the door and walked in.

"The bag is under the work bench," the Power of Knowing told him.

That's where I saw it. He looked again. *The duffle isn't there.* Adam couldn't believe it.

"Stay calm, my Son," Shaddy whispered.

Adam bent low and looked farther back under the bench to where the sides met the wall. There, in the corner, pushed behind some paint cans, was the USN sea bag of the United States Navy.

Adam moved the cans carefully and smiled. In one of those worst scenarios a guy can have, he could see himself kick over a bucket of paint and leave red footprints all the way back to the foot of the bell tower ladder at the church.

That is not going to happen. He was confident of that. He was no longer a scared kid with no home, no family, and no backbone, hiding in the shadows and moving around only in the dark. He would not stay silent any longer. Not that he would make any noise, but everybody was going to hear him.

He grabbed hold of the top of the duffle and carefully removed the bag. He thought of the infant's hands and tiny fingers. *I will not return the carving with as much as a small scratch on the wood.*

After he withdrew the bag, each paint can was carefully replaced exactly as he had found them. He lifted the duffle into his arms like a new daddy would lift his son, opened the side door to the garage, and stepped out. He was not in the clear yet. He was still in the Phillips' yard. He had to be able to walk away from the house, with the bag, without being seen.

"Hide in our darkness," the shadows offered. "We will make your deception complete. No one will see you. You will do wonders within our gloom. No one will know you."

"Walk boldly, My Son," Shaddy directed. "Do not listen to them. I am the way."

With his head held high, Adam gently pulled the door behind him and strolled down the concrete drive just like he lived there.

He had rounded the snowy edge of the drive and was back onto the sidewalk when he heard a car coming in the distance. *The sound carries far on the icy air,* he remembered. He was thankful for that blessing. It was like a warning siren. He fixed his eyes like flint on the prize that was ahead. He was going to return the Christ Child carving to its home.

Adam crossed the street and walked up the steps of the library just like any other patron in search of a good book for the weekend. As before, once inside, he turned, watched from the windows and waited a few minutes. He was suddenly aware that his breathing was heavy. He had felt no fear when he rescued the carving. Now, after the danger had passed, his body seemed to say, *What just happened? What did I do?*

No cars had passed on Maplecrest since he left the Phillips' garage, walked the block or so to the library and went in. He couldn't see how anyone could make an association between him and the house at 1220. He started to open the library door then noticed a car pull into the Phillips' driveway. Adam waited. A man got out, closed the car door and walked right into the house without knocking. *I guess Mr. Phillips is home now. Thank you, Shaddy.*

Adam stepped out of the library as if he were one of their most benevolent patrons, a friend of the library he would be called. With confidence and courage, he walked down the steps and back to Cranberry Street with the Baby Jesus in his arms. Pops carried him the same way when he was very little. Adam wondered why he remembered that.

When he got to the parsonage beside the church, he studied the scene before he approached. The days were short. Late afternoon shadows were beginning to gather, envelope the house and tuck the day under the bushes. Inside, the kitchen light was already on. As Adam watched, someone turned off one of the living room lights. Through the window to the left of the door, he could see Pastor Silverman move from the couch in the living room to the dining room table.

Adam walked down the sidewalk on the other side of the street where the buildings cast even longer shadows. He walked five yards beyond the Silverman's house, crossed the street and then doubled back so he could approach the porch past the living room window, not the dining room.

Shaddy, let me give this Christ Child back to the church anonymously. Take away my fear.

Quietly, cautiously, but with smooth confidence, he stepped up two steps and then onto the porch. *Thank you, Shaddy, for cement. Concrete doesn't creak.* He set the sea bag beside the front door. *Now, how do I get away?*

Adam rang the doorbell. Then, with a great flying leap, he soared over the porch railing and landed in the bushes.

"What is this?' Pastor Silverman questioned as he opened the door.

"What is it, Dear?" Mrs. Silverman stepped onto the porch beside him.

"I don't know," he said, then stooped to untie the sea bag. "Connie, will you just look." He carefully pulled the top of the duffle down until the rich glow of the Christ Child's arms reached up and out.

"Honey," Connie Silverman's eyes filled with tears, "it's home. The Christ Child is home. It's a miracle."

The boy didn't breathe a word. He saw all the joy he could ever imagine while on his knees in the evergreens. He was filled with amazement.

Adam saw the joy the return of the carving brought but he could only rejoice in silence.

Chapter 30

The Crèche is Full Again

Adam had gone back into the church, hungry as always and tired. He had eaten a sandwich Mrs. Gunderman had provided earlier. Mr. G. had suggested the food, but didn't tell his wife that Adam would have little to eat since the holidays had nearly passed. All the special meals and treats that were part of the celebration would be over too. Only the New Year's party was left.

He was thankful for Mrs. G.'s generosity. He had no money. The four dollars he had earned for cutting up the tree was great, but his wallet was missing. The leather billfold had to be in the belfry but he couldn't find it. How was that possible? He certainly didn't have dresser drawers to lose stuff in.

Adam's legs felt heavy as he trudged through the empty, dim church. He could hear the wind pick up outside and was glad he wasn't on the streets. But, he wasn't home either. Except for his cleaning day at the farm, he hadn't been home in months.

Out of habit, he started up the ladder to the bell tower and pushed the door open. Ice peppered the small window like a sand storm. Adam shivered. He didn't know if he was too hungry or too tired to hold any heat in his body, but he was cold. The thought of being sick and alone in the dark bell tower, like a hobo crouched down in a doorway or along a railroad track, crowded into his thoughts. That made his body chill more violently. He looked around his wretched garret. With no light at that hour of the evening, he couldn't see if the little hummingbird had come back.

He dragged his blanket and pillow back down the ladder. "Mr. G. knows I'm living here," he spoke out loud to the rough beams and bare floor. "I might as well get warm tonight, before they find me frozen stiff someday."

He pulled his bedding into the youth room where a couch and some overstuffed chairs made a cozy place for the high school kids to meet. The scent of buttered popcorn from the last Youth meeting still hung in the air.

Adam spread the blanket on the sofa and threw himself onto his new bed. He could have turned on the light, but he had gotten used to the darkness. With no light, he didn't have to see how alone he was.

Why has God forgotten all about me? He thought the same thoughts that had no answers. *Why has he left me utterly alone? Why can't I be thankful for what I have?*

He had placed the sandwich on the side table and broke off a corner. "Good," he whispered to the wind. Then his eye caught sight of something that had been there all along. An upright Philco radio stood on the floor across the room. Could it be? Would he actually hear another's voice as he lay on the couch with Mrs. Simington's quilt pulled over him?

Adam pushed one of the station selection buttons on the Philco and then curled up on the sofa. He broke off another piece of sandwich and closed his eyes. A singer was just finishing a song from a recent movie, *The Picture of Dorian Gray.*

"Goodbye, little yellow bird," the song began. Adam sat up and listened. The song finished with the lyrics, "in a cage of gold."

Birdcage. The word leaped in Adam's mind and would not let him go. He got up, went into the church kitchen and prepared a saucer of fresh sugar water. He took the dish back up the ladder but didn't even go to the top. The belfry was cold and dreary. He simply scooted the plate across the floor from the opening.

"Little Hummer, you may leave me, Pops may desert me, Fritzy may turn on me, but, Bright One, I will not abandon you."

• • •

"What is that?" Adam spoke into the darkness of the night. If he had been in the bell tower, he would not have heard the sound. In the Senior High Sunday School room, every creak grated on his ears.

Probably nothing. This time he didn't speak out loud. He turned over and pulled the pillow over his ears.

Bang!

What the . . .? That is not nothing. That is something. He sat up and listened to the blackness all around him. Thud! *Someone else is in this church.*

Adam slowly lowered one sock-covered foot to the floor. *I cannot just lay here and wait for someone to bash me in the head.* Thoughts raced through his mind he had never thought of before. *What would happen to Moms if Pops and I were both gone? Pops, where are you?*

Adam was angry, confused and scared all at the same time. As one emotion rolled and crashed into another, his stomach churned and fell with them. *How can I do this?*

241

He sat down on his couch-bed. *Maybe the intruder won't hear me if I'm really quiet. Maybe it's those two idiots who took the carving in the first place.*

Adam realized he was holding his breath. He finally exhaled. There was a closet across the room from his bed. He could hide in there, but he couldn't bring himself to do that. *Hide again? Not this time.*

He cautiously got up and crossed the room with silent steps. Then he thought of Good King Wenceslas and laughed bitterly. There was no heat in the floor he walked on. There were no footprints to walk in. There was no pillar of light by night or cloud of dust by day. There was silence. There was nothing.

Then I have nothing to lose. A stream of light cast a plumb line on the floor through the slightly opened door that led into the hallway. If he opened the door, he would no longer be able to hide in the shadows. *I have been hiding in the dark for months now. I know I will be exposed out in the open, but I don't care.* He knew that the thought of exposure had two meanings but that was okay with him.

If the tiny hummingbird can endure a long flight across the gulf, I can walk out that door. Mr. G. had said, "Adam, you can endure what you are dealt."

The boy followed the light and pushed gently. He held his breath until he thought his lungs would explode. The door hinges might squawk and announce his presence. That could not happen.

Silence, Shaddy, silence.

"Silence and peace, my son," the spirit reassured him.

He pulled on the doorknob and waited for a sound. There was nothing. He stepped into the Agnes Coffee Lounge and looked around. The large room was not totally dark. The street-lamp flooded the floor across to the crank-up door which was open. He could see no one. Silently, like kittens' paws on the kitchen linoleum, he crept closer to the sanctuary.

His eyes took a while to adjust to the lesser light. When he crossed into the sanctuary, he slowly made his way to the altar where the crèche still stood. The scene had announced a miraculous birth that Adam had not truly celebrated. He expected to see the doll from the nursery in the manger.

"Isn't he beautiful?" Pastor Silverman suggested. "Come closer, Adam."

"No, thank you," Adam shrunk from the scene.

"The Christ Child is for you too, Adam. Come."

Adam crawled near the scene of love on his knees. His heart was full. There, in the straw lay the beautiful wooden carving, with a glow of chestnut gold. Two chubby arms reached dimpled hands to the boy who stood over the place where the Baby Jesus lay. That was his first sight of the Christ Child carving. He hadn't even opened the bag when he returned the duffle.

Pastor Silverman spoke softly. "A long time ago, Adam, Alfred Gunderman helped an angry, disbelieving young boy to trust. Mr. G. vowed to stand with that boy, and Alfred believes in you too. You have a mother and people who will stand beside you. Now look, our carving has returned."

Adam could not take his eyes from the Christ Child in the manger as it reached out to him. He touched the small hand of the babe who represented all the love in the world. Tears rolled down Adam' cheeks.

"I know. I know, Adam. I've been there. Adam Shoemaker's name is written on God's heart from this moment on."

"Schumacher, Pastor," Adam smiled as he touched the glowing face in the manger. "Make sure God spells it right. My name is Adam Schumacher."

Chapter 31

Sunday Blessings

Sunday, December 30, 1945

It was Sunday morning again but Adam didn't awaken in the cold, drafty belfry. He studied his surroundings for a moment then recognized the youth room where he had fallen asleep. Sunbeams were streaming through the double pane windows that faced the front of the church.

"Yikes," he said out loud as he jumped to his feet. "Folks will start coming for church in half an hour."

He straightened the room and gathered up the blankets and pillow he had dragged down from the belfry the evening before. He would have to wash up in the small men's restroom and then hurry up the belfry ladder to dress for the day. Then he stopped.

Fritzy will be here. Will she talk to me or pretend I'm not here?

Adam washed and scrambled up the ladder, found some clothes but struggled for a moment as he hurried to dress. His arm refused to slip into his shirt sleeve as he heard voices downstairs. He fussed with the buttons then pulled on the dress shoes Mrs. Bremen had given him and hurried down the ladder that led to the main floor.

"Adam," Pastor gasped. "I am so sorry, my boy. When I left the house, I told my wife I'd be right back. I darted out of here last evening and forgot you would be sleeping here alone—again."

"That's all right. I've been sleeping here alone for months. I've gotten used to it."

"Well, it's not all right with me. You should be in a house, in a proper room. You'll sleep in our guest room tonight. My wife will never forgive me if I left you over here alone again."

"I don't want to put you out. I ..." Adam stopped. Fritzy and her family had come in for services, but his eyes were on her alone. What would she do? What would she say?

"Hi," she said as she stomped the snow off her boots.

"Hi."

"Is that all you two can say?" Jimmy Bremen smiled and nudged Adam's arm.

"No, that is not all I have to say," Fritzy stated flatly as she turned up her nose. "But, Adam and I have all day to talk about it. Don't we Adam?"

"I hope so."

"Of course we do. We have all day. You'll come to dinner at our house; we'll play games and—talk."

"I'm sorry I..."

"No Adam, I'm sorry. I shouldn't have gotten mad at you. I didn't even know the whole story. Now, that's all that needs to be said. I don't want to talk anymore about it." She put her gloves in her pocket and unbuttoned her coat as they walked into the sanctuary.

The Christmas decorations were still in place as the holiday season lasted through New Year's Day. Adam looked at every bright ornament, red bow and gold streamer that was in the room. His artistic heart could never get enough color to satisfy his need for beauty. They sat quietly in a pew on the right side of the room. Adam knew that Mr. G. would want him to roll up the large wall again at the end of the service. He had settled into a pattern of responsibilities and it felt good.

The organ music began to play as the people took their seats. Suddenly, Fritzy threw her hand to her mouth and gasped in amazement. She jumped to her feet, hurried to the front of the sanctuary and stopped beside the manger which was still overstuffed with fragrant hay. The rough, wooden trough now cradled the precious carving of the infant Jesus.

"Adam," she whispered hoarsely. "He's back."

News spread from person-to-person throughout the large room. "The carving has returned," they said in hushed tones.

Adam came forward and put his hand on her shoulder. "He's beautiful—just like you said."

"It's a miracle," she whispered. "I know it's a miracle."

A low gurgle and gulp, and the shuffling of feet were heard from the balcony off to the left as the two thieves leaned as far forward as possible to see this miracle that had happened. Freddy and Buddy jabbed each other in the ribs until they nearly fell out of the balcony.

"I know what you're thinking boys," Pastor Silverman smiled as he looked at the two balcony buzzards. "We are all amazed. I think it is a miracle that the carving has been returned to us. Come—let us all gather around as close as we can and rededicate this carving as an instrument of Christmas joy."

Pastor Silverman raised his hands and gestured for all the people to come closer. "Those who need to rest can sit on the front pews." Then he laughed, "There's plenty of room. Those rows are rarely used."

Adam looked up to see what Buddy and Freddy would do. Would they join in the celebration? No. They slumped in their seats, jammed their hands in their pockets and sulked through the rest of the service.

"Let us pray," the pastor began.

They need a lot of prayer, Adam thought as he bowed his head. *Sorry God. Who am I to criticize others?*

• • •

After services, Adam had another great time at the Bremans' house. The meal was delicious and he ate his full. He even beat Fritzy in games of dominoes.

As he started to leave, Mrs. Breman stuffed his pockets with a few extra chicken legs wrapped in waxed paper and a large piece of chocolate cake with whipped chocolate icing placed on one of Mrs. Breman's china plates covered with more waxed paper.

"You can return the plate when you pick up Fredericka for the party," she smiled. "Wish I had something to send a glass of milk in. Cake and milk go together."

"Thank you, Ma'am. I'll be sleeping at the pastor's house tonight. They may have a little extra milk."

"I imagine they do," she agreed. "We enjoyed your company today."

"Thanks again," Adam burst with truth. Then he turned to Fritzy. "See you tomorrow."

"See you tomorrow," she agreed.

At the end of the day, he slept the night in Pastor Silverman's guestroom. He was warm and comfortable and no one even knew it was he who had returned the carving. He was accepted for who he was, not a hero, not a basketball star, for just being Adam Schumacher.

Chapter 32

New Year's Eve

Monday, December 31, 1945

Adam **woke up** the next morning in the Silvermans' guest room. He shook his head and tried to clear his thinking. The events of the previous day gathered around the edges of his mind.

"Adam?" Pastor Silverman tapped on the bedroom door.

"Yeah?"

"May I come in?"

"Sure." Adam pulled the covers over him again, sat up and leaned on his elbow.

"A couple of people have been by to see you this morning."

"How did they know where to find me?"

"Actually, Frederica Breman stopped. She said you two had seen each other yesterday. I guess she also knew you had been living in the church's bell tower."

"Yeah, I guess. I'm that crazy boy that lives with the bats in the belfry."

"Speaking of bats in the belfry, you know what I found over there this morning? I hope you don't mind. I had gone up the ladder to get your school books, clothing and stuff. Look what I found."

Pastor Silverman reached around into the hallway and brought in B.B. Brumble's basket-purse turned birdcage. The basket was covered with a white cloth.

Adam's breath caught in his throat. Many things tumbled through his mind and B.B.'s basket was another wad to choke on. The little hummer was gone. He didn't realize until that moment how much the little ruby throated hummingbird meant to him.

"So you found the basket?" Adam was sure. Once he was found with the silly purse, no one would believe or trust him.

"That's right. I found it," Pastor said.

"Pastor Silverman—"

"This is the most appropriate use of B.B.'s bag I can think of."

"It's okay that I had the purse?" Adam was confused. If everything was all right, then why did the pastor confront him with the bag now?

"Okay? Of course, Adam. The basket-purse was there for the taking." He pulled one of Mrs. Silverman's card-table cloth covers from the top of the cage. There in the center of the basket was the little hummingbird.

Adam leaped from the bed and grabbed the cage. "How did he survive? How is this possible? I thought the little guy was either gone or dead."

He pulled the cage close to his face and studied the bird from every angle. Great tears of joy and other feelings he had stuffed away to deal with another time, rolled down Adam's cheeks. He looked over the bright red throat and the little green feathers and saw how proud the bird looked.

The hummer appeared to be healthy and strong. Suddenly, he began chirping his long, "Look at me, aren't I great" song.

"He's showing off," Adam grinned. "He is amazing." He looked again at the little bird. "I'm shocked, Pastor?" He hitched up the basketball sweats he had used as pajamas bottoms, took the birdcage and sat down on the edge of the bed. He couldn't take his eyes off his only roommate, as small and amazing as the hummer was.

"How could any of these things happen? Adam, I don't know. I'm not the author of any of this. I just know there are so many little miracles that gather around us each day; we would trip over them if we saw them all. Most of us see only a few in a lifetime."

"And some of us miss them all," Adam admitted. How many miracles in his life had he missed?

"You said Fritzy was here?"

"She left a card she had made. Trust me. I didn't look at the message. She said she had made the card last evening. She wanted you to have it right away. I guess you two have a date for the New Year's Party. She also said to remind you that you had promised." The pastor waited for Adam to reply.

"Oh, and here is her card," Pastor offered.

Adam took the envelope and withdrew the handmade card. There were two verses with a hand drawn cover, just like a card from Woolworth's. The cover had a watercolor painting of a ruby throated hummingbird, signed by Fritzy. Inside, the words sounded like they had been written just for him. He thought about all that had happened recently. He saw the path he had walked written within the ten lines of Fritzy's poem.

God bless you with–
Truth to speak
The home you seek
Grace for living
A cause for giving.

For This New Year:
I wish you peace to share
Those who care
A song to sing
And hummingbirds in the spring.

Adam brushed a tear away with the back of his hand. "I wasn't sure I would be able to take her to the party. I don't have any money. I lost my billfold on my way back from Mr. and Mrs. Breman's house."

"Now, that is another thing. A man stopped by and asked if I knew where the Schumacher family lived. I said I had just met Adam Schumacher Saturday evening." Pastor paused to let Adam have time to remember the miracle of that night in the church.

"Did you tell him?" Adam's muscles trembled again as he prepared for another flight.

"Well, yes," Pastor said. "Isn't that okay, Adam? He had been driving slowly along the streets he had seen you on before. About a block and a half from here, he spotted your wallet on a small stretch of sidewalk that had been cleared of snow. He gave it to me."

"I have met him. I don't know who he is. Do you know where he is now?"

"He said he had to get home. He had taken a few days out of his Christmas vacation already, trying to find the Schumacher family. But, he had to go back home. He needed to be with his family for a few days before his children went back to school after Christmas vacation."

"What did he want—besides giving back the billfold? I saw him around town long before he found my wallet."

"He had a message for you and your mother. That's all he wanted. He claimed he shouldn't give the information to anyone but the Schumacher family. He said that someone had told him that a man, believed to be your father, William

Schumacher, had been found in an Army hospital. He said the source was reliable. Your father has evidently been there since a Prisoner of War camp was liberated at the end of the war. The man, your father, doesn't remember his own name, but a patient in the same ward, said he thought he recognized him. No one would believe the other patient because he had memory lapses too. Sergeant Smith said your dad had no identification on him and the VA wouldn't notify you or your mom without proper I.D. They wouldn't want to make a mistake. The man, thought to be your dad, was thin and ill but getting stronger. The war buddy of mine said he had picked these up off the battlefield at the Battle of the Bulge. They were found near where your father had been when the enemy dragged him away. Sergeant Smith wanted you and your mother to have them."

Pastor Silverman reached in his pocket and pulled something out. He took the bird from Adam and put the cage on a table in front of a window.

"This is for you and your mom," he said as he dropped Will Schumacher's Army dog-tags into Adam's hand.

"Oh no! The man in the blue car had these all along? Where is he? Where's Pops?"

"Sergeant Smith left his name, address and phone number. He said he would like you and your mom to write to him. He can make arrangements for you two to meet the man believed to be William Schumacher." The pastor handed the card with the contact information to a stunned young man, the newly renamed Adam Schumacher.

I will go with you, My Son. I'll help you find your father, Shaddy blew into Adam's ear with certainty.

"I will find him. I know I will find Pops as soon as spring comes. Thank you, Reverend." Adam grabbed the pastor and held onto the dog-tags. They were the only reality he had known in months. They were not a fantasy. They were a truth about Pops he could live with.

253

"I did nothing, Son. You should thank God." Pastor patted the boy's shoulders then added. "I saw no suit among your clothes in the belfry. You're going to need one for the party."

"But—"

"Sounds to me like you promised Fritzy Breman you would take her to the party, and she is an awful nice girl to back out on your promise." He didn't give Adam a chance to protest but continued, "I have a suit hanging in the back of my closet that I have not worn in years. I guess I kept the suit of clothes to remind me of how slim I was at one time. My wife can take in the pants a little for you."

Could it be? Had I actually witnessed a miracle and almost didn't see it? He looked at the hummer and the wallet and the dog tags and wondered how much more proof he would need?

Chapter 33

Finding Surprise Blessings

"Get your coat, Adam." Pastor Silverman came into his kitchen a half hour later. He grabbed his car keys off the counter as the boy finished a bowl of corn flakes.

"Sir?"

"I made a few phone calls while you dressed and ate. I'm taking you out to the sanitarium to pick up your mother. I'm supposed to move you two into Gunderman's guest space today like you and Mrs. G. talked about." Pastor put his arm through the sleeve of his coat, flipped the toaster side up, and popped the corner of the dry bread in his mouth.

"What?" Adam was stunned.

"I hope I haven't over stepped my bounds, Adam, but you said your mother could come home when the house was ready for her. I talked to her on the telephone and asked if she would like to stay at the Gundermans' until summer break, along with you of course." Silverman looked the boy up and down. Adam had said nothing.

"What did she say?" Adam was cautious. He had lived the fabrication for so long, he had made lies his new reality. Would he be able to meet the day with the truth?

"I explained the guest space and the small amount of money, and she said she would love to move in. Gundermans would help her and she would help them. She said she knows Mrs. Gunderman a little, and she thinks you could help Mr. Gunderman in the yard and around the place."

"So, she can finally get out of that place?"

"Like I said, Adam, get your coat. We're going out to pick her up."

The ride to the sanitarium was a blur of color and buildings. Soon they came to open fields that slept under a blanket of white. Winter wheat was visible in some fields not completely covered with snow. Adam was happy to see the green that peppered the ground again.

"The sanitarium is just up here," Adam pointed, "around the next bend. Trust me, I have walked this road so many times, I've named all of the trees."

The red brick building was old. "The whole place looks sterile." Young Schumacher studied the structure from the basement window wells to the attic roof.

Adam had mixed emotions about the place. On the one hand, he sure missed Moms and had been feeling desperately alone, cold, sad, and defeated. For all of that, he hated the West Slope Tuberculosis Hospital. Yet, he knew he had to be grateful to the sanitarium for making Moms well again.

Pastor pulled his car to a stop in the circular drive just outside the entrance. They got out and Adam approached the front door a few steps ahead of the pastor. He didn't like the looks of the place. He hurried past the facade and went quickly inside where the Christmas decorations made the interior a little more cheery. Adam had just been there two days before, but he was much too cold and wet on Christmas Day to appreciate the entrance except for the warmth. Was Christmas just Tuesday past? How could that be possible? Time usually flew by, but recent days were in slow motion.

"I will be so glad when Moms gets out of here."

"Yes, I am sure you will be, but you'll have to admit, this facility was a blessing to your mother. The hospital was here when she became sick and was in need of nursing care."

"This pile of bricks and stone?" Adam couldn't believe what he was hearing. The sanitarium—a blessing? How?

"Blessings come in different sizes and packages. Miracles are recognized with the heart not the eyes, Son."

"How in the world could this place be anything except—" Adam stepped aside and allowed the pastor to enter the Sanitarium Director's office.

"Good morning, Mr. Fairfield," Adam greeted the man with more maturity than most fifteen-year-olds. "This is Pastor Silverman from the church on Cranberry Street." Adam heard himself mocking the director in his head. Then, he realized that the man had nothing but nice things to say to him. Ridicule and negative self-talk did no one any good.

The two men shook hands. "I'm happy to finally meet you, Sir," the director smiled. "I was glad to talk to you on the telephone and make these arrangements for the Shoemaker family. Bridget Shoemaker is a brave and wonderful woman."

"Schumacher, Sir. Our name is Schumacher." Adam spoke firmly and assuredly. He had been confused about many things in the last months, but of that fact he was sure.

"Yes, Son, thank you." Fairfield smiled. "All is ready for your mother's transfer to the Gundermans' place. Mr. and Mrs. Gunderman tell me that you and your mother will have a separate entrance, a nice completely outfitted bathroom, a good sized bedroom, and living room, complete with furniture and radio. I believe, Son, you will sleep on the couch. Is that all right with you?"

Adam was stunned. "Is it all right? If the ceiling rafters are enclosed; if there is running water with a bathroom, heat and electricity and a finished floor, it is more than all right. The place is a castle."

257

Adam stopped and thought of all his blessings. Maybe he had been missing miracles. "That sounds just fine to me. In fact, the couch sounds great." Adam continued to study the two men.

Adam had more questions than he had answers. *Why on earth would anyone do anything so nice for Moms and me? Life isn't usually like that. Besides, I still have a lot of luggage. Wherever I live, there has to be room for a funny little basket purse and small bird.*

"The arrangement is fair. You and your mother would live there in exchange for her being on the property when Mrs. Gunderman is at work. You will shovel snow now in the winter and mow the grass in the spring. Are you sure that is all okay with you? You play a part in making this work, Young Man."

"I am happy to be able to help get a safe place for Moms." Adam felt a few inches taller. "Yep, it is very okay with me."

Adam was stunned beyond words to express. He was actually helping his mother to have advantages she had not had before. There was nothing but hard work on the farm and in the clan in which she had grown up. The gypsy ways were primitive. At the same time, he would be helping himself escape from the belfry.

"Then, if you will excuse me, I will go get your mother and help her with her belongings."

As soon as the director was out of the office, Adam's attention snapped back to Silverman. "It all sounds great, Pastor, but how in the world can this place be a blessing or a miracle like you said?"

"Your mother is alive, isn't she, Adam? She's coming home today, is she not? She is a well woman. She just has to regain her strength and try not to catch a cold. Isn't that a miracle? Her treatment happened here. Here in 1945, fifty percent of people, who do not receive treatment for tuberculosis, die."

• • •

Adam was excited about the little apartment behind Mr. and Mrs. Gunderman's house. "Isn't the place wonderful, Moms?" He was proud. Finally, he was able to take care of Moms through his hard work and new friends.

"It is so good to see you again, Bridget." Arletta greeted her old friend with open arms. "You haven't been to club in years."

"There's always something that has to be done on the farm, Arletta. But, it is so very good to see you today."

"This is great," Adam whispered in amazement. The apartment was everything Alfred and Arletta had described, and more. "The furniture all looks new," Adam observed out loud and then wished he hadn't. He didn't want to sound ungrateful.

"Mother Gunderman only lived a few months after we moved her in here," Arletta smiled. "We bought everything new for her, and she purchased a lot too, like new pots and pans and decorations." Mrs. G. seemed proud as she showed Adam and his mother around their home.

"Did she die here?" Again, Adam couldn't believe his thoughts were not kept to himself.
For a man of few words, all of the wrong ones were tumbling out of the back of his mind.

"Adam!" Moms gave a little smack to her son's shoulder and looked down, away from Mrs. G.

"Now that is an honest concern." The corners of Mrs. G.'s mouth gave away her stifled laugh. "No, Adam. As a matter of fact, Mother Gunderman came into our house and tried to get a book from a high shelf there in our living room, and fell. Her hip broke when she landed on the floor and she

259

had to go to the hospital. Like some older people, her hip healed, but the rest of her body just finally gave out."

"I'm sorry." Adam cringed inside. *What are you, Schumacher, a four-year-old?*

"I like the question though. It shows me you're thinking." Arletta smiled and looked around. "I forgot the extra coffee pot, Bridget. Let me run into the house and get it."

"Certainly," Moms smiled and took in everything in the little apartment.

"Adam, this is wonderful!" She hugged her son with all the strength she was gaining. "This has all come about because of your hard work. I am so proud of you."

"Thanks, Moms, but we won't be a real family until Pops comes home." Adam tried to keep a happy face while thoughts of Pops' absence tried to spoil their blessing.

"Adam—maybe Pops can't come home. Even if that's true, we are still a family."

"Moms, what's wrong with me? I've been so excited about your hospital release, I haven't told you yet. Pastor Silverman said a man came by trying to find Pops' family. The man had been all over Middletown looking for us. I saw him a couple of times, but I didn't know who he was and didn't trust him. Pastor said the man told him he thinks Pops is alive but has lost his memory."

Adam led his mother over to the sofa. "You have to hear this while sitting down," he said as he helped her onto the sofa.

"Moms, Pops doesn't know anyone or even his own name. Someone saw him in a VA hospital here in the Eastern part of United States. His dog tags were missing, and he couldn't be officially identified until an Army buddy thought he recognized him."

"Adam, how can that be?" Bridget put her hands over her face, then whispered again, "How can that be, Adam?"

"I don't know, but I met the man, Moms. He seemed to show up everywhere. When he couldn't talk to me or you, he looked up Pastor Silverman. He said his name is Sergeant Smith. He gave Pastor these." Adam held out the prize to his mother.

"Your daddy's dog tags?" Bridget Schumacher took the small tags on the metal beaded chain and clutched them to her chest. "Do you think—? Could your daddy have been alive all this time, sick and lost inside his mind?"

"Yes, Moms, I do. I think Pops is still alive. I will be sixteen in April and I can get my driver's license. This spring, I'm going to go find Pops. Sergeant Smith said Pops had been released from a POW camp and was taken to a hospital. That hospital is here in the states. I'll keep driving until I find him. I'll look up that Sergeant and he'll lead me to Pops. I know he will."

"But, Adam, the money for gas? Where will you get money for food and gas and shelter?"

"Shelter is no problem. I've learned I don't need a bed to sleep in. I'll save some of the money from my job at the church to get me started. I can work my way from town to town. If hummingbirds can fly south, I can drive east."

Chapter 34

A Near Catastrophe

Adam settled Moms in the little apartment and he could breathe again. He could be a real fifteen-year-old and enjoy a party for the first time since before the war.

That evening, the door to the bathroom in the little cottage opened and a young man in a brown suit, white shirt, striped tie and brown leather shoes stepped out. His grin exposed his feelings of relief and joy.

Moms raised the reclining chair she was enjoying to its full, upright position. "Adam, look at you. You look great!"

"Thanks Moms," he smiled as he straightened his tie. "Are you sure you're going to be alright if I'm gone this evening?"

"I don't need to be tucked in, you know," she chuckled.

"Promise you won't wait up for me. I would feel really guilty if you lost a minute of sleep."

"Adam, what I do is not your fault. What Pops does, or doesn't do, is not your fault. You are fifteen, and you deserve a night out just like the other kids at school. Don't begrudge me the privilege, and I do mean the privilege, of waiting up for my son." Moms smiled and opened her arms for a proper goodbye hug and kiss, just like normal people, in normal times would do.

"I love you Moms," Adam said as he leaned over and kissed his mother on the cheek.

"How are you going to get over to the Stafford house?"

"I didn't want to put her out, but I'm going to let Mrs. G. drive me over. Fritzy and I have a ride from there."

"That's right," Moms remembered. "Arletta said she was so excited about being able to participate in the evening's fun. She can't go to the party. She said she needs to stay with Alfred. But, she'll take you over and be able to drop off her shower gift for Sarah Jane while she's there. The whole town is excited about the parties—the kids at the high school and the parents at Alma Stafford's house."

Adam said goodbye, left the cottage and walked up the sidewalk to the kitchen door where Mrs. Gunderman stood peeling potatoes for their dinner. "Come on in, Adam," she said as she gestured for him to open the door and enter. "My hands are busy," she laughed.

"Is that Adam?" Alfred called from his chair by the front room window.

"It's me, Mr. G." he responded.

"Come in here so I can see you," he playfully commanded.

As the boy walked from the kitchen into the living room the small smile on Alfred's face spread into a full grin. "Say, you clean up real good, don't ya?"

"Thank you, Sir."

"Mrs. Gunderman," Alfred called toward the kitchen, "this boy is as ready as a man can get. Dinner will wait. You'd best run him over before Fritzy Breman calls and wonders if we've kidnapped her date."

"That could happen," Arletta chuckled. "Adam, if you'll pick up that package for me there on the chair, I'll get my coat."

"It's a coffee pot, don't ya know," Alfred added. "The misses loves her Maxwell House."

"Yes Sir," Adam agreed as he retrieved the wrapped present from the chair.

As they road over to the New Year's Eve party and Shower, Adam had something he had to say. "Mrs. G., I cannot thank you enough for your generous charity to our family."

"Charity? Adam, this is not charity. Don't you know the sign of a good friendship is when you think you're getting more out of the relationship than the other person? I'm as happy you and your mom are living there as you are, maybe more."

Adam thought about the truth of friendships as they drove the remaining few blocks to the party house. Once they got there, they were immediately greeted by more smiling faces.

• • •

"Adam, I'm glad you're here. Come on in. Good to see you too, Arletta. Would you like some eggnog?" Mr. Stafford shook Adam's hand and nearly pulled him into the house. It was Monday evening and the New Year's Eve party at the school would start soon.

"Yes, thank you Willard," Mrs. Gunderman said. "I'll find Alma and then help myself."

"I don't think so, thank you," Adam smiled shyly. "We'd best be going."

"You look like a fine gentleman, my Boy," Willard said.

"Thanks, Sir." Adam stepped into the room flooded with color and light.

The Breman family was all at the Stafford home for their New Year's Eve party. This year, it was also a wedding shower for Fritzy's sister, Sarah Jane. It seemed like the entire membership of the Cranberry Street Church, and many others from all over town, were there. At least the adults were. The high schoolers came long enough to meet their friends and then head off to the school Gym for their party. Mr. Breman was one of the chaperones and Mrs. Breman would join him after Sarah's shower.

The Stafford home was hung with white crepe paper bells and gold and blue bows. They were woven in and out of the Christmas decorations. Adam wasn't much interested in wedding colors, but he had to admit, the house looked nice.

Adam's total focus turned to the round, claw-footed table that had been moved in from the library. The Staffords invited guests to place any shower gifts on that round oak table in the middle of the room. There was already a huge pile of presents wrapped in white, blue and gold paper. The whole thing sat on a round floral area carpet with a fringed edge that was placed over the Persian rug.

Adam wasn't fooled for a minute. He knew the table straddled the eighteen inch hole in the floor he and Mr. Stafford had cut a few days before. Adam remembered every detail. He knew that Mr. Stafford had braced the floor with two-by-eight inch lumber that partnered with those floor joists that had to be cut in order to get out the last rat. He knew it was safe but he still worried. Mrs. Stafford would have been horrified if someone fell through the floor at her fancy party.

As he stood there that evening, he gave a little sniff test and smiled. As he stared at the table, Fritzy came over.

"Don't worry," she soothed. "It looks great. It seems like Grandma planned for the table to be in the middle of the room all along."

"Do the sprawling claw feet spread out enough to cover the entire hole? I would die if the table and everything on it fell through and landed on a giant spider web below—or worse yet, a rat's nest."

"Spiders?" Fritzy shuddered.

"Don't worry," Adam teased. "Bet I knocked down enough spider webs to knit a sweater with the threads."

"Adam, stop!" she demanded. "I'll be seeing spiders riding on the backs of large rats in my dreams for a month."

"Adam," Mr. Stafford interrupted, "it looks fine doesn't it. And, thank goodness, it smells good too."

"Yes, Sir. It looks and smells great." Adam studied the table a minute longer. "Sir, is the table usually crooked or is there something else going on?

"Crooked, my Boy, no." Mr. Stafford turned and stared at the table, buried under a mountain of gifts.

"Do you think—? No, it couldn't happen."

Suddenly the table slipped a little more and leaned slightly farther toward Adam. He and Mr. S. were transfixed by the scene before them.

"Do you think it will collapse?" the boy whispered. He knew what that could mean.

"No—it wouldn't dare. My dear wife wouldn't allow it."

Adam squatted down next to the table foot and studied the problem. "Mr. Stafford," he whispered and motioned for the older man to meet him near the floor. "It looks like the glass ball in this claw foot is cracking."

Another pair of eyes joined them as they investigated the bottom of the table leg. "Wow," Charlie Baker's little brother got down on his hands and knees and gasped. "If that heavy table falls, the whole thing could crash through the floor." His eyes sparkled, "It would land in a heap in the basement."

"Crawl space," Adam corrected, "trust me, I know."

"Mrs. Stafford may never forgive me, Adam, if that whole thing collapsed after all." Mr. S. shook his head in disbelief.

"What on earth—" Mrs. Stafford gasped as she approached the center of the room. Then, she drew her white lace handkerchief up to her face. "Well, this just cannot happen."

The two rat-hunters looked at each other and back at Mrs. S.

She turned and, with a wave of her fancy handkerchief, she rallied all those in the house to come to her side. "My friends, we have an impending catastrophe in our midst. My momma's beautiful oak table is losing its grip. I'm afraid some of Sarah Jane's lovely gifts will be damaged if our table collapses."

She was a gracious lady who had no problem admitting that the ancestral table might fall apart before her eyes. But, she did not want anyone to know about the large rats' nest that had been below the carpet. That would have been disgraceful.

"If all of you will help move the gifts to the dining room table, we will serve our desserts from the sideboard." She nodded at her husband and Adam with a silent cue.

"We'll pass them along and you all can place them on the other table," Mr. S. smiled.

The idea of having people line up and pass the presents along from person to person sounded cleaver but Adam knew the truth. Fritzy's grandparents did not want a lot of people around the table at one time. They feared it would add too much weight to the floor beneath the table.

He was amazed by the game the people made out of a possibly embarrassing situation. Like the bucket brigade of an old fire company, friends and family lined up and passed each gift, hand over hand, and gently laid them on the other table.

"Observe, my Boy. Our women can accomplish anything with a smile and a wave of their lace."

"So I see," Adam watched and then allowed a broad smile to take over his face as he realized a truth. *A person can't be shamed or embarrassed if they choose not to accept the shame.*

"Charlie and Barbara are here to pick you two up." Mr. Breman called to them from the front door. "You two want to come in?"

"No thank you, Coach. Barb is waiting in the car."

Fritzy got her coat and joined Adam near the door.

"You both go ahead, Fritzy," her father said. "I'll help finish up with the presents, then I'll be right over. Mom will follow later."

"Thanks Daddy."

"Thank you, Sir," Adam joined in.

"No, Adam, I think we all owe you a big thank you. It is wonderful to have you around. We can depend on you. And now, the Gundermans can depend on you and your mom, too. It is a wonderful after-Christmas blessing, don't you think?" Coach Breman assured him.

"Yes, Sir, a very big blessing," he agreed and in his head, he thanked Shaddy.

Chapter 35

A Celebration of Life and Strength

"You look pretty, Frederica Breman," Adam smiled as they walked around the gym floor at the party.

"This place looks wonderful," Barbara said excitedly. "Do you two mind if Charlie and I walk around and see all the games?"

"Of course not, Barb," Fritzy agreed. "We're going to take it all in at our own pace, too."

Kids played BINGO and won amazing prizes at one table, at least Adam thought they were. As they watched, he saw one boy win a new pearl-handled pocket knife and a friend of Fritzy's scored a bottle of French cologne.

"Let me smell," Fritzy asked. Then, she took a little whiff of the cologne. "The perfume smells amazing," she said.

"This is great!" Adam said as he looked all around.

"The parents have gone all out to make the party special. The war is over. The dads and moms are home now. Many of them were gone for two or three years. Daddy said the party is so grand because the entire city of Middletown wanted to play for an evening—with all the lights on. They wanted a fun night, not for themselves, but for their children.

271

They wanted them to have all the fun that had been denied them. The chaperon list had tripled as returning dads wanted to spend those precious hours with their children."

"Well, you still look great," Adam said again.

"Thank you, kind sir," Fritzy blushed at Adam's compliment. Then her eyes darted around the room in excitement. "Look, a scavenger hunt!"

Adam picked up a list to search for the first item in the hunt. "Find the female with one green eye and one blue eye."

"What?" Fritzy puzzled. "I've lived here all my life, and I don't know anyone with one blue eye and one green eye. Skip that one. Maybe we'll happen on her later. Let's look around some more."

"Okay. Let's go over there." Adam's eyes caught an amazing sight. "They put up a bowling alley—with three lanes."

"How did they do that?" Fritzy ran over to the newly installed alleys. "They're bowling in their stocking feet."

Adam liked the sound the fabric in Fritzy's red taffeta dress made as she moved beside him. If not for the Christmas holidays, he may have forgotten how special girls looked in party clothes.

"Well, what do you think?" Coach Breman burst with pride as the two got over to the lanes.

"About what?" Adam stumbled. His mind was still on Fritzy's dress.

"How? Why?" Fritzy stammered as she looked at the glistening hardwood of the alleys.

"Sorry for the secrecy, Frederica. We were hoping to have the alley ready by tonight, but we had no guarantee. I didn't want to disappoint you. Principal Sparrow and I decided to add bowling as an activity by rolling up old parachutes to make the lanes but no gutters. Sign up for your turn to play," the coach beamed.

"If bowling isn't your choice, people over there are shooting baskets. They are trying to win a prize for making three baskets in a row from the top of the key. There are folk dances in the corner near the cafeteria. Some kids over there are having fun painting Christmas ornaments," he pointed.

"The room is full of stuff, all kinds of games and fun and . . . Fritzy, listen to the music. This is great!" Adam looked around every corner of the gym. "Wow, Coach, this is amazing!"

"I will leave you two young people to your own fun. There are hot dogs, cokes, potato salad, cupcakes and everything that goes with them in the cafeteria."

"Let's just walk around for a while and look at everything." Adam took Fritzy's hand as they cruised the room. They stopped at the dart board. A sign read, "Break three balloons and win a prize."

"Look over there, Adam—a cake walk. Walk around the chairs until the music stops and win a cake," Fritzy's eyes flashed with excitement as she took in all the games.

"I could use a cake," Adam started, but then thought he'd better drop the topic of food.

"Whatever you want, Adam. All the games are free and so is the food."

"Free? I like those prices," Adam laughed.

"Isn't it wonderful that the Christ Child was returned," Fritzy beamed. "The congregation didn't even respond to the ransom demand. A note, actually stuck right in the baby's hand, said, 'The carving belongs to the people of the Church on Cranberry Street, not to me.' It is a miracle, Adam. A real miracle."

"I never believed in miracles before."

"And now?"

"So many things have happened. So many things have changed." He thought for a moment then remembered with excitement. "Did I tell you, the little hummingbird came back?"

"That's wonderful! I think he came back because you've changed. They say hummingbirds won't stick around if there is

273

hatred or ugliness around them. Maybe that has changed, too. Maybe you're happier."

Adam thought of the bitterness he had felt and the anger he had harbored toward his father. All the bad feelings were gone, and he hadn't even realized when they left. Then he thought of the Christ Child in the manger and the freedom he has felt since he knelt there at the occupied manger and the infant occupied his heart.

"I am happier. I can feel joy all the way down to my shoes. Or, maybe I should say, Jim's shoes. Thank your mother again for me."

"Adam, they aren't Jim's shoes now, any more than they would belong to the Bon Ton if you had bought them there. They are yours now. Straighten up and own them." She gave him a playful jab to his arm as she emphasized the point she was making. "Get over the woo-is-me complaints."

"Thanks. I'm not going to feel sorry for myself, and I'm not going to be Mr. Woo any more. Self-pity only makes me confused and weak."

From off to the side, two silly boys pushed and pulled at each other. They really didn't watch where they were going.

"Look at those two. They've already made fools out of themselves to my thinking. What will they do next?"

Then the boys turned sharply, ran into Fritzy and nearly knocked her down. She stumbled into Adam who was happy to catch her before she fell.

"Hey, watch where you're going," Adam spoke firmly to the roughnecks.

"Says who?" One of the boys shot back.

"Me—you just heard me." Adam snapped quickly. One of the boys turned so Adam could see his face. Then the other good-for-nothing turned as well.

"Well, well, look who's here," Adam smirked at the two. "I thought you two weren't coming to the party."

"Where'd ya get the idea we wouldn't come?" Freddy growled out. "We're just as good as you. We have homes. At least we don't live in a belfry," Buddy smirked.

"Never mind them, Adam. Let's go on." Fritzy took his arm and tried to nudge him away.

"Right, Adam," Buddy mocked, "let the little lady lead you around by the nose."

"At least I have a friend, Buddy. What do you call Freddy? Your litter-mate? You guys are always rolling around like little mutts." Adam smiled sarcastically.

"Mutts are we? We have families and houses. I've heard you live in the rafters of the church on Cranberry Street. That's where the Christ Kid was stolen. I think the robbery was an inside job," Buddy yelled.

"Destroy him," the shadows hissed with menacing delight. "Their lives belong to you. You know their deep secret." The darkness oozed out of the corners and moved across the floor, inviting Adam to watch them, to let them in.

"No," Adam protested.

"No what?" Fritzy questioned.

"No—nothing, Fritzy. I—see—."

"See what? Two stupid boys?" Fritzy looked at the two, then she added, "The theft was an inside job. The carving was taken from the inside to the outside, moron."

"Moron? Me? Looks like the resident bat in the belfry would have heard something that night," Buddy insisted again.

"They deserve to be broken. They are lost to us anyway," the shadows touched each boy on the shoulder. "They will let us in."

"Shadows be gone!" Adam ordered and the shadows dissolved into the corners, always there, always waiting.

"Be gone?" Freddy laughed. "Are you trying to cast a spell on us?"

"If I were, you would have felt it by now," Adam stated as one with authority.

275

"I wish you two—" Adam began then stopped. "No," he stopped again. He would not wish.

"Adam, are you alright?" Fritzy asked.

"Yes, I'm fine. I'm just having an argument with myself," he admitted.

"Let us touch her," the shadows begged in chorus as they moved out of hiding. "She is beautiful."

"No," Adam demanded again. This time he stepped forward and put himself between Fritzy and the darkness.

"What is that smell?' Fritzy recoiled.

"You can smell the foul odor?" Adam gasped. He would have to get Fritzy away from the dark corner quickly.

"Yes," she held her hand to her nose and mouth. "Can't you smell that?"

"Yes, Fritzy, I smell it, but I had hoped you wouldn't." Adam put his hand on her shoulder to lead her away.

"Where do you think you're going?" Buddy demanded and pushed his fingers into Adam's shoulder.

"We will give you the power to break them. Their lives will be ruined beyond repair. You know what happened that night in the storage room. We were there," evil's argument grew in strength with each dark thought.

"My Son," Shaddy whispered even though he was not called. "You will have what you need when you need it."

Adam smiled and brushed Buddy's hand from his shoulder like an unwanted fly at a picnic. "I need to talk to you two."

He turned to Fritzy and apologized. "The boys and I will step into the hallway. I want you to go find your dad and I'll meet you there." He squeezed her hand and pointed the way out of the room.

"You've been caught now, haven't you, Belfry Brat," Freddy giggled as they bounced into the hall, expecting an easy win in the game they were playing.

"I heard Pastor Silverman say something interesting you guys would want to know before you carry this prank any farther." Adam smiled and moved in closer to the two wimps who only cowered and slunk back.

"What do we care?" Buddy asked sheepishly.

"Will, I think you guys will care a lot. The Navy duffle bag the carving was in had a few smudges of fresh yellow paint on the outside. I am sure, if the police wanted to, they could go from house to house and check for freshly painted walls and maybe even used paint cans—maybe out in the garage."

Buddy and Freddy closed their eyes in unison, like they had both seen the last scene of a bad movie. "Are they going to?" Freddy questioned.

"Shut up, Stupid," Buddy jabbed at his cohort in crime.

"They will, if this streak of burglary and lies doesn't stop. I happen to know some of the policemen, and they are descent guys. I think they'd like to let all of this go away. Do you think you're done with this mess?" Adam stepped a little closer and got in their faces. "Well?"

"I'm done with it all. It wasn't—"

"Freddy, are you going to shut up?" Buddy demanded.

"No, I am not. Do you want me to talk more, Buddy?" Freddy's back stood a little straighter, and he grew a little taller.

"I thought you might decide to do the right thing, Freddy." Adam turned to leave. He heard Buddy smack Freddy again. "Freddy, if he gives you any trouble, the officer's name is Overton. He knows me. Oh, and, I think you lost your pocket knife, Buddy. The one with the B.P. initials on it. It was nearly swallowed by a rat. I would hate to think that someone was responsible for putting all those rats in my friend's basement."

Buddy said nothing more, but took two steps away from Freddy.

Adam smiled again and went back into the gym, leaving the two hoodlums to fight out their own power struggle.

Adam felt that he had been brought back from darkness into the light. He too had refused self-serving greed. He had chosen truth.

Back at the bowling alley, Adam took Fritzy's hand for a moment. "Fritzy—"

"Adam, what was that all about? I'm confused," she confessed.

"Let's talk about something else." He took a deep breath and cleared his thoughts. "I have some great news. This spring—I'll be gone for a while. Right before school is out for Easter vacation, I'll get my driver's license. I'm going to go find my Pops. Over Spring Break, I will follow up on some leads."

"How do you know where to look?"

"The VA hospitals are the only clues I have right now, but I will write some letters through the rest of the winter and try to get a trail on his whereabouts. A Sergeant Smith has made contact with us."

"Adam, that is so exciting. Are you going to fly? You've flown before," she chuckled.

"Ha ha," Adam mocked.

"Seriously, I'll really miss you, but I know you can do this."

"Now, how do you know I'll be able to find him?"

"The Indians say that a hummingbird symbolizes timeless joy and the Nectar of Life."

"That's what the Indians say?"

"It is," she agreed. "The hummingbird is a symbol for accomplishing things which seem impossible."

"Accomplish the impossible? Another miracle?"

"Some say, the hummingbird will teach you how to find the miracle of joyful living from your own circumstances. Your life, Adam, is filled with miracles, if you'll just recognize them."

"I am beginning to see them. I'm beginning to see them everywhere."

For This New Year -
I wish you peace to share
Those who care
A song to sing
And hummingbirds in the spring.

Resources

Martin, Hugh and Blane, Ralph (1943). Have Yourself a Merry Little Christmas. From the film *Meet Me in St. Louis*

www4.brainyquote.com. (Accessed January 8, 2011)

http://tobaccodocuments.org. The Jack Benny Show, NBC, December 30, 1945. (Accessed January 7, 2011)

www.hummingbirdworld.com. (Accessed January 7, 2011)

www.funtrivia.com. Goodbye Little Yellow Bird, words and music by C. W. Murphy. (Accessed January 7, 2011)

OTHER BOOKS BY DORIS GAINES RAPP

Novelette:

    News at Eleven (Glo Magazine - Serialized Jan, Feb, March, and April 2015 Expanded to: *News at Eleven – A Novel*

Novels:

    Escape from the Shadows
    Length of Days – The Age of Silence
    Length of Days – Beyond the Valley of the Keepers
    Length of Days – Search for Freedom
    Escape from the Belfry –First Edition
    Smoke from Distant Fires
    Hiawassee – Child of the Meadow
    News at Eleven – A Novel

Collection:

    Christmas Feathers, one of eight short stories in a wonderful collection titled, ***Christmases Past***

Children's:

    Lincoln's Christmas Mouse

Non-Fiction:

    Waiting for Jesus in a Can't Wait World – Advent 2014
    Prayer Therapy of Jesus
    Promote Yourself

Internet Presence:

    www.prayertherapyrapp.blogspot.com
    www.dorisgainesrapp.blogspot.com
    Website: www.dorisgainesrapp.com
    Facebook: Doris Gaines Rapp – Author Page

About the Author

Doris Gaines Rapp, Ph.D. is a writer by birth, psychologist and teacher by education and experiences. She creates fictional characters that live in several centuries and loves the stories she tells. As a psychologist, she understands the people who appear on her computer screen; she laughs with them, cries with them, and triumphs over adversity with them. They are real and full of life. All of her works have at their heart a Christian world view.

Rapp also writes on the non-fiction topics of self-publishing with an encouragement to promote yourself and your work; as well as Prayer Therapy, learning to pray specifically so God can answer prayers specifically.

She speaks on several topics:

Voices of Assertiveness within My Novels
Write About What You Know
Prayer Therapy
Promote Yourself
Know Your Own History
Live All of Your Life
Step Out of Your Comfort Zone

Dr. Rapp is a former counseling center director of Taylor University, Upland, IN and Bethel College, Mishawaka, IN. She currently writes and speaks full time. She and her pastor husband have survived rearing six children. They live in Indiana.

www.ingramcontent.com/pod-product-compliance
Lightning Source LLC
Chambersburg PA
CBHW070430120726
47910CB00003B/723